特蒐多益聽力與閱讀模擬試題　累積字彙力邁向金色證書殿堂

NEW TOEIC
關鍵金色字彙1200

Essential Vocabulary for the New TOEIC
1200 Words You Need to Know

第二版

書林編輯部◎編著

國家圖書館出版品預行編目資料

New TOEIC 關鍵金色字彙 1200 = Essential Vocabulary for the New TOEIC: 1200 Words You Need to Know/ 書林編輯部編著. -- 二版. -- 臺北市：書林出版有限公司, 2024.12
　　面；　公分. --（應試高手 ; 46）
ISBN 978-626-7605-03-5（平裝）

1.CST: 多益測驗 2.CST: 詞彙

805.1895　　　　　　　　　　　　　113017312

應試高手 46

NEW TOEIC 關鍵金色字彙 1200，第二版
Essential Vocabulary for the New TOEIC: 1200 Words You Need to Know

編　　　著	書林編輯部
執 行 編 輯	張雅雯
校　　　對	王建文‧李虹慧
英 文 顧 問	Lynn Sauvé
出 版 者	書林出版有限公司
	100臺北市羅斯福路四段60號3樓
	Tel (02)2368-4938‧2365-8617　　Fax (02)2368-8929‧2363-6630
台北書林書店	106臺北市新生南路三段88號2樓之5　Tel (02) 23658617
學校業務部	Tel (02) 2368-7226‧(04) 2376-3799‧(07) 229-0300
經銷業務部	Tel (02) 2368-4938
發 行 人	蘇正隆
郵　　　撥	15743873‧書林出版有限公司
網　　　址	http://www.bookman.com.tw
經 銷 代 理	紅螞蟻圖書有限公司
	台北市內湖區舊宗路二段121巷19號
	Tel (02) 2795-3656(代表號)　Fax (02) 2795-4100
登 記 證	局版臺業字第一八三一號
出 版 日 期	2024年12月二版初刷
定　　　價	350元
I　S　B　N	978-626-7605-03-5

欲利用本書全部或部分內容者，須徵得書林出版有限公司同意或書面授權。

掃描封面 QR code，點選資訊欄中的「資源下載」，即可下載全書音檔！

Table of Contents

認識多益測驗 ii

Chapter 1　Personnel 人事

1.1　Recruitment 徵聘人員 2
1.2　Employment 就業 10
1.3　Promotion 升遷 17
1.4　Salaries & Benefits
　　 薪資福利 22

Exercises 28

Chapter 2　Organization 組織

2.1　Enterprise 企業 32
2.2　Company Structure
　　 公司架構 40

Exercises 46

Review 1 47

Chapter 3　Office Life 辦公室生活

3.1　Supplies & Equipment
　　 用品設備 54
3.2　At the Office 辦公室 64
3.3　Meeting & Presentation
　　 會議與簡報 77
3.4　Building 建築物 88

Exercises 95

Chapter 4　Sales & Marketing 業務行銷

4.1　Advertising 廣告 98

4.2　Marketing 行銷 108

Exercises 121

Review 2 123

Chapter 5　Business Trip 商務旅行/出差

5.1　Air Travel 搭飛機 130
5.2　Accommodation 膳宿 .. 140
5.3　Schedule Arrangement
　　 行程規劃 146
5.4　Transportation 交通運輸 152

Exercises 157

Chapter 6　Social Events 社交活動

6.1　Dining 用餐 160
6.2　Art & Music
　　 藝術與音樂 166
6.3　Plays & Movies
　　 戲劇與電影 171
6.4　Leisure & Hobbies
　　 休閒與嗜好 174

Exercises 179

Review 3 181

Chapter 7　Finance 財務

7.1　Accounting 會計 188
7.2　Assets 資產 195

Exercises 200

Chapter 8 Purchasing & Logistics 採購與後勤

8.1   Purchasing 採購 204
8.2   Logistics 後勤 211

Exercises 219

Review 4 221

Chapter 9 Production 生產

9.1   Equipment 設備 228
9.2   Production 生產 235

Exercises 248

Chapter 10 Legal Affairs & Tax 法務與稅務

10.1 Contract 合約 252
10.2 Legal Affairs 法務 257
10.3 Tax 稅務 260

Exercises 266

Review 5 269

Answer key 275

認識多益測驗

什麼是多益測驗？

　　TOEIC 測驗全名為 Test of English for International Communication（國際溝通英語測驗），係針對非母語人士設計之英語能力測驗，測驗分數反映受測者在國際職場環境中與他人以英語溝通的熟稔程度。參加本測驗毋需具備專業的知識或字彙，測驗內容以日常使用之英語為主。多益測驗的題型設計面向職場，於 1979 年開辦，歷經 2006、2018 年改新制，至今全球每年有超過 700 萬人報考，台灣報考人數超過 30 萬。考生年齡以 21 至 25 歲四成佔多數，其次為兩成 20 歲以下考生。全球已有 160 個國家施測，並有超過 14,000 家的企業、學校或政府機構採用為衡量標準，是全球最廣泛且英語能力衡量測驗之一。

多益測驗的內容

　　多益的設計，以職場的需要為主。測驗題目從全世界各地職場的英文資料中蒐集而來，題材多元化，包含各種場合與情境。

一般商務	契約、談判、行銷、銷售、商業企劃、會議
製造業	工廠管理、生產線、品管
金融／預算	銀行業務、投資、稅務、會計、帳單
企業發展	研究、產品研發
辦公室	董事會、委員會、信件、備忘錄、電話、傳真、電子郵件、辦公室器材與傢俱、辦公室流程
人事	招考、雇用、退休、薪資、升遷、應徵與廣告
採購	比價、訂貨、送貨、發票
技術層面	電子、科技、電腦、實驗室與相關器材、技術規格
房屋／公司地產	建築、規格、購買租賃、電力瓦斯服務
旅遊	火車、飛機、計程車、巴士、船隻、渡輪、票務、時刻表、車站、機場廣播、租車、飯店、預訂、脫班與取消
外食	商務／非正式午餐、宴會、招待會、餐廳訂位
娛樂	電影、劇場、音樂、藝術、媒體
保健	醫藥保險、看醫生、牙醫、診所、醫院

多益測驗方式

第一大類：聽力

總共有一百題，共有四大題。考生會聽到各種各類英語的直述句、問句、短對話以及短獨白，然後根據所聽到的內容回答問題。聽力的考試時間大約為四十五分鐘。

- 第一大題：照片描述 6 題（四選一）
- 第二大題：應答問題 25 題（三選一）
- 第三大題：簡短對話 39 題（四選一）
- 第四大題：簡短獨白 30 題（四選一）

第二大類：閱讀

總共有一百題，題目及選項都印在題本上。考生須閱讀多種題材的文章，然後回答相關問題。考試時間為七十五分鐘，考生可在時限內依自己能力調配閱讀及答題速度。

- 第五大題：句子填空 30 題（四選一）
- 第六大題：段落填空 16 題（四選一）
- 第七大題：單篇閱讀 29 題（四選一）
  多篇閱讀 25 題（四選一）

考生選好答案後，要在與題目卷分開的答案卷上劃卡。雖然答題時間約為兩小時，但考試時考生尚須在答案卷上填寫個人資料，並簡短的回答關於教育與工作經歷的問卷，因此真正待在考場內時間會較長。

多益測驗計分方式

考生用鉛筆在電腦答案卷上作答。考試分數由答對題數決定，再將每一大類（聽力類、閱讀類）答對題數轉換成分數，範圍在 5 到 495 分之間。兩大類加起來即為總分，範圍在 10 到 990 分之間。答錯不倒扣。

多益成績與英語能力參照

TOEIC 成績	語言能力	證照顏色
905~990	英文能力十分近似於英語母語人士，能夠流暢有條理表達意見、參與談話，主持英文會議、調和衝突並做出結論，語言使用上即使有瑕疵，亦不會造成理解上的困擾。	金色 (860~990)
785~900	可有效地運用英文滿足社交及工作上所需，措辭恰當、表達流暢；但在某些等定情形下，如：面臨緊張壓力、討論話題過於冷僻艱澀時，仍會顯現出語言能力不足的情況。	藍色 (730~855)
605~780	可以英語進行一般社交場會的談話，能夠應付例行性的業務需求，參加英文會議，聽取大部份要點；但無法流利的以英語發表意見、作辯論，使用的字彙、句型也以一般常見為主。	綠色 (470~725)
405~600	英文文字溝通能力尚可，會話方面稍嫌辭彙不足、語句簡單，但已能掌握少量相關語言，可以從事英語相關程度較低的工作。	棕色 (220~465)
255~400	語言能力僅僅侷限在簡單的一般日常生活對話，同時無法做連續性交談，亦無法用英文工作。	橘色 (10~215)
10~250	只能以背誦的句子進行問答而不能自行造句，尚無法將英文當作溝通工具來使用。	

NEW TOEIC 關鍵金色字彙 1200 使用說明

1. 英文字彙通常有多個意思，本書採用該字於多益考試中最常測驗的意思及用法，幫助集中學習，有效準備多益測驗。

2. 本書每頁均有此虛線，其作用在於方便讀者複習字彙，沿著虛線向外摺頁，可立即小試身手，隨時測驗學習成效。

3. 當您做完第一次測驗時，可在第一個方塊中註記測試結果（如沒有問題，可於方塊上打 ✔；還需要再加強，就在方塊上打 ✘，您可以依照自己的習慣加上符號或日期，記錄學習成果）。第二個方塊的使用方式同上。

4. 本書中的中文例句保留該字的英文，此一編排方式可讓您於中文例句中再次記憶該字的用法及意思，學習效果加乘。

考前 30 天衝刺計畫

☐ **Day 1** ■ 1.1 Recruitment 　ability~switch 實力累積： 49 words	☐ **Day 2** ■ 1.2 Employment 　accurately~workplace ■ 1.3 Promotion 　assignment~respect 實力累積： 118 words	☐ **Day 3** ■ 1.4 Salaries & Benefits 　allowance~welfare 實力累積： 153 words + Exercises
☐ **Day 4** ■ 2.1 Enterprise 　access~vote 實力累積： 203 words	☐ **Day 5** ■ 2.2 Company Ranking 　administrator~worker ■ 3.1 Supplies & Equipment 　acquainted~documentary 實力累積： 251 words + Exercises + Review 1	☐ **Day 6** ■ 3.1 Supplies & Equipment 　email~whiteboard 實力累積： 296 words
☐ **Day 7** ■ 3.2 At the Office 　appointment~post 實力累積： 352 words	☐ **Day 8** ■ 3.2 At the Office 　print~website ■ 3.3 Meeting & Presentation 　advance~inquire 實力累積： 400 words	☐ **Day 9** ■ 3.3 Meeting & Presentation 　interrupt~workshop 實力累積： 438 words
☐ **Day 10** ■ 3.4 Building 　architecture~utility 實力累積： 478 words + Exercises	☐ **Day 11** ■ 4.1 Advertising 　absorb~potential 實力累積： 525 words	☐ **Day 12** ■ 4.1 Advertising 　preliminary~trend ■ 4.2 Marketing 　aggressive~management 實力累積： 577 words
☐ **Day 13** ■ 4.2 Marketing 　market~wealthy 實力累積： 612 words + Exercises + Review 2	☐ **Day 14** ■ 5.1 Air Travel 　am~landing 實力累積： 660 words	☐ **Day 15** ■ 5.1 Air Travel 　Lost and Found~turbulence ■ 5.2 Accommodation 　accomodation~voucher 實力累積： 709 words

NEW TOEIC 認識多益測驗

NEW TOEIC 關鍵金色字彙1200

Day 16 ■ 5.3 Schedule Arrangement accelerate~visit 實力累積： 746 words	**Day 17** ■ 5.4 Transportation avenue~wheel 實力累積： 774 words + Exercises	**Day 18** ■ 6.1 Dining attend~tray 實力累積： 814 words
Day 19 ■ 6.2 Art & Music antique~violinist ■ 6.3 Plays & Movies attractive~theater 實力累積： 858 words	**Day 20** ■ 6.4 Leisure & Hobbies acquaintance~vegetarian 實力累積： 884 words + Exercises + Review 3	**Day 21** ■ 7.1 Accounting accountant~yearly 實力累積： 928 words
Day 22 ■ 7.2 Assets afford~tenant 實力累積： 952 words + Exercises	**Day 23** ■ 8.1 Purchasing approve~vend 實力累積： 991 words	**Day 24** ■ 8.2 Logistics airmail~X-ray 實力累積： 1037 words + Exercises + Review 4
Day 25 ■ 9.1 Equipment advanced~wire ■ 9.2 Production amazing~industrial 實力累積： 1099 words	**Day 26** ■ 9.2 Production invention~technician 實力累積： 1147 words + Exercises	**Day 27** ■ 10.1 Contract agreement~term ■ 10.2 Legal Affairs accumulate~stressful 實力累積： 1198 words
Day 28 ■ 10.3 Tax advantage~violation 實力累積： 1227 words + Exercises + Review 5	**Day 29** ■ Review Chapter 1~4 總計複習： 612 words	**Day 30** ■ Review Chapter 5~10 總計複習： 615 words

Chapter 1
Personnel 人事

A company's Personnel Department is responsible for recruiting new employees. Job openings with requirements are posted at the beginning of the hiring process. Interviews are then conducted with qualified candidates with the appropriate education and skills. When new employees are hired, they are informed about the company's working hours, benefits, and travel allowances. Companies may reward outstanding employees with raises, bonuses, or promotions.

Chapter 1 Personnel 人事

New TOIEC 1200

1 Recruitment 徵聘人員 ①

能力   1 **ability** [ə`bɪlətɪ] *n.*

例 This job requires the **ability** to speak both English and French.

這份工作需要英法語 ability。

學術的   2 **academic** [ˌækə`dɛmɪk] *adj.*

例 We are looking for an office administrator with a solid **academic** background.

我們正在找具有紮實 academic 背景的行政人員。

口音，腔調   3 **accent** [`æksɛnt] *n.*

例 Our company is looking for native English speakers with a British **accent**.

本公司徵求英語母語人士，且具有英國 accent。

成就；專長   4 **accomplishment** [ə`kamplɪʃmənt] *n.*

例 Being able to speak English fluently is one of Amy's many **accomplishments**.

會說一口流利的英文是艾美眾多 accomplishments 之一。

適用於   5 **applicable** [`æplɪkəb!] *adj.*

例 This training is **applicable** to new employees.

這項訓練 applicable 新進員工。

6   **application** [ˌæpləˈkeʃən] *n.*　　申請表

　　例　If you want to work here, you need to fill out this **application**.

　　　　如果你想要在這工作，必須填寫這份 application。

7   **apply for** [əˈplaɪ ˈfɔr] *v. phr.*　　申請

　　例　Many graduates **apply for** internships at big corporations.

　　　　許多畢業生會 apply for 到大公司實習。

8   **attachment** [əˈtætʃmənt] *n.*　　附件

　　例　I emailed my résumé as an **attachment**.

　　　　我以 attachment 形式寄出履歷表。

9   **background** [ˈbækˌɡraʊnd] *n.*　　背景，學經歷

　　例　Candidates need to have a **background** in law to be considered for the position.

　　　　應徵該職位的人必須有法律 background。

10 **candidate** [ˈkændəˌdet] *n.*　　（競選或求職的）候選人

　　例　Over one thousand **candidates** are competing for the position.

　　　　超過一千名 candidates 在競爭這個職位。

11 **capable** [ˈkepəbḷ] *adj.*　　有能力，能夠

　　例　Jack is **capable** of juggling many tasks at the same time.

　　　　傑克 capable 同時處理多件工作。

證書	12 **certificate** [sə`tɪfəkɪt] *n.*
	例 A **certificate** in English will help you find a better job.
	擁有英文 certificate 可以幫你找到較好的工作。

首要的	13 **chief** [tʃif] *adj.*
	例 Betty always considers her multicultural background her **chief** asset.
	貝蒂一直認為多元文化背景是她最 chief 本錢。

勝任	14 **competent** [`kɑmpətənt] *adj.*
	例 It's too early to say if he is **competent** enough to do this job.
	要說他是否能 competent 這份工作還言之過早。

教育	15 **education** [ˌɛdʒə`keʃən] *n.*
	例 Applicants need to have a master's degree in **education**.
	應徵者必須具備 education 碩士學位。

耐力，耐久力	16 **endurance** [ɪn`djʊrəns] *n.*
	例 The position requires a lot of overtime, so don't apply if you don't think you have the **endurance**!
	這份工作常需要加班，如果你沒有 endurance 的話就別應徵了！

熱忱，熱情	17 **enthusiasm** [ɪn`θjuzɪˌæzəm] *n.*
	例 She has a lot of **enthusiasm** for the new product line.
	她對新產品系列投注很多 enthusiasm。

18 **experience** [ɪkˋspɪrɪəns] *n.*   經驗

例 You need to have enough work **experience** to get the job.
你需要足夠的工作 experience 才能獲得該職位。

19 **expert** [ˋɛkspɝt] *n.*   專家，行家

例 Tina is the **expert** when it comes to accounting.
蒂娜是位會計 expert。

20 **expertise** [ˌɛkspɝˋtiz] *n.*   專長，技能

例 David's **expertise** is in computer programming.
寫電腦程式是大衛的 expertise。

21 **fit** [fɪt] *v.*   適合

例 This candidate's qualifications **fit** the position perfectly.
這位應徵者的資格非常 fit 這個職位。

22 **hire** [haɪr] *v.*   聘僱，僱用

例 The company has stopped **hiring** people due to their tight budget.
這家公司因為預算緊縮而不再 hiring 人了。

23 **impressive** [ɪmˋprɛsɪv] *adj.*   令人印象深刻的

例 In order to get a job interview, you need to have an **impressive** résumé.
為了能有面試的機會，你必須寫份 impressive 履歷。

代替，取代	24	**instead** [ɪnˋstɛd] *adv.*
		例 More and more companies prefer outsourcing work **instead** of hiring new people.
		越來越多的公司傾向以將工作外包 instead 雇用新人。
求職者	25	**job hunter** [ˋdʒɑbˋhʌntɚ] *n.*
		例 Many **job hunters** have difficulty finding a job they like.
		許多 job hunters 很難找到他們喜歡的工作。
…活，勞動	26	**labor** [ˋlebɚ] *n.*
		例 The warehouse position isn't suitable for applicants who can't endure hard **labor**.
		倉庫人員一職不適合做不了粗 labor 的人。
執照，許可證	27	**license** [ˋlaɪsn̩s] *n.*
		例 You need to have a special **license** to drive the truck.
		你要有特別的 license 才能駕駛卡車。
獲得	28	**obtain** [əbˋten] *v.*
		例 You need to obtain a certified copy of your diploma to complete your application.
		你需要 obtain 一份經校方認證的學歷證明副本以完成申請。
職缺	29	**opening** [ˋopənɪŋ] *n.*
		例 We have several **openings** in the HR division.
		我們人資部門有一些 openings。

| 30 | **panel** [ˋpænl̩] *n.* | 專門小組，評判的小組 |

> 例 The **panel** of interviewers decided that none of the candidates were qualified for the position.
> 面試官 panel 決定，應試者中無人能勝任此職位。

| 31 | **portfolio** [portˋfolɪˏo] *n.* | 作品集 |

> 例 When applying for a graphic designer position, a well-organized **portfolio** is essential.
> 應徵美術設計時，一定要備好完整的 portfolio。

| 32 | **postpone** [postˋpon] *v.* | 延遲，延緩 |

> 例 We can't **postpone** the deadline any longer.
> 我們無法再 postpone 截止期限了。

| 33 | **prerequisite** [priˋrɛkwəzɪt] *n.* | 必要條件；前提 |

> 例 Previous experience in sales is a **prerequisite** for this job.
> 具備銷售相關經驗是這項工作的 prerequisite。

| 34 | **profession** [prəˋfɛʃən] *n.* | （需專門技能的）行業，職業 |

> 例 Sally has made up her mind to go into the teaching **profession**.
> 莎莉下定決心要從事教書的 profession。

| 35 | **profile** [ˋprofaɪl] *n.* | 概述 |

> 例 This applicant's résumé matches the **profile** for a position in accounting, not sales.
> 該名應徵者的履歷符合會計部門的職務 profile，而非業務部門。

7

資格，限定條件	36 **qualification** [ˌkwɑləfəˈkeʃən] *n.*
	例 If you don't meet the **qualifications**, don't apply for the position.
	如果不符合該工作的 qualifications，就別應徵了。

合格的	37 **qualified** [ˈkwɑləˌfaɪd] *adj.*
	例 After years of training, Holly is finally a **qualified** doctor.
	經過多年的訓練，荷莉終於成為 qualified 醫生。

辭職，辭掉	38 **quit** [kwɪt] *v.*
	例 It isn't wise to **quit** your job with the economy (being) so unstable.
	經濟情況不穩定，quit 你的工作是很不明智的。

推薦	39 **recommend** [ˌrɛkəˈmɛnd] *v.*
	例 Fred is highly **recommended** as a good assistant.
	佛瑞德極受 recommended，譽為稱職的助理。

招募，招聘	40 **recruit** [rɪˈkrut] *v.*
	例 The company is **recruiting** new people.
	這家公司在 recruiting 新人。

招聘人員	41 **recruiter** [rɪˈkrutɚ] *n.*
	例 Karen is the **recruiter** you should talk to if you are looking for a job.
	凱倫是 recruiter，如果你要找工作，可以找她談談。

42 **reference** [ˈrɛfərəns] *n.*   推薦，介紹

☐ 例 Some companies ask applicants for a **reference** letter.
☐   有些公司會要求應徵者提供 reference 信。

43 **reject** [rɪˈdʒɛkt] *v.*   拒絕

☐ 例 Greg's application was **rejected**.
☐   葛雷格的申請遭到 rejected 了。

44 **require** [rɪˈkwaɪr] *v.*   需要

☐ 例 This job **requires** knowledge of various computer programs.
☐   這份工作 requires 懂各種電腦程式。

45 **requirement** [rɪˈkwaɪrmənt] *n.*   必要條件

☐ 例 You won't be considered for the position if you don't meet the **requirements**.
☐   若你不具備該職缺的 requirements，是不會列入考慮的。

46 **résumé** (resume) [ˌrɛzjʊˈme] *n.*   履歷表

☐ 例 You should always keep your **résumé** updated in case you decide to look for a new job.
☐   你的 résumé 要常更新，以為未來想找新工作時做準備。

47 **seek** [sik] *v.*   尋找，尋求

☐ 例 The company is **seeking** someone who can handle customers overseas.
☐   這家公司在 seeking 能應對海外客戶的人員。

技巧，技藝	48 **skill** [skɪl] *n.*
	例 Driving a bulldozer takes special **skills**.
	駕駛推土機需要特殊的 skills。
改變，轉換	49 **switch** [swɪtʃ] *v.*
	例 It's hard to **switch** career paths when you reach middle age.
	當你到了中年就很難 switch 職業跑道了。

2　Employment 就業 ②

正確無誤	50 **accurately** [ˋækjərɪtlɪ] *adv.*
	例 Be sure you write the names **accurately** on each envelope.
	請確認每個信封上姓名均書寫 accurately。
有野心的，有雄心的	51 **ambitious** [æmˋbɪʃəs] *adj.*
	例 Jerry is very **ambitious** in his career.
	傑瑞對他的事業非常 ambitious。
職業，生涯	52 **career** [kəˋrɪr] *n.*
	例 It took my younger sister a long time to choose a **career**.
	我妹妹花了很長的時間才決定好她的 career。
挑戰，艱鉅任務	53 **challenge** [ˋtʃæləndʒ] *n.*
	例 It will be a **challenge** to have the task completed in two days.
	要在兩天內完成這項工作會是項 challenge。

54 **communication** [kəˌmjunəˈkeʃən] *n.*   溝通

例 Make sure all **communication** with our clients is accurate.
請確保我們與客戶的 communication 無誤。

55 **database** [ˈdetəˌbes] *n.*   資料庫

例 All employee information is stored in a **database**.
所有的員工資料皆儲存於 database 中。

56 **description** [dɪˈskrɪpʃən] *n.*   說明，描述

例 Job **descriptions** provide information about employee responsibilities.
工作內容 descriptions 記載了員工的職務責任。

57 **devote** [dɪˈvot] *v.*   獻身，致力

例 Mr. Lin has **devoted** ten years to the company as a forklift operator.
林先生 devoted 於這家公司擔任堆高機操作員已有十年的時間。

58 **duty** [ˈdjutɪ] *n.*   責任

例 The company has a **duty** to the shareholders.
該公司對股東負有 duty。

59 **duties** [ˈdjutɪz] *n.*   職責

例 Fulfilling guest needs is one of the concierge's **duties**.
滿足顧客需求是旅館服務台人員的 duties 之一。

• duty 意思為「職責」時，需為複數

11

雇用	60	**employ** [ɪmˋplɔɪ] *v.*
		例 That international airline **employed** over a hundred people this year.
		那家國際航空公司今年 employed 超過一百位員工。

受雇者，員工	61	**employee** [ˌɛmplɔɪˋi] *n.*
		例 Due to the economic recession, many **employees** have been let go.
		因為經濟衰退，許多 employees 都給辭退了。

雇主，老闆	62	**employer** [ɪmˋplɔɪɚ] *n.*
		例 Maria's **employer** rejected her request for additional vacation time.
		瑪麗亞的 employer 拒絕她增加休假時間的請求。

受雇，就業	63	**employment** [ɪmˋplɔɪmənt] *n.*
		例 The **employment** rate has increased by two percent since last year.
		自去年起，employment 率已上升兩個百分點。

全部，整個	64	**entire** [ɪnˋtaɪr] *adj.*
		例 The **entire** staff has gone on strike due to unfair treatment.
		Entire 員工為不平等待遇而集體罷工。

開除，解雇	65	**fire** [faɪr] *v.*
		例 Due to David's poor work performance, he was **fired** last week.
		大衛因為工作表現不佳，上週遭到 fired。

66 **flexible** [ˋflɛksəbl̩] *adj.* 有彈性

　　例 My working hours are pretty **flexible**.
　　　 我的工作時間非常 flexible。

67 **freelance** [ˋfriˌlæns] *n. adj.* 自由業者（的）

　　例 We hired a **freelance** photographer for the photo shoot.
　　　 我們聘請了一名 freelance 攝影師來拍攝照片。

68 **handbook** [ˋhændˌbʊk] *n.* 手冊

　　例 Please check the employee **handbook** for information about extending business trips for vacation.
　　　 有關將商務旅行延長為休假之事宜，請查閱員工 handbook。

69 **in charge** [ɪnˋtʃɑrdʒ] *phr.* 負責，執掌

　　例 Katie is **in charge** of the Editing Department.
　　　 凱蒂 in charge 編輯部門。

70 **income** [ˋɪnˌkʌm] *n.* 收入，所得

　　例 With two **incomes**, the couple can easily purchase a large home.
　　　 因為有兩份 incomes，這對夫妻才能輕鬆購買一間大房子。

71 **interview** [ˋɪntɚˌvju] *n.* 面試，面談

　　例 I have a job **interview** tomorrow afternoon.
　　　 我明天下午有一個工作 interview。

Chapter 1 人事

13

參加面試者	72 **interviewee** [ˌɪntɚvjuˋi] *n.*
	例 Most **interviewees** are nervous during interviews.
	許多 interviewees 在面試過程中會感到緊張。

主持面試者	73 **interviewer** [ˋɪntɚˌvjuɚ] *n.*
	例 The **interviewer** asked some difficult questions during the job interview.
	那位 interviewer 在面試時問了許多刁鑽的問題。

使用，佔據	74 **occupy** [ˋɑkjəˌpaɪ] *v.*
	例 Robert's volunteer work at the hospital **occupies** most of his spare time.
	羅伯特在醫院的志工服務 occupies 了他大部分的閒暇時間。

職前講習	75 **orientation** [ˌɔrɪɛnˋteʃən] *n.*
	例 All new employees must attend an **orientation** session.
	所有的新進員工都必須參加 orientation。

全體人員，職員	76 **personnel** [ˌpɝsnˋɛl] *n.*
	例 We should ask **personnel** from both departments to attend the meeting.
	我們應該都請那兩個部門的 personnel 參與會議。

精確的，明確的	77 **precise** [prɪˋsaɪs] *adj.*
	例 It is important to be very **precise** when communicating instructions to employees.
	下達員工的指示要 precise 是很重要的。

78 **probation** [pro`beʃən] *n.* 　　　　　　試用期，考察期

例 In Taiwan, new employees must go through a three-month **probation** period before being officially hired.

在台灣，新進員工在正式任用前必須通過三個月的 probation。

79 **resign** [rɪ`zaɪn] *v.* 　　　　　　辭職

例 The general manager was forced to **resign** from his position.

總經理被迫 resign。

80 **resignation** [ˌrɛzɪg`neʃən] *n.* 　　　　　　辭職

例 Joshua put his **resignation** letter on the manager's desk last night before he left the office.

喬舒亞昨晚下班前，將他的 resignation 信放在經理辦公桌上。

81 **retire** [rɪ`taɪr] *v.* 　　　　　　退休

例 Most people **retire** at 65.

大部分的人都在六十五歲的時候 retire。

82 **satisfy** [`sætɪsˌfaɪ] *v.* 　　　　　　滿意

例 I have to make sure that my boss is **satisfied** with my work before I leave the office.

我必須在下班之前確定老闆 satisfied 我的工作成果。

83 **sufficient** [sə`fɪʃənt] *adj.* 　　　　　　足夠的，充足的

例 Our team doesn't have **sufficient** support to finish the project.

我們的團隊缺乏 sufficient 支援來完成這項計畫。

15

任務，工作	84 **task** [tæsk] *n.*
	☐ 例 Monica can handle multiple **tasks** at the same time.
	☐ 莫妮卡能夠同時處理好幾件 tasks。

受訓者	85 **trainee** [tre`ni] *n.*
	☐ 例 I helped show the **trainees** how to use the photocopier.
	☐ 我協助向 trainees 演示如何使用影印機。

訓練人員	86 **trainer** [`trenɚ] *n.*
	☐ 例 A **trainer** in each department is responsible for getting new employees ready for the job.
	☐ 各部門裡的 trainer 要負責帶新人熟悉工作。

訓練，培訓	87 **training** [`trenɪŋ] *n.*
	☐ 例 It takes years of **training** to be a good doctor.
	☐ 要成為一位好醫師得花上多年的 training。

調動	88 **transfer** [træns`fɚ] *v.*
	☐ 例 Patricia wants to **transfer** to another department.
	☐ 派翠西亞想 transfer 到另一個部門。

拒絕	89 **turn down** [`tɝn `daʊn] *v. phr.*
	☐ 例 I **turned down** a job offer to go work for another company yesterday.
	☐ 我昨天 turn down 跳槽到別家公司工作的機會。

90 **workforce** [ˋwɝkˌfɔrs] *n.* 職場

例 After graduation from high school, some people join the **workforce** rather than attend college.

有些人高中畢業後選擇進入 workforce，不繼續讀大學。

91 **workload** [ˋwɝkˌlod] *n.* 工作量

例 Employees in the factory are unhappy with their current **workload**.

工廠員工對他們目前的 workload 不滿意。

92 **workplace** [ˋwɝkˌples] *n.* 工作場所

例 It is important to dress professionally in the **workplace**.

在 workplace 穿著正式是很重要的。

3 Promotion 升遷 ③

93 **assignment** [əˋsaɪnmənt] *n.* 工作，任務

例 Jennifer always completes her **assignments** by the deadline.

珍妮佛總是能在期限內完成 assignments。

94 **celebrate** [ˋsɛləˌbret] *v.* 慶祝

例 We are going out tonight to **celebrate** Tina's promotion.

我們今晚要去 celebrate 蒂娜獲得升遷。

恭喜	95 **congratulation** [kənˌgrætʃəˋleʃən] *n.*
	☐ 例 **Congratulations**! Our boss really liked your ideas on how to boost sales.
	Congratulations! 老闆很喜歡你增加銷售的辦法。
	• congratulation 意思是「恭喜」或「祝賀」時，需為複數

任命，指定	96 **designate** [ˋdɛzɪgˌnet] *v.*
	☐ 例 Jason was **designated** the leader of the production team.
	傑森受 designated 為該生產團隊的主管。

選舉，投票選出	97 **elect** [ɪˋlɛkt] *v.*
	☐ 例 The board of directors **elected** Johnson as the new CEO.
	董事會已 elected 出強森來擔任新任執行長。

評估	98 **evaluate** [ɪˋvæljʊˌet] *v.*
	☐ 例 The factory manager is **evaluating** staff performance this month.
	工廠經理會在這個月 evaluating 員工的工作績效。

傑出，優異	99 **excellent** [ˋɛksḷənt] *adj.*
	☐ 例 Mary does an **excellent** job organizing staff events.
	瑪麗處理員工事務的表現非常 excellent。

執行，主管	100 **executive** [ɪgˋzɛkjʊtɪv] *adj.*
	☐ 例 Kate is the **executive** editor in this publishing company.
	凱特是這家出版社的 executive 編輯。

18

101 **feedback** [ˈfɪd͵bæk] *n.* 　　　　　　　　回饋

例 Martin asked his boss for **feedback** on his performance.

馬丁請他老闆就他的工作表現給予 feedback。

102 **hard-working** [ˈhɑrdˈwɝkɪŋ] *adj.* 　　努力工作的

例 Bella is a **hard-working** employee. It's no wonder (that) she got a raise so soon.

貝拉是個 hard-working 員工。難怪她沒多久就加薪了。

103 **incompetent** [ɪnˈkɑmpətənt] *adj.* 　　無能，不勝任

例 Missing deadlines all the time makes Dave look **incompetent**.

戴夫老是無法按時完成工作，顯得他很 incompetent。

104 **leader** [ˈlidɚ] *n.* 　　　　　　　　　　領導者

例 As the **leader** of this project, you have to assign each of us our tasks.

身為這項專案的 leader，你必須指派工作給我們。

105 **leadership** [ˈlidɚ͵ʃɪp] *n.* 　　　　　　領導才能

例 Strong **leadership** skills will help you move ahead in this company.

擁有強大的 leadership 能讓你在公司出頭天。

106 **nominate** [ˈnɑmə͵net] *v.* 　　　　　　提名，推薦

例 Ms. Jackson has been **nominated** for Manager of the Year.

傑克森女士受 nominated 為年度最佳經理。

傑出的，出色的	107 **outstanding** [`aʊt`stændɪŋ] *adj.*
	例 Among all the résumés,, Heather's was the most **outstanding**.
	在所有的履歷表中，海瑟的是最 outstanding。

表現；績效	108 **performance** [pɚ`fɔrməns] *n.*
	例 Our boss was disappointed with our team's **performance**.
	老闆對我們團隊的 performance 感到失望。

職位，職務	109 **position** [pə`zɪʃən] *n.*
	例 What **position** do you hold in the company you are currently working for?
	你在目前任職的公司擔任何種 position ？

進展	110 **progress** [`prɑgrɛs] *n.*
	例 Please give me regular updates on the **progress** of the project.
	請定期告訴我這項計畫的最近 progress。

有希望	111 **promising** [`prɑmɪsɪŋ] *adj.*
	例 The business relationship between those two companies looks **promising**.
	那兩間公司的合作關係看來很 promising。

晉升	112 **promote** [prə`mot] *v.*
	例 After the annual evaluation, the CEO will announce who will be **promoted** to production manager.
	在年度考核後，執行長將宣布誰會 promoted 為生產部經理。

113 **promotion** [prə`moʃən] *n.*   晉升，升遷

    例 Larry has been waiting for a **promotion** for years.
        賴瑞等 promotion 等很久了。

114 **prosperity** [prɑs`pɛrətɪ] *n.*   興旺

    例 I wish your company success and **prosperity**.
        祝你的公司成功與 prosperity。

115 **pursue** [pɚ`su] *v.*   追求，致力於

    例 John has decided to **pursue** a singing career after high school.
        約翰決定在高中畢業之後 pursue 歌唱生涯。

116 **reliable** [rɪ`laɪəbl] *adj.*   可靠的

    例 William is considered the most **reliable** employee in the company.
        威廉應算是公司裡最 reliable 員工。

117 **reputation** [ˌrɛpjə`teʃən] *n.*   名譽，名聲

    例 You may ruin your **reputation** if you are always behind schedule.
        你會因為老是無法趕上期限而壞了自己的 reputation。

118 **respect** [rɪ`spɛkt] *n.*   尊敬，敬重

    例 Good leaders are able to earn the **respect** of the staff.
        好的主管要能贏得下屬的 respect。

Chapter 1 人事

4 Salaries and Benefits 薪資福利 ④

津貼，補助 | 119 **allowance** [əˋlaʊəns] *n.*

例 Our company offers each division an **allowance** for stationery.
公司配給各部門購買文具的 allowance。

協助，支援 | 120 **assistance** [əˋsɪstəns] *n.*

例 Without your **assistance**, I never would've finished the job on time.
若沒你的 assistance，我不可能準時完成工作的。

福利 | 121 **benefit** [ˋbɛnəfɪt] *n.*

例 That law firm provides very good employee **benefits**.
那家律師事務所提供非常好的員工 benefits。

獎金，紅利 | 122 **bonus** [ˋbonəs] *n.*

例 In Taiwan, employees receive an annual **bonus** before Chinese New Year.
在台灣，員工會在農曆年前收到年終 bonus。

賠償；補償 | 123 **compensate** [ˋkɑmpənˌset] *v.*

例 The injured construction worker will be **compensated** by the insurance company.
保險公司會 compensated 那位受傷的建築工人。

賠償，賠償金 | 124 **compensation** [ˌkɑmpənˋseʃən] *n.*

例 Victims of the industrial accident will be paid at least three million dollars in **compensation**.
工業事故的受害者將至少獲得三百萬的 compensation。

125 **concern** [kən`sɝn] *n.* 關心的事

例 Having our products delivered on time is one of our biggest **concerns**.

將貨品準時送達是我們最 concerns。

126 **contest** [`kantɛst] *n.* 比賽，競賽

例 The two sales teams are working day and night to win the **contest**.

這兩個行銷團隊日以繼夜的工作要贏得 contest。

127 **data** [`detə] *n.* 資料，數據

例 The **data** from the employee survey showed that most staff members would prefer a longer lunch break.

員工調查報告的 data 顯示，大多數的職員寧可午餐休息時間長一點。

128 **deadline** [`dɛd͵laɪn] *n.* 最後期限，截止期限

例 The project has to be completed by the **deadline**.

這個專案一定要在 deadline 內完成。

129 **deal with** [`dil`wɪθ] *v. phr.* 應付，處理

例 Receptionists often need to **deal with** customer complaints.

接待員常常要 deal with 客人的抱怨。

130 **earn** [ɝn] *v.* 賺

例 Tom **earned** a lot of money by selling clothing online.

湯姆靠在網路上賣衣服 earned 了不少錢。

利潤，收益 | 131 **earnings** [ˋɝnɪŋz] *n.*

例 The biotechnology company just detailed its first fiscal quarter **earnings**.

這家生技公司剛公佈了他們的第一會計季度的 earnings。

效率 | 132 **efficiency** [əˋfɪʃənsɪ] *n.*

例 Mark's **efficiency** at work allows him to complete many tasks in a short amount of time.

馬克的工作 efficiency 讓他可以在短時間內完成多項工作。

有效率的 | 133 **efficient** [əˋfɪʃənt] *adj.*

例 It would be a more **efficient** use of time to have the photocopier staple the papers together rather than do it yourself.

用影印機裝訂紙張要比你自己做來得 efficient 多了。

努力 | 134 **effort** [ˋɛfɚt] *n.*

例 Nick has put a lot of **effort** into the project since he started it last year.

尼克自去年啟動這項計畫以來投注了不少 effort。

差事 | 135 **errand** [ˋɛrənd] *n.*

例 Our manager's assistant is always running personal **errands** for her.

我們經理的助理老是要幫她處理私人 errands。

24

136 **pass** [pæs] *n.* 通行證，入場證

例 Our company will issue you a **pass** for the fitness room.
公司將會發給你健身房的 pass。

137 **pay** [pe] *v.* 支付

例 This job doesn't **pay** much, so I have to find a part-time job.
這份工作 pay 的薪水不高，所以我必須再找一份兼職工作。

138 **pension** [ˋpɛnʃən] *n.* 退休金，養老金

例 When I retire, I will have to survive on a small **pension**.
我退休之後，只能靠著微薄的 pension 度日。

139 **permission** [pɚˋmɪʃən] *n.* 許可

例 I asked my boss for **permission** to take a vacation day next week.
我向老闆要求下週休假的 permission。

140 **productive** [prəˋdʌktɪv] *adj.* 富有成效；多產

例 Some people are more **productive** in the morning.
有些人在早上工作比較 productive。

141 **raise** [rez] *n.* 加薪

例 After working a year for the company, Fran asked her boss for a **raise**.
在公司工作滿一年之後，法蘭向老闆要求 raise。

25

減少，降低 | 142 **reduce** [rɪ`djus] *v.*

例 My company is planning to **reduce** the number of staff members.

我的公司正計畫 reduce 職員人數。

減少，降低 | 143 **reduction** [rɪ`dʌkʃən] *n.*

例 There was a dramatic **reduction** in profits for many companies last year.

許多公司的收益在去年均大幅 reduction。

退還，償還 | 144 **refund** [rɪ`fʌnd] *v.*

例 My company will **refund** all food purchases made on the trip.

我的公司會 refund 我所有於出差期間購買食物的錢。

補償 | 145 **reimburse** [ˌriɪm`bɝs] *v.*

例 I don't think the company will **reimburse** me for any alcoholic beverages consumed on the trip.

我不認為公司會 reimburse 給我出差時飲酒的花費。

度假勝地 | 146 **resort** [rɪ`zɔrt] *n.*

例 The conference is being held at a four-star **resort**.

本會議將在一間四星級的 resort 舉行。

責任 | 147 **responsibility** [rɪˌspɑnsə`bɪlətɪ] *n.*

例 It's my **responsibility** to go through every detail of this project.

把關這計畫的每個細節是我的 responsibility。

148 **reward** [rɪˋwɔrd] *v.* 獎勵，獎賞

□ 例 The company **rewarded** Tom's good work performance by giving him a bonus.
□ 公司發獎金給湯姆以 rewarded 他的優異表現。

149 **salary** [ˋsælərɪ] *n.* 薪水，薪資

□ 例 The **salary** they offered for the position was much lower than I thought it would be.
□ 他們對這職位提出的 salary 比我預期的低很多。

150 **wages** [ˋwedʒɪz] *n.* 工資，薪水

□ 例 Jane's **wages** aren't high enough to support her lifestyle.
□ 珍的 wages 不足以負擔她的生活方式。

151 **weekday** [ˋwik͵de] *n.* 平日（週一至週五）

□ 例 The office is only open on **weekdays**.
□ 這間辦事處只有 weekdays 營業。

152 **weekend** [ˋwik͵ɛnd] *n.* 週末

□ 例 Most employees have **weekends** off.
□ 大部分受雇者 weekends 都不用上班。

153 **welfare** [ˋwɛl͵fɛr] *n.* 福利

□ 例 We need to cut costs for the **welfare** of the company.
□ 我們必須刪減公司的 welfare 支出。

Chapter 1 人事

Exercises

請從選項中,選出最適當的答案完成句子。

1. Being able to speak a foreign language well is quite a(n) _____. It takes a long time and it takes hard work.

   (A) requirement   (B) employment   (C) compliment   (D) accomplishment

2. We are glad to inform you that your _____ for the job vacancy has been accepted.

   (A) education   (B) indication   (C) implication   (D) application

3. Human beings are _____ of jealousy at birth; in other words, jealousy is inborn.

   (A) capable   (B) dependable   (C) susceptible   (D) reliable

4. This car sells well because of its _____ and reliability; it lasts a long time and has few mechanical problems.

   (A) endurance   (B) persistence   (C) insistence   (D) resistance

5. Her male colleagues were eager to help Lisa repaint her apartment, but their _____ waned when they were told Lisa wouldn't be home during the repaint.

   (A) suspension   (B) intension   (C) enthusiasm   (D) patience

6. Employ and _____ are synonyms; they mean the same thing.

   (A) hint   (B) clue   (C) hire   (D) hide

7. If you are applying for a job, you need to send your _____ and autobiography.

   (A) realization   (B) repentance   (C) resume   (D) requirement

8. Jim decided to join the _____ after high school rather than going to college.

   (A) market   (B) workforce   (C) fair   (D) exhibition

9. A _____ force was assigned to rescue the victims in the war zone.

   (A) work   (B) task   (C) job   (D) business

10. To know more about the candidate, the _____ asked him a few personal questions.

    (A) interviewer (B) supplier (C) buyer (D) performer

11. You can call on me on either Friday or Saturday; I'm _____.

    (A) deductible (B) flexible (C) determinable (D) indispensable

12. An employer has the right to dismiss an employee during _____ for unsuitability.

    (A) interview (B) employment (C) probation (D) suspension

13. Email is the most popular form of office _____ today.

    (A) skill (B) challenge (C) experience (D) communication

14. The secretary was fired; the manager considered her _____.

    (A) extraordinary (B) extra (C) insufficient (D) incompetent

15. Alan has worked here for five years. He wants to ask his manager for a _____ next month.

    (A) promotion (B) respect (C) resignation (D) leadership

16. You take up a(n) _____ with a certain organization when you start a job there.

    (A) celebration (B) election (C) position (D) application

17. Make no more complaints. All the losses you suffered have been _____ for.

    (A) depended (B) compensated (C) recommended (D) suspended

18. The government's new housing project will _____ a lot of people.

    (A) attempt (B) accept (C) perform (D) benefit

19. The hourly _____ working at a convenience store is around NT$ 100.

    (A) wage (B) increase (C) decrease (D) bill

20. You can improve your _____ by planning in advance and by doing important things first.

    (A) adequacy (B) sufficiency (C) efficiency (D) fluency

Chapter 2
Organization 組織

An organization is a group of individuals with specific roles and responsibilities who collaborate to achieve a common goal. Administration, for example, is essential for managing a company's daily operations. The CEO at the headquarters is responsible for making significant decisions that impact branches, subsidiaries, and franchises, thereby facilitating the company's business growth. Stockholders invest in the company and have the right to vote on major decisions affecting the enterprise.

Chapter 2 Organization 組織

New TOEIC 1200

1　Enterprise 企業 ⑤

使用權　154 **access** [`æksɛs] *n.*

例 Temporary employees do not have **access** to building security codes.
短期僱員沒有大樓安全碼的 access。

稱呼　155 **address** [ə`drɛs] *v.*

例 Our boss insists that we **address** him by his first name.
我們老闆堅持要我們直接 address 他的名字。

行政　156 **administration** [əd͵mɪnə`streʃən] *n.*

例 The **administration** in the company is disorganized.
這家公司的 administration 一塌糊塗。

採取，接納　157 **adopt** [ə`dɑpt] *v.*

例 If we **adopt** a positive attitude, we may be more productive at work.
如果我們 adopt 樂觀的態度，在工作上也許會更具生產力。

建議，忠告　158 **advice** [əd`vaɪs] *n.*

例 Could you give me some **advice** on how to prepare for my interview?
您能否給我一些如何準備面試的 advice 嗎？

159 **against** [əˋgɛnst] *prep.* 　　　　　　反對

☐ 例 There were many employees who were **against** the parking increase.

有許多員工 against 調漲停車費。

160 **allocate** [ˋælə͵ket] *v.* 　　　　　　分配；分派

☐ 例 Each employee is **allocated** a certain number of photocopies.

每個員工都 allocated 一定數量的影印本。

161 **allow** [əˋlaʊ] *v.* 　　　　　　允許，許可

☐ 例 The office employees are **allowed** to smoke on the balcony.

辦公室的員工 allowed 到陽台抽菸。

162 **apprentice** [əˋprɛntɪs] *n.* 　　　　　　學徒，見習生

☐ 例 Our company is open to hiring **apprentices**.

我們公司在徵求 apprentices。

163 **branch** [bræntʃ] *n.* 　　　　　　分公司

☐ 例 The other **branch** has more employees.

其他 branch 僱用的員工人數更多。

164 **build** [bɪld] *v.* 　　　　　　建立；發展

☐ 例 Over the past few years, we have **built** up our clientele.

過去幾年來，我們已經 built 自己的客群。

生意；營業；公司	165	**business** [ˈbɪznɪs] *n.*
	☐ 例	I heard the **business** was in trouble.
	☐	我曾聽說 business 出了問題。
生意人，商人	166	**businessperson** [ˈbɪznɪsˌpɝsn̩] *n.*
	☐ 例	He wants to be a **businessperson**, just like his father.
	☐	他想要成為 businessperson，一如他的父親。
中心，中心點	167	**center** [ˈsɛntɚ] *n.*
	☐ 例	My desk is in the **center** of the office.
	☐	我的辦公桌位在辦公室的 center。
打卡上班	168	**clock in** [ˈklɑk ˈɪn] *v. phr.*
	☐ 例	What time do you usually **clock in**?
	☐	你通常幾點 clock in？
打卡下班	169	**clock out** [ˈklɑk ˈaʊt] *v. phr.*
	☐ 例	I **clocked out** a little early today.
	☐	我今天稍微提早 clocked out。
委員會	170	**committee** [kəˈmɪtɪ] *n.*
	☐ 例	The **committee** will be meeting after work to discuss the staff party.
	☐	Committee 下班後要開會，一起討論職員派對。
公司	171	**company** [ˈkʌmpənɪ] *n.*
	☐ 例	The **company** has been in business for over twenty years.
	☐	這家 company 已經經營二十幾年了。

172 **competitor** [kəmˋpɛtətɚ] *n.*　　競爭者，對手

例 I heard our biggest **competitor** is going out of business.

我聽說我們最大的 competitor 即將要結束營業。

173 **compliance** [kəmˋplaɪəns] *n.*　　遵守

例 We need your company's **compliance** in order for us to continue with the deal.

我們需要貴公司的 compliance，以利繼續這項交易。

174 **comprehensive** [ˌkɑmprɪˋhɛnsɪv] *adj.*　　廣泛的，全面的

例 The document gave new employees a **comprehensive** overview of the company.

這份文件讓新進職員對公司有 comprehensive 概觀。

175 **consider** [kənˋsɪdɚ] *v.*　　考慮

例 The owner of the shop is **considering** whether or not to close his business.

這家店的老闆正 considering 要不要結束營業。

176 **contact** [ˋkɑntækt] *n.*　　人脈

例 Peter has a lot of **contacts** within the industry.

彼得在業界擁有許多 contacts。

177 **council** [ˋkaʊnsl̩] *n.*　　議會；委員會

例 The **council** decided against the plans to expand the office.

council 決定駁回擴建辦公室的計劃。

部門	178 **department** [dɪˋpɑrtmənt] *n.*
	例 The entire **department** was asked to begin dressing more professionally at work.
	整個 department 員工在職場上要開始穿得更專業些。

部門，科，課	179 **division** [dɪˋvɪʒən] *n.*
	例 Tracy works for a small **division** within the company.
	崔西在公司裡一個小小的 division 裡工作。

企業；公司	180 **enterprise** [ˋɛntɚˏpraɪz] *n.*
	例 The product will contribute greatly to the success of our **enterprise**.
	這項產品將帶來巨大貢獻，助我們 enterprise 邁向成功。

建立，確定	181 **establish** [əˋstæblɪʃ] *v.*
	例 We need to **establish** the qualities we are looking for in an employee before conducting interviews.
	在舉行面試之前，我們需要先 establish 想找何種特質的員工。

執行者，主管	182 **executive** [ɪgˋzɛkjʊtɪv] *n.*
	例 The **executives** are having a lunch meeting.
	Executives 正舉行午餐會議。

擴展，擴張	183 **expansion** [ɪkˋspænʃən] *n.*
	例 There are rumors of company **expansion** floating around the office.
	辦公室裡正流傳著公司要 expansion 的傳言。

184 **founder** [ˈfaʊndɚ] *n.* 創辦人

　例　The **founder** of the company gave a speech at the business dinner.
　　　該公司 founder 在商業晚宴上發表演說。

185 **franchise** [ˈfræntʃaɪz] *n.* 加盟店；加盟權

　例　They are opening a new **franchise** in Miami.
　　　他們在邁阿密要開一家新的 franchise。

186 **headquarters** [ˈhɛdˈkwɔrtɚz] *n. pl.* 總部；總公司

　例　Our **headquarters** are downtown.
　　　我們的 headquarters 位於市中心。

187 **in-house** [ˈɪnˌhaʊs] *adj.* 內部的

　例　We will use our **in-house** editor to look over the document.
　　　我們會請公司 in-house 編輯來檢閱文件。

188 **initiate** [ɪˈnɪʃɪˌet] *v.* 開始（一項計畫等）

　例　The company decided to **initiate** a new project last month.
　　　這家公司在上個月決定 initiate 一項新計畫。

189 **operation** [ˌɑpəˈreʃən] *n.* 經營，營運

　例　The company has only been in **operation** for about five years.
　　　這公司的 operation 僅五年左右。

| 機構；組織 | 190 | **organization** [ˌɔrɡənaɪˈzeʃən] *n.* |

例 The **organization** was established over three decades ago.

該 organization 已經成立三十多年之久。

| 人員配置 | 191 | **placement** [ˈplesmənt] *n.* |

例 The **placement** of the intern in our division was a bad decision.

在我們部門中安排實習生 placement，是很糟糕的決定。

| 政策，方針 | 192 | **policy** [ˈpɑləsɪ] *n.* |

例 The **policy** is being revised by the supervisors.

Policy 正在主管的手上進行修改。

| 基本信條，原則 | 193 | **principle** [ˈprɪnsəpl] *n.* |

例 You can be creative as long as you follow company **principles**.

只要好好遵循公司的 principles，你可以盡情發揮創意。

| 改革，改良 | 194 | **reform** [rɪˈfɔrm] *v.* |

例 We have to **reform** the filing system to help us save time.

我們必須 reform 檔案管理系統以便節省時間。

| 資源；資產 | 195 | **resource** [rɪˈsɔrs] *n.* |

例 Employees are the most important **resource** at this company.

員工是本公司最重要的 resource。

196 **significant** [sɪgˋnɪfəkənt] *adj.* 重大的

例 The people who broke into the office did **significant** damage to the staff room.

闖入辦公室的人給教師休息室帶來 significant 破壞。

197 **stockholder** [ˋstɑkˌholdɚ] *n.* 股東

例 **Stockholders** share in the profits of the company.

Stockholders 可以共享公司所獲的盈餘。

198 **staff** [stæf] *n.* 職員

例 Our company has a **staff** of forty-five people.

本公司有四十五位 staff。

199 **subsidiary** [səbˋsɪdɪˌɛrɪ] *n.* 子公司

例 That company is a **subsidiary** of our competitor.

那家公司是同業的 subsidiary。

200 **system** [ˋsɪstəm] *n.* 系統；制度

例 The **system** in place isn't as effective as it could be.

現行的 system 未如預期的有效。

201 **team** [tim] *n.* 團隊

例 Employees should treat each other like members of a **team**.

員工對待彼此應如同一個 team 的成員。

各式各樣的   202 **various** [ˈvɛrɪəs] *adj.*

例 There are **various** ways we can improve organization in the office.

有 various 方式可讓我們來改善公司的組織。

投票，表決   203 **vote** [vot] *v.*

例 Everyone **voted** to go to that restaurant for the annual staff party.

大家 voted 決定好了員工年度聚餐要去那家餐廳。

2 Company Structure 公司架構 (6)

主管，（機構的）管理人   204 **administrator** [ədˈmɪnəˌstretɚ] *n.*

例 Ms Bailey is the **administrator** in our office.

貝立小姐是我們辦公室的 administrator。

助理，助手   205 **assistant** [əˈsɪstənt] *n.*

例 Mr. Roberts is looking for an **assistant** to help him with the administrative work.

羅伯茲先生正徵求 assistant 協助處理行政事務。

查帳員，稽核員   206 **auditor** [ˈɔdɪtɚ] *n.*

例 An **auditor** is coming to examine the company financial records.

有一位 auditor 要來檢視公司的財務紀錄。

老闆，上司   207 **boss** [ˈbɔs] *n.*

例 Our **boss** is in San Francisco on business till next Wednesday.

我們 boss 到舊金山出差了，下週三才回來。

40

208 **CEO** [ˋsiˋiˋo] *n.*　　　　　　　執行長

例 The new **CEO** from England is ready to make big changes in the company.

來自英國的新任 CEO 準備在公司做出重大改革。

209 **chairperson** [ˋtʃɛrˌpɝsn̩] *n.*　（會議或委員會的）主席

例 The **chairperson** asked for everyone's attention.

Chairperson 要在場大家專心聽他發言。

210 **code** [kod] *n.*　　　　　　　密碼

例 Only permanent employees have the security **code** to enter the building.

只有全職員工有進入大樓的安全 code。

211 **colleague** [ˋkɑlig] *n.*　　　　同事

例 My **colleagues** invited me out for a drink after work.

我的 colleagues 邀我下班後喝一杯。

212 **consultant** [kənˋsʌltənt] *n.*　顧問

例 Nick works in our office as an English **consultant**.

尼克在我們公司擔任英文 consultant。

213 **coworker** [ˋkoˌwɝkɚ] *n.*　　同事

例 I usually go for a drink with my **coworkers** on Fridays.

我通常會在週五跟 coworkers 小酌一番。

41

減少，降低	214 **decrease** [dɪˋkris] *v.*
	例 In order to make more profit, we have to **decrease** costs.
	為了要增加利潤，我們得要 decrease 成本。

副經理	215 **deputy manager** [ˋdɛpjətɪˋmænɪdʒɚ] *n.*
	例 Janet has a great chance at being promoted to **deputy manager**.
	珍娜很有機會升為 deputy manager。

工程師，技師	216 **engineer** [ˌɛndʒəˋnɪr] *n.*
	例 The **engineers** work in a separate office from administration.
	Engineers 的辦公室和行政管理部門分開。

全體教師	217 **faculty** [ˋfæk!tɪ] *n.*
	例 The entire **faculty** will have to attend the meeting this afternoon.
	Faculty 都要出席今天下午的會議。

前任的，以前的	218 **former** [ˋfɔrmɚ] *adj.*
	例 The **former** president contributed a lot to the company.
	那位 former 總經理對公司貢獻良多。

總經理	219 **general manager** [ˋdʒɛnərəl ˋmænɪdʒɚ] *n.*
	例 Ellen hopes to be promoted to **general manager** one day.
	艾倫希望有天能當上 general manager。

220 **government** [ˈgʌvə·nmənt] n. 政府
  例 It is said the **government** will increase the tax rate for foreign companies.
  聽說 government 將調升外資公司的稅率。

221 **increase** [ɪnˈkris] v. 增加
  例 Sales have **increased** a lot since last quarter.
  銷售量自上一季以來已 increased 不少。

222 **manager** [ˈmænɪdʒə·] n. 經理
  例 Being a **manager** is not as easy as people think.
  當 manager 不是大家想的那麼簡單。

223 **newcomer** [ˈnjuˌkʌmə·] n. 新來者，新人
  例 Please welcome company **newcomer** Alison to our team.
  請大家歡迎公司的 newcomer 愛麗森加入團隊。

224 **peer** [pɪr] n. 同儕
  例 I find it uncomfortable when I'm asked to evaluate the performance of my **peers**.
  要我評比 peers 的工作表現讓我感到很不自在。

225 **position** [pəˈzɪʃən] n. 職位，職務
  例 What **position** do you hold in the company you are currently working for?
  你在目前任職的公司擔任何種 position？

43

總經理；	226 **president** [ˋprɛzədənt] *n.*
董事長；	例 **Presidents** in large corporations make important decisions on a daily basis.
社長	大企業的 presidents 每天都要做出重大決策。

程式設計師	227 **programmer** [ˋprogræmɚ] *n.*
	例 A computer **programmer** will be at the office this morning to help employees who are experiencing difficulty.
	電腦 programmer 今天早上會到公司協助有困難的員工。

業務人員	228 **salesperson** [ˋselz͵pɝsn̩] *n.*
	例 If you decide to become a **salesperson**, be prepared to work long hours.
	如果你要當 salesperson，就要有長時間工作的心理準備。

秘書	229 **secretary** [ˋsɛkrə͵tɛrɪ] *n.*
	例 Ms. Jones has been Mr. Smith's **secretary** for years.
	瓊斯小姐已經擔任史密斯先生的 secretary 許多年了。

（級別或地位）高的，資深的	230 **senior** [ˋsinjɚ] *adj.*
	例 Nicole is the most **senior** employee in her company.
	妮可是她公司裡最 senior 員工。

231 **supervisor** [ˈsupɚˌvaɪzɚ] *n.* 主管；監督者

例 Nina's **supervisor** doesn't mind when she's late for work.

妮娜的 supervisor 不介意她上班遲到。

232 **typist** [ˈtaɪpɪst] *n.* 打字員

例 Renee was a **typist** before she went back to college.

瑞妮回到校園前的工作是 typist。

233 **vice president** [ˈvaɪsˈprɛzədənt] *n.* 副總經理

例 Everyone is wondering who is going to be promoted to **vice president** of the company.

大家都在猜誰會升到 vice president 的職位。

234 **worker** [ˈwɝkɚ] *n.* 工作者，工人

例 Many **workers** have left the factory since it went under new ownership.

自從這間工廠換東家之後，許多的 workers 都離開了。

Exercises

請將符合字義的單字填入空格。

| executive | staff | division | position |
| secretary | advice | branch | founder |

1. related to managing businesses and making decisions _____.

2. a suggestion about what someone should do _____.

3. a job in a company or organization _____.

4. a group of people who work for an organization _____.

5. someone who establishes a business or organization _____.

6. a smaller office of a company in a different location _____.

7. an assistant who schedules appointments for a boss _____.

8. a department _____.

Review 1

I Photographs (30)

Look at the pictures below and listen to the statements. Then choose the statement that best describes what you see in the picture.

1. (A) (B) (C) (D)   2. (A) (B) (C) (D)

II Conversations (31)

You will hear some conversations between two people. Listen to the conversations and answer the questions below.

Questions 3-5

3. Where is this conversation most likely taking place?
   (A) At a job interview.
   (B) At a resume writing class.
   (C) At Sunray Industries.
   (D) At a print shop.

4. Where does the man learn about the woman's former employer?
   (A) From Sunray Industries.
   (B) From her resume.
   (C) From her project manager.
   (D) From her friends.

5. What was the woman's last job about?
   (A) Taking calls from customers.
   (B) Managing office resources.
   (C) Managing new projects.
   (D) Interviewing new workers.

Questions 6-7

6. What does the man suggest to avoid the traffic jam?
   (A) Leaving at night.
   (B) Being late for the concert.
   (C) Taking a two-week vacation.
   (D) Leaving earlier than planned.

7. Why is it hard for the woman to take Friday off?
   (A) She is about to quit her job.
   (B) Her boss is on vacation.
   (C) Her boss expects everyone to follow the rules for taking leave.
   (D) She has too much work to do.

III Short Talks ㉜

You will hear some short talks given by a single speaker. Listen to the short talks and answer the questions below.

Questions 8-9

8. According to the talk, what should one plan for before an interview?
   (A) Adding experience to your resume.
   (B) Getting the result you want.
   (C) Becoming a better person.
   (D) Being talkative at the interview.

9. According to this talk, how should one answer questions?
   (A) With only the truth.
   (B) However you want.
   (C) With what they want to hear.
   (D) With a "yes" or a "no."

Questions 10-11

10. Which of these statements is NOT true?
    (A) The club only interviewed one candidate.
    (B) Michael used to play baseball for the Bears.
    (C) Michael starts his new job today.
    (D) Everyone in the organization likes Michael.

11. What is said about Michael?
    (A) He has been the manager of the club for the last two years.
    (B) He has a lot of experience.
    (C) He is the president of the team.
    (D) He managed another team.

IV Incomplete Sentences

A word or phrase is missing in each of the sentences below. Four answer choices are given below each sentence. Select the best answer to complete the sentence.

12. This parking lot is for _____ of this building only!
    (A) candidates   (B) opportunities   (C) products   (D) employees

13. Thousands of cancer patients have _____ from the new drug.
    (A) overcame   (B) benefited   (C) interviewed   (D) fulfilled

14. Mr. Parker quit his job and started his own company after his request for a _____ and a pay raise was rejected by his employer.
    (A) promotion   (B) career   (C) resume   (D) performance

15. Thank you for your _____ in this matter.
    (A) career   (B) cooperation   (C) culture   (D) vacation

16. Smith _____ in Singapore two years ago.
    (A) live   (B) lives   (C) lived   (D) living

17. The sunny weather we have been enjoying _____ to stay around for a few more days.
    (A) will   (B) shall   (C) does   (D) is going

18. Mr. Flake bought _____.
   (A) his son a toy car
   (B) a toy car his son
   (C) a toy car to his son
   (D) a toy car at his son

19. I left my glasses in the office _____ I was here earlier.
   (A) or   (B) when   (C) and   (D) which

V Reading Comprehension

In this part, you will read a selection of texts. Each text is followed by several questions. Select the best answer for each question and mark the letter (A), (B), (C), or (D).

Questions 20-21 refer to the following memo.

July 4, 2010
Memo
To: All Employees of State Bank, Downtown Branch

Susan Newman has been promoted to Secretary of the Board of Directors of State Bank. Ms. Newman has been with the bank for more than 10 years. She always exceeds the expectations of her co-workers and managers. Today's promotion is a result of her excellent performance. Please join me in congratulating Ms. Newman.

Matt Weinstein
Manager, Human Resources

20. What is the purpose of this memo?
   (A) To let Susan Newman know that she was promoted.
   (B) To let the Board of Directors know that Susan Newman was promoted.
   (C) To let the employees of the bank know that Susan Newman was promoted.
   (D) To let the employees know that the bank just hired a new secretary.

21. Why was Ms. Newman promoted?

   (A) She has worked for the bank for many years.

   (B) Her managers are very happy with her performance.

   (C) She worked in her last position for ten years.

   (D) The bank wanted to hire a newcomer.

Questions 22-23 refer to the following memo.

Memo: To all department managers
Re: Overtime costs

Because we are trying to keep costs down in the coming winter, all managers need to keep overtime under 70 hours per week. Last winter, our overtime costs were more than we had planned. If overtime hours are more than 70 hours in your department, contact HR immediately and we will give you more staff to help with the work.

If this winter is as busy as last winter, and we can keep costs down, we will all enjoy another successful year!

Thanks,

Don

22. What is the purpose of this memo?

   (A) To hire new employees.

   (B) To work 70 hours a week.

   (C) To thank managers for their hard work.

   (D) To keep overtime costs down.

23. What can you say about this company?

   (A) It is a hotel.

   (B) It is losing money.

   (C) Winter is a busy time of the year.

   (D) It has more than 70 employees.

VI Text Completion

Read the text that follows. A word or phrase is missing in some of the sentences. For each blank, four answer choices are given. Select the best answer to complete the text.

The Daily Gregorian is (24)_____ hard-working, high-energy people to sell subscriptions to our newspaper. The Daily Gregorian has been reporting the news to this area for over 60 years, as well as providing a place for community announcements and advertisements from local businesses.

(25)_____ you have a good personality, you can make money merely by speaking with people about our newspaper. There are two types of (26)_____ – telephone sales and door-to-door sales.

Most people in this community who are not current subscribers have simply let their subscriptions end and are waiting for someone to (27)_____ them and help them to re-subscribe. You could be that person! Send your (28)_____ to **jobs@dailygregorian.com** today!

24. (A) reducing (B) enriching (C) hiring (D) notifying
25. (A) If (B) Yet (C) But (D) And
26. (A) requests (B) positions (C) advancement (D) resources
27. (A) enrich (B) respect (C) attach (D) contact
28. (A) memo (B) resume (C) candidate (D) attachment

Chapter 3
Office Life 辦公室生活

Office life involves the daily business activities and interactions that ensure the workplace operates efficiently. To assist employees in completing their tasks, they are provided with essential supplies and equipment, such as laptops, photocopiers, and stationery. Regular briefings and meetings keep employees informed, with charts often used to present data. When a company expands, it may need to relocate the office to a high-rise building with greater capacity. This offers employees the chance to personalize their workspace, which in turn helps enhance productivity.

Chapter 3 Office Life 辦公室生活

New TOEIC 1200

1 Supplies & Equipment 用品設備 ⑦

熟悉　　　235 **acquainted** [əˋkwentɪd] *adj.*

例 I'm sure the computer program will be easy once I get **acquainted** with it.
我相信一旦我對電腦程式 acquainted 後，它也就不難了。

冷氣機　　236 **air conditioner** [ˋɛr kənˋdɪʃənɚ] *n. phr.*

例 The **air conditioner** runs all day in hot weather.
天氣炎熱時，air conditioner 整天開著。

佈告欄　　237 **bulletin board** [ˋbʊlətn̩ ˌbɔrd] *n. phr.*

例 Please put the information about the parking fee increase on the **bulletin board**.
請在 bulletin board 上張貼停車費漲價的消息。

名片　　　238 **business card** [ˋbɪznɪs ˌkɑrd] *n.*

例 Every employee in the office is provided with **business cards** to give to clients.
公司提供每名員工 business cards，以便能發給客戶。

櫥，櫃　　239 **cabinet** [ˋkæbənɪt] *n.*

例 There is no more room in the **cabinet** to store office supplies.
Cabinet 裡已經沒有多餘的空間存放辦公用品。

240 **calculator** [ˋkælkjəˌletɚ] *n.* 計算機

例 Could I borrow your **calculator** to add up these totals?

我可以借你的 calculator 好合計總數嗎？

241 **cart** [kɑrt] *n.* 手推車，購物車

例 Sheila filled her **cart** with supplies for the office.

席拉在 cart 裡裝滿了辦公用品。

242 **carton** [ˋkɑrtn̩] *n.* 紙箱

例 The **carton** contained damaged merchandise.

Carton 裡放了損壞的商品。

243 **cartridge** [ˋkɑrtrɪdʒ] *n.* （墨水）匣

例 Could you please order a new ink **cartridge** for the printer?

能請您訂購新的列表機墨水 cartridge 嗎？

244 **clipboard** [ˋklɪpˌbɔrd] *n.* 帶夾筆記板

例 Judy attached her paper to a **clipboard** so she could write while standing.

茱蒂把紙夾在 clipboard 上，這樣她才能站著寫字。

245 **computer** [kəmˋpjutɚ] *n.* 電腦

例 My **computer** is too slow to go on the Internet.

我的 computer 上網速度太慢。

Chapter 3 辦公室生活

會議室　　246 **conference room** [ˈkɑnfərəns ˌrum] *n. phr.*

例 The **conference room** can seat up to sixteen people.

這間 conference room 能容納十六個人。

影印機　　247 **copier** [ˈkɑpɪɚ] *n.*

例 Jeffery jammed the **copier** about an hour ago.

傑佛瑞一小時前把 copier 卡紙了。

電線　　248 **cord** [kɔrd] *n.*

例 The printer stopped working because the **cord** was unplugged.

因為 cord 遭拔除，印表機停止了運作。

工商名錄　　249 **directory** [dəˈrɛktərɪ] *n.*

例 The office name could not be located in the **directory**.

Directory 中找不到該公司的名字。

光碟　　250 **disk** [dɪsk] *n.*

例 Robert backed-up his files on a **disk**.

羅伯特將檔案備份在 disk 上。

紀錄片　　251 **documentary** [ˌdɑkjəˈmɛntərɪ] *n.*

例 That **documentary** was shown at the last conference I attended.

我上次參加的會議播放了那部 documentary。

252 **e-mail** [`i͵mel] *n.*　　　　　　　　　電子郵件

□ 例 Please be sure to keep your **e-mails** professional.
□ 　　請務必讓您的 e-mails 顯示專業性。

253 **envelope** [`ɛnvə͵lop] *n.*　　　　　　信封

□ 例 Don't forget to seal the **envelopes** before you
□ 　　mail them.
　　　把信寄出前，別忘了將 envelopes 封好。

254 **environment** [ɪn`vaɪrənmənt] *n.*　　環境

□ 例 We are using recycled paper to help save the
□ 　　**environment**.
　　　我們使用回收紙來幫忙拯救 environment。

255 **equipment** [ɪ`kwɪpmənt] *n.*　　　　設備

□ 例 The **equipment** in the factory is really old.
□ 　　這家工廠的 equipment 非常老舊。

256 **eraser** [ɪ`resɚ] *n.*　　　　　　　　橡皮擦

□ 例 Could I borrow your **eraser**?
□ 　　能借我你的 eraser 嗎？

257 **extension number** [ɪk`stɛnʃən ͵nʌmbɚ] *n. phr.*　　分機號碼

□ 例 Could you please give me Robert Smith's
□ 　　**extension number**?
　　　您能給我羅伯特・史密斯的 extension number
　　　嗎？

| 設施，設備 | 258 **facility** [fəˋsɪlətɪ] *n.*

□ 例 The building's **facilities** include underground parking and a fitness room.
□ 這大樓的 facilities 包括地下停車場以及一間健身房。

傳真 | 259 **fax** [fæks] *v.*

□ 例 The secretary **faxed** the receipt to the client.
□ 該秘書將收據 faxed 給客戶。

檔案 | 260 **file** [faɪl] *n.*

□ 例 The **files** are located in the cabinet behind the water cooler.
□ Files 就放在飲水機後面的櫃子裡。

檔案夾，資料夾 | 261 **folder** [ˋfoldɚ] *n.*

□ 例 I put the information for each client in a separate **folder**.
□ 我把要給每位客戶的資料放在不同的 folder 裡。

家具 | 262 **furniture** [ˋfɝnɪtʃɚ] *n.*

□ 例 The **furniture** in the office is a little outdated.
□ 辦公室裡的 furniture 有些過時了。

硬體 | 263 **hardware** [ˋhɑrdˌwɛr] *n.*

□ 例 My computer **hardware** is a little outdated.
□ 我電腦的 hardware 有些老舊。

264 **headphone** [ˋhɛdˌfon] *n.*   耳機

☐ 例 If you need to listen to audio files in the office,
☐　　 please use **headphones**.
　　 如果您需要在辦公室裡聽音訊檔案，請使用 headphones。

265 **instruction** [ɪnˋstrʌkʃən] *n.*   操作指南，使用說明

☐ 例 The **instructions** were not included in the box.
☐　　 Instructions 並未附在箱子裡。

266 **internal** [ɪnˋtɝnl] *adj.*   內部的

☐ 例 How much **internal** memory does your
☐　　 computer have?
　　 你電腦的 internal 記憶容量為何？

267 **internet** [ˋɪntɚˌnɛt] *n.*   網際網路

☐ 例 Employees are prohibited from surfing the
☐　　 **internet** at work.
　　 員工不得在工作時隨意瀏覽 internet。

268 **laptop** [ˋlæpˌtɑp] *n.*   筆記型電腦

☐ 例 I left my **laptop** on the bus.
☐　　 我把 laptop 忘在公車上了。

269 **letter** [ˋlɛtɚ] *n.*   信，函件

☐ 例 It is faster to send a **letter** by air than by land.
☐　　 空運 letter 比寄陸運還要迅速。

Chapter 3 辦公室生活

59

印有箋頭
（公司行號
名稱地址）
之信紙

270 **letterhead** [ˋlɛtɚˏhɛd] *n.*

☐ 例 Employees are asked to write all letters to clients on company **letterhead**.

公司要求員工一律使用公司的 letterhead 寫信給客戶。

清單，目錄

271 **list** [lɪst] *n.*

☐ 例 Please make a **list** of the office supplies you need.

請將您所需的辦公用品列在 list 上。

標誌

272 **logo** [ˋlogo] *n.*

☐ 例 Our company **logo** is green and black.

本公司的 logo 是綠黑兩色。

郵件

273 **mail** [mel] *n.*

☐ 例 Jason's nephew sorts **mail** in the mail room.

傑森的姪子在郵務室分發 mail。

手冊，指南

274 **manual** [ˋmænjʊəl] *n.*

☐ 例 The **manual** said to let the laptop battery drain completely before recharging.

Manual 寫著要讓筆記型電腦的電池完全耗盡後，才可再次充電。

會議室

275 **meeting room** [ˋmitɪŋ ˏrum] *n. phr.*

☐ 例 Unfortunately, the **meeting room** is already booked.

很遺憾地，meeting room 已經有人預約了。

276 **memo** [ˋmɛmo] *n.* 　　備忘錄

例 The **memo** was sent out to all supervisors and managers within the company.

Memo 已送到公司內部所有主管與經理的手上。

277 **notice** [ˋnotɪs] *v.* 　　注意到

例 If you **notice** me leaving a little early today, it is because I have a doctor's appointment.

如果你 notice 我今天有點早退，那是因為我有預約看醫生。

278 **office** [ˋɔfɪs] *n.* 　　公司，辦公室

例 The **office** is moving to a larger space on another floor of the building.

Office 將搬遷至同棟大樓裡空間較大的樓層。

279 **office supplies** [ˋɔfɪs səˋplaɪz] *n. phr.* 　　辦公用品

例 Please let me know what **office supplies** you need and I will order them for you.

請告知我您所需的 office supplies，我將會為您訂購。

280 **paperwork** [ˋpepɚˏwɝk] *n.* 　　文書工作，書面作業

例 Christine's position requires a lot of **paperwork**.

克莉絲汀的職位需要做很多的 paperwork。

281 **partition** [parˋtɪʃən] *n.* 　　隔板，分隔物

例 Employee desks are separated by **partitions**.

員工的座位都是用 partitions 隔開的。

電話號碼　　282 **phone number** [ˋfon ˌnʌmbɚ] *n. phr.*

例　My **phone number** is on my business card.
我的名片上面有我的 phone number。

影印本　　283 **photocopy** [ˋfotoˌkɑpɪ] *n.*

例　How many **photocopies** do you want me to make?
你要我影印幾份 photocopies？

記事本　　284 **planner** [ˋplænɚ] *n.*

例　I'm not sure when I'm available because I left my **planner** at home.
我不確定我什麼時候有空，因為我把 planner 忘在家裡了。

印表機　　285 **printer** [ˋprɪntɚ] *n.*

例　The printer only **prints** in black and white.
這台 printer 只能列印出黑白兩色。

處理器　　286 **processor** [ˋprɑsɛsɚ] *n.*

例　This computer **processor** is slow and needs to be updated.
這台電腦 processor 太慢了，需要更新。

投影機　　287 **projector** [prəˋdʒɛktɚ] *n.*

例　The **projector** is often used to present data during meetings.
Projector 經常在會議時用來呈現數據資料。

288 **report** [rɪˋpɔrt] *n.*　　　　　　　　　　　報告

　　例　The year-end **report** will be available next week.
　　　　下星期年終 report 將會出爐。

289 **scanner** [ˋskænɚ] *n.*　　　　　　　　　　掃描機

　　例　We only have one **scanner** in the office.
　　　　我們辦公室裡只有一台 scanner。

290 **screen** [skrin] *n.*　　　　　　　　　　　螢幕

　　例　Please turn off your computer **screen** when you are not sitting at your desk.
　　　　離開座位時，請關閉電腦的 screen。

291 **stamp** [stæmp] *n.*　　　　　　　　　　　郵票

　　例　Don't forget to put a **stamp** on each envelope.
　　　　別忘了在每個信封上貼上 stamp。

292 **stationery** [ˋsteʃənˏɛrɪ] *n.*　　　　　　　文具

　　例　Please only use the **stationary** with the new logo.
　　　　請只使用有新標誌的 stationary。

293 **substitute** [ˋsʌbstəˏtjut] *n.*　　　　　　　替代品

　　例　We don't have any sugar **substitute** for the coffee in the staff room.
　　　　我們的員工休息室裡沒有任何咖啡用的糖 substitute（代糖）。

Chapter 3　辦公室生活

打卡鐘，
計時鐘

294 **time clock** [ˋtaɪm ˌklɑk] *n. phr.*

例 Companies depend on the **time clock** to keep track of the hours their employees work.

公司依靠 time clock 來查看職員的上班時間。

語音信箱

295 **voicemail** [ˋvɔɪsˌmel] *n.*

例 I have six messages in my **voicemail** that I haven't listened to yet.

我的 voicemail 裡有六通尚未聽取的留言。

白板

296 **whiteboard** [ˋhwaɪtˌbɔrd] *n.*

例 You can use the **whiteboard** in the conference room during your presentation.

你可使用會議室裡的 whiteboard 進行簡報。

2 At the Office 辦公室 (8)

預約，
見面的約定

297 **appointment** [əˋpɔɪntmənt] *n.*

例 Marianne asked her manager if she could leave a few minutes early so she could attend a doctor's **appointment**.

瑪莉安娜向她的經理要求早退，以便能赴上醫師的 appointment。

安排，整理

298 **arrange** [əˋrendʒ] *v.*

例 Please **arrange** the files alphabetically.

請將檔案按照英文字母的順序來 arrange。

299 **arrangement** [əˋrɛndʒmənt] *n.* 佈置，整理

例 The **arrangement** of these files is confusing.

這些檔案的 arrangement 令人混淆。

300 **aspect** [ˋæspɛkt] *n.* 面向

例 There are a few **aspects** about my position that I like and a few I don't.

我喜歡我這職位的一些 aspects，但也有一些是我不喜歡的。

301 **assemble** [əˋsɛmbl] *v.* 收集，彙集

例 Can you help me **assemble** these handouts?

你能幫我 assemble 這些傳單嗎？

302 **attach** [əˋtætʃ] *v.* 附上，加上

例 Don't forget to **attach** your resume to the email.

請別忘了隨電子郵件 attach 您的履歷表。

303 **categorize** [ˋkætəgəˌraɪz] *v.* 分類

例 Please **categorize** the files according to purpose.

請將檔案按其目的 categorize。

304 **available** [əˋveləbl] *adj.* 有空

例 Are you **available** to meet after lunch?

午餐後你 available 碰個面嗎？

Chapter 3 辦公室生活

65

| 瀏覽，隨便翻閱 | 305 **browse** [braʊz] *v.*
例 I've been **browsing** the classified section for new job opportunities.
我一直以來都在 browsing 分類廣告，找新的工作機會。

| 打電話 | 306 **call** [kɔl] *v.*
例 I took a message and told the client you would **call** her back.
我記下客戶的留言並說你會回 call 給她。

| 來電者 | 307 **caller** [ˋkɔlɚ] *n.*
例 An unknown **caller** left a disrespectful message on the company answering machine.
有個不知名的 caller 在公司的電話答錄機上留下無禮的留言。

| 小心，謹慎 | 308 **caution** [ˋkɔʃən] *n.*
例 Walk with **caution**, the floors have just been mopped.
走路要 caution，地板才剛擦過。

| 手機 | 309 **cell phone** [ˋsɛl ˌfon] *n. phr.*
例 We have a strict no-**cell-phone** policy in the office.
我們公司有個「禁止使用 cell phone」的規定。

| 拿走 | 310 **collect** [kəˋlɛkt] *v.*
例 Please be sure to **collect** all your belongings before leaving the conference room.
離開會議室前，請記得 collect 您所有的隨身物品。

311 **connection** [kə`nɛkʃən] *n.* 　　連接

例 Our office internet **connection** is not working today.
今天我們公司網路的 connection 壞掉了。

312 **consecutive** [kən`sɛkjətɪv] *adj.* 　　連續的，不斷的

例 Julia has been absent for five **consecutive** days.
茱莉亞已經 consecutive 五天缺席了。

313 **conservative** [kən`sɝvətɪv] *adj.* 　　保守的

例 Our boss tends to be very **conservative** with his investments.
我們老闆對於他的投資持非常 conservative 態度。

314 **constructive** [kən`strʌktɪv] *adj.* 　　有建設性的

例 I don't want to hear what you think about my presentation unless it is **constructive**.
我不想聽你對我報告的看法，除非是 constructive。

315 **control** [kən`trol] *v.* 　　控制

例 If you are not in a good mood, it is important to try to **control** yourself at work.
在職場上，心煩時能 control 你的脾氣很重要。

316 **convince** [kən`vɪns] *v.* 　　說服

例 Margret is trying to **convince** me to go to the two-day conference with her.
瑪格麗特正試著 convince 我跟她一起參加為期兩日的會議。

副本	317 **copy** [ˈkɑpɪ] *n.*
	例 Could you please make me twenty **copies** of this document?
	能請你幫我把這份文件印二十份 copies 嗎？

通信，通信聯繫	318 **correspondence** [ˌkɔrəˈspɑndəns] *n.*
	例 I have been maintaining **correspondence** with the CEO since we were introduced years ago.
	自從幾年前我與執行長經人介紹認識後，我們就一直維持 correspondence。

辯論，討論	319 **debate** [dɪˈbet] *v.*
	例 The manager and supervisor **debated** over the length of employee break times.
	經理與主管 debated 關於員工休息時間的長短。

決定	320 **decision** [dɪˈsɪʒən] *n.*
	例 The final **decision** on the project has not yet been made.
	這計畫尚未定下最後的 decision。

宣佈，聲明	321 **declaration** [ˌdɛkləˈreʃən] *n.*
	例 My boss made a **declaration** that she would retire by the end of the year.
	我老闆做了個 declaration，她會在年底退休。

委派；授權	322 **delegate** [ˈdɛləˌget] *v.*
	例 I **delegated** part of my work to Judy.
	我將部份工作 delegated 給茱蒂。

323 **detach** [dɪ`tætʃ] *v.* 分開，分離

例 It is important to **detach** yourself from work related stress when you go home.
回家後，能把自己從工作壓力中 detach 很重要。

324 **dial** [`daɪəl] *v.* 撥（號）

例 I accidentally **dialed** the wrong number.
我不小心 dialed 錯誤的號碼。

325 **digital** [`dɪdʒɪtl] *adj.* 數位（的）

例 I left my new **digital** camera on the bus.
我把新買的 digital 相機遺留在公車上了。

326 **disposal** [dɪ`spozl] *n.* 丟棄；處置

例 Please only use the garbage can for **disposal** of items that cannot be recycled.
此垃圾桶只用於 disposal 不能回收的垃圾。

327 **download** [`daʊn͵lod] *v.* 下載

例 My manager asked me to **download** this program onto her computer.
我的經理要我 download 這程式到她的電腦裡。

328 **election** [ɪ`lɛkʃən] *n.* 選舉

例 An **election** will be held next month.
下個月將舉行 election。

Chapter **3** 辦公室生活

69

裝進，（隨函）附寄	329	**enclose** [ɪn`kloz] *v.*
		例 Don't forget to **enclose** a copy of the invoice in the envelope for the customer.
		別忘了在信封裡 enclose 要給客戶的發票。
執行，實施	330	**enforce** [ɪn`fɔrs] *v.*
		例 We have many rules in the office, but they are rarely **enforced**.
		我們公司有許多規定，卻很少 enforced。
提高	331	**enhance** [ɪn`hæns] *v.*
		例 Could you help me **enhance** the clarity of this image?
		您能幫我 enhance 影像的清晰度嗎？
登記，報名	332	**enroll** [ɪn`rol] *v.*
		例 I **enrolled** in a yoga class to help me de-stress after work.
		我 enrolled 瑜珈課來抒解工作壓力。
註冊／報名人數	333	**enrollment** [ɪn`rolmənt] *n.*
		例 **Enrollment** in the adult swimming class is much higher than last year.
		成人游泳班的 enrollment 比去年成長很多。
外部的，外接的	334	**external** [ɪk`stɝnl] *adj.*
		例 You should back up your files on an **external** hard drive.
		你應該把檔案備份到 external 硬碟。

335 **focus** [ˈfokəs] *v.*　　　　　　　　　集中於，專注於

例　There is too much talking in the office for me to **focus** on my work.

辦公室裡人聲嘈雜，我沒辦法 focus 在工作上。

336 **forward** [ˈfɔrwɚd] *v.*　　　　　　　轉寄；發送

例　Could you please **forward** me the email the manager sent to staff?

能請您將經理發給員工的電子郵件 forward 給我嗎？

337 **highlight** [ˈhaɪˌlaɪt] *v.*　　　　　　強調

例　Our boss **highlighted** a few important ideas we learned at the conference.

我們老闆 highlighted 一些我們在會議上學到的重要概念。

338 **implement** [ˈɪmpləˌmɛnt] *v.*　　　　執行，實施

例　Employees were asked to **implement** the new process immediately.

員工被要求立刻 implement 幾個新步驟。

339 **incoming** [ˈɪnˌkʌmɪŋ] *adj.*　　　　　新來的

例　The **incoming** manager has a lot of experience.

Incoming 經理閱歷豐富。

340 **in regard to** [ɪn rɪˈgɑrd tu] *phr.*　　關於

例　I would like to speak with you **in regard to** your frequent absences from work.

我想跟你談談 in regard to 你時常請假的事。

安裝　　　　341 **install** [ɪn`stɔl] *v.*

例　Could you help me to **install** this software on my computer?
能請您幫我把這軟體 install 到我的電腦上嗎？

留言　　　　342 **leave a message** [`liv ə `mɛsɪdʒ] *v. phr.*

例　If I don't answer my phone, please **leave a message**.
如果我沒有接電話，就請你 leave a message。

提到，提及　343 **mention** [`mɛnʃən] *v.*

例　Don't forget to **mention** the boss when you thank the staff for their hard work.
當你感謝辛勤的工作人員時，別忘了 mention 我們的老闆。

留言　　　　344 **message** [`mɛsɪdʒ] *n.*

例　I had five **messages** waiting for me on my answering machine.
我的電話答錄機裡有五通未聽的 messages。

監控，監督　345 **monitor** [`manətɚ] *v.*

例　Our supervisor **monitors** the work of employees very closely.
我們的主管密切 monitors 員工工作。

建立人脈，
互相交往　　346 **network** [`nɛt͵wɝk] *v.*

例　Conferences offer working professionals a great opportunity to **network**.
研討會提供在職的專業人員 network 的絕佳機會。

72

347 **note** [not] *n.*   筆記

　　例 Please take **note** of anything you think should be shared at the next meeting.

　　請寫 note 記下任何你覺得應該在下次會議裡分享的事情。

348 **online** [ˌɑn`laɪn] *adv.*   連線，在線上

　　例 Employees should not chat with their friends **online** during work hours.

　　員工不應在工作時間 online 跟朋友聊天。

349 **opinion** [ə`pɪnjən] *n.*   意見

　　例 What is your **opinion** of the new company logo?

　　你對公司的新標誌有何 opinion？

350 **path** [pæθ] *n.*   路徑，途徑

　　例 My supervisor told me I was on the right **path** with my work.

　　我的主管跟我說我的工作正走在正確的 path 上。

351 **plug** [plʌg] *v.*   插上，接通電源

　　例 Could you help me **plug** my computer in?

　　您能幫我把電腦 plug 嗎？

352 **post** [post] *v.*   張貼

　　例 Could you please **post** the details of the workshop on the bulletin board?

　　能麻煩您在佈告欄上 post 研討會的細節嗎？

列印　　　353 **print** [prɪnt] v.

　　　　　☐　例　I **printed** two copies of the document.
　　　　　☐　　　我 printed 了兩份文件。

確認；重申　354 **reaffirm** [ˌriəˋfɝm] v.

　　　　　☐　例　I called the client back to **reaffirm** the details.
　　　　　☐　　　我回電給客戶，reaffirm 細節部分。

收到　　　355 **receive** [rɪˋsiv] v.

　　　　　☐　例　I haven't **received** the parcel you sent last week.
　　　　　☐　　　我還沒 received 你上星期寄出的包裹。

認可，認出　356 **recognize** [ˋrɛkəɡˌnaɪz] v.

　　　　　☐　例　I hope that people **recognize** our involvement in
　　　　　☐　　　this charity.
　　　　　　　　我希望人們能 recognize 我們在這場賑濟上的貢
　　　　　　　　獻。

回收利用　357 **recycle** [riˋsaɪk!] v.

　　　　　☐　例　Please **recycle** all scrap paper in the office.
　　　　　☐　　　請將辦公室裡的廢紙 recycle。

參考，參照　358 **refer to** [rɪˋfɝ tu] v.

　　　　　☐　例　If you aren't sure how to assemble the shelf,
　　　　　☐　　　**refer to** the manual.
　　　　　　　　如果你不確定要怎麼組裝架子，那就 refer to 說明
　　　　　　　　書吧。

359 **reminder** [rɪˋmaɪndɚ] *n.*　　　　　　　　提醒函

例 Employees were sent a **reminder** to turn off their computers at night.

員工們都收到 reminder，提醒晚上電腦都要關機。

360 **replace** [rɪˋples] *v.*　　　　　　　　更換

例 The batteries in my camera need to be **replaced**.

我相機裡的電池需要 replaced。

361 **reply** [rɪˋplaɪ] *n.*　　　　　　　　回覆

例 I am waiting for the client's **reply** to my email.

我在等客戶對我電子郵件的 reply。

362 **response** [rɪˋspɑns] *n.*　　　　　　　　回覆

例 I accepted the proposal in my email **response**.

我在電子郵件的 response 裡接受了提議。

363 **restriction** [rɪˋstrɪkʃən] *n.*　　　　　　　　限制，約束

例 Staff members are under many **restrictions** while in the office.

在公司裡，職員受到許多 restrictions。

364 **rule** [rul] *n.*　　　　　　　　規定，章程

例 There are no official **rules** in the office.

辦公室裡沒有正式的 rules。

75

（傳）送　　365 **run** [rʌn] *v.*

☐　例 Could you please **run** these papers to the human
☐　　 resources department?

　　　能麻煩您把這些文件 run 到人力資源部門嗎？

掃描　　　366 **scan** [skæn] *v.*

☐　例 My client asked me to **scan** the receipt and email
☐　　 it to him.

　　　我的客戶要求我 scan 收據並以電子郵件寄給他。

監督，管理　367 **supervisory** [ˌsupɚˋvaɪzərɪ] *adj.*

☐　例 Employees in **supervisory** positions need to go
☐　　 through extensive training.

　　　在 supervisory 職位的員工需要經過充份的訓練。

舉行；發生　368 **take place** [ˋtekˋples] *v. phr.*

☐　例 When will the next meeting **take place**?
☐　　下次會議將於何時 take place？

內文，文字　369 **text** [tɛkst] *n.*

☐　例 Please read the **text** carefully before sending.
☐　　在寄出前，請仔細閱讀 text。

分析解決　　370 **troubleshoot** [ˋtrʌblˌʃut] *v.*
（問題）

☐　例 After **troubleshooting** the problem, Jim gave up
☐　　 trying to find a solution.

　　　在 troubleshooting 後，吉姆就放棄了尋找解決方
　　　案。

371 **update** [`ʌpdet] *n.*　更新；最新訊息

例 My manager likes to receive regular **updates** on the progress of the project.

我的經理喜歡按時收到案子進度的 updates。

372 **website** [`wɛb͵saɪt] *n.*　網站，網頁

例 The company **website** was designed by the boss's son.

公司的 website 是老闆的兒子所設計的。

3　Meeting & Presentation 會議與簡報 9

373 **advance** [əd`væns] *adj.*　預先的

例 We always have meetings without **advance** notice.

我們每次開會都不會收到 advance 通知。

374 **afterward** [`æftəwəd] *adv.*　之後，後來

例 We are planning on going to the conference and then going for dinner **afterward**.

我們計畫出席會議，afterward 再去吃晚餐。

375 **agenda** [ə`dʒɛndə] *n.*　記事簿；議程

例 Patricia wrote the meeting time in her **agenda**.

派翠西亞在她的 agenda 上寫下開會的時間。

376 **agreement** [ə`grimənt] *n.*　同意書，協議書

例 Henry signed the **agreement** after the meeting.

亨利在會議後簽下了 agreement。

替代的，可供選擇的	377 **alternative** [ɔl`tɝ·nətɪv] *adj.*
	例 Maybe there is an **alternative** solution to the problem.
	也許會有解決這問題的 alternative 方案。

宣佈，發表	378 **announce** [ə`naʊns] *v.*
	例 My boss **announced** his plans to retire this afternoon.
	今天下午，我老闆 announced 他的退休計畫。

宣佈，通知	379 **announcement** [ə`naʊnsmənt] *n.*
	例 An emergency **announcement** was made over the speaker system.
	一項緊急的 announcement 透過廣播系統發佈。

掌聲	380 **applause** [ə`plɔz] *n.*
	例 Please hold your **applause** until the end of the speech.
	請將你們的 applause 留待至演說的尾聲。

爭吵，爭論	381 **argue** [`argjʊ] *v.*
	例 It is rude to **argue** in front of guests.
	在賓客面前 argue 是沒禮貌的。

注意	382 **attention** [ə`tɛnʃən] *n.*
	例 It was brought to my **attention** that you have been late 3 days this week.
	你這星期已經遲到三天，引起了我的 attention。

383 **attn** *n. (abbr.)* 　注意（attention 的縮寫）

例 The fax that came in this morning read, "**attn**: all staff members."

今天早上進來的傳真上面寫著：「attn：所有職員」。

384 **brief** [brif] *adj.* 　短暫的；簡短的

例 I hope the staff meeting is **brief**.

我希望員工會議 brief 就好。

385 **briefing** [ˋbrifɪŋ] *n.* 　簡報

例 The manager gave us a **briefing** on our new clients before the meeting began.

在會議開始前，經理就為我們做了新客戶的 briefing。

386 **chart** [tʃart] *n.* 　圖表

例 The manager used many **charts** throughout his presentation.

經理在整個報告中大量使用 charts。

387 **comment** [ˋkɑmənt] *v.* 　評論，發表意見

例 Frank asked us to **comment** on the quality of his presentation.

法蘭克請我們 comment 他簡報的品質。

388 **conclusion** [kənˋkluʒən] *n.* 　結論，決定

例 I've come to the **conclusion** that I am not suited for this position.

我下了一個 conclusion，我不適合這個工作。

Chapter 3 辦公室生活

79

同意，贊成　389 **concur** [kənˋkɝ] *v.*

例 James **concurred** with the boss's opinion.
詹姆士 concurred 他老闆的意見。

主持；帶領　390 **conduct** [kənˋdʌkt] *v.*

例 Sarah is not comfortable **conducting** meetings.
莎拉對於要 conducting 會議感到不自在。

商談，協商　391 **confer** [kənˋfɝ] *v.*

例 The manager needed to **confer** with the CEO before making a decision.
經理需要先與執行長 confer 才能做出決定。

（正式）會議　392 **conference** [ˋkɑnfərəns] *n.*

例 The **conference** is held at the same location every year.
每年的 conference 都在相同的地點舉行。

有信心　393 **confident** [ˋkɑnfədənt] *adj.*

例 Michelle is **confident** about the proposal she will be presenting at tomorrow's meeting.
蜜雪兒對於要在明天會議中提出的提案很 confident。

集會，代表大會　394 **congress** [ˋkɑŋgrəs] *n.*

例 I'm going to attend the **congress** of our representatives from across the country this afternoon.
今天下午我將出席一場全國公司代表 congress。

80

395 **consensus** [kən`sɛnsəs] *n.* 共識

例 We have come to a **consensus** that the department needs to be reorganized.
我們已達成 consensus，要重新打理那個部門。

396 **convention** [kən`vɛnʃən] *n.* 會議，大會

例 The **convention** was cancelled this year.
今年的 convention 取消了。

397 **disapproval** [ˌdɪsə`pruvl] *n.* 不贊成

例 Our boss expressed her **disapproval** of the project at the last meeting.
我們老闆在上回會議中對這企劃案表示 disapproval。

398 **discipline** [`dɪsəplɪn] *n.* 紀律

例 If you are going to work from home, you have to have a lot of **discipline**.
如果你打算在家工作，你就必須建立許多 discipline。

399 **discuss** [dɪ`skʌs] *v.* 討論

例 My supervisor told me that she had some items she wanted to **discuss** with me.
我主管說她要跟我 discuss 一些事項。

400 **inquire** [ɪn`kwaɪr] *v.* 詢問

例 I will contact the hotel to **inquire** about the fees for booking the conference room.
我會聯絡飯店 inquire 預定會議室的費用。

中斷，打斷	401 **interrupt** [ˌɪntəˈrʌpt] *v.*
	☐ 例 The meeting was **interrupted** by the fire alarm.
	☐ 會議因火災警報而 interrupted。

介紹	402 **introduction** [ˌɪntrəˈdʌkʃən] *n.*
	☐ 例 We will begin the meeting by making some **introductions**.
	☐ 我們的會議將由一些 introductions 開啟序幕。

議題	403 **issue** [ˈɪʃʊ] *n.*
	☐ 例 The most important **issues** should be discussed first.
	☐ 最重要的 issues 應優先討論。

項目	404 **item** [ˈaɪtəm] *n.*
	☐ 例 We have six important **items** on the agenda for the staff meeting.
	☐ 我們議程上有六項重要的 items 要在員工會議上進行討論。

演講，講課	405 **lecture** [ˈlɛktʃɚ] *n.*
	☐ 例 The **lecture** was very informative.
	☐ 這堂 lecture 讓人增廣見聞。

演講者；講師	406 **lecturer** [ˈlɛktʃərɚ] *n.*
	☐ 例 The **lecturer** spoke for almost two hours straight.
	☐ Lecturer 講了幾乎整整兩小時。

407 **lunch meeting** [ˋlʌntʃˌmitɪŋ] *n. phr.* 午餐會議

☐ 例 The **lunch meeting** will be held in the restaurant downstairs.
☐ Lunch meeting 將在樓下的餐廳舉行。

408 **marker** [ˋmɑrkɚ] *n.* 標記；馬克筆

☐ 例 Jill drew on the graph with a green **marker** to indicate the rise in sales.
☐ 吉兒在圖表上以綠色 marker 表示銷售量的上升。

409 **material** [məˋtɪrɪəl] *n.* 素材，資料

☐ 例 The **materials** used in the presentation held the interest of the people at the meeting.
☐ 報告中使用的 materials 抓住與會者的興趣。

410 **meeting** [ˋmitɪŋ] *n.* 會議

☐ 例 The **meeting** will start at 2:30.
☐ Meeting 將於兩點三十分開始。

411 **minute** [ˋmɪnɪt] *n.* 分鐘

☐ 例 How many **minutes** do we have until we can leave the office?
☐ 我們還有多少 minutes 才能離開辦公室？

412 **minutes** [ˋmɪnɪts] *n.* 會議記錄

☐ 例 Our boss was angry that no one took **minutes** at the meeting.
☐ 我們老闆對於沒有人在會議中寫 minutes 非常生氣。

Chapter 3 辦公室生活

83

反對，異議	413 **objection** [əb`dʒɛkʃən] *n.*
	例 Several staff members raised **objections** to the plan.
	好幾個職員對此計畫提出 objections。

對手，對方隊	414 **opposition** [ˌɑpə`zɪʃən] *n.*
	例 The **opposition** leader at the debate spoke first.
	辯論時，opposition 的領隊先發言。

部分	415 **part** [pɑrt] *n.*
	例 Every employee has an important **part** to play in the company.
	公司裡的每個員工都扮演很重要的 part。

參與者	416 **participant** [pɑr`tɪsəpənt] *n.*
	例 How many **participants** will be at the workshop tomorrow?
	明天的專題研討會將會有多少 participants 出席？

出席，在場	417 **presence** [`prɛzn̩s] *n.*
	例 The manager's **presence** made everyone nervous.
	經理的 presence 讓每個人都很緊張。

出席的，在場的	418 **present** [`prɛzn̩t] *adj.*
	例 How many people will be **present** at the meeting?
	有多少人會 present 會議？

84

419 **presentation** [ˌprɛznˈteʃən] *n.* 報告,演示

例 The **presentation** lasted over two hours.
Presentation 進行了兩個小時以上。

420 **proceed** [prəˈsid] *v.* 繼續進行

例 Does anyone have any questions before we **proceed**?
在我們 proceed 之前,有任何人要提出問題嗎?

421 **propose** [prəˈpoz] *v.* 提議,建議

例 I have an idea I would like to **propose** to the boss.
我想向老闆 propose 一個想法。

422 **purpose** [ˈpɝpəs] *n.* 目的

例 The **purpose** of this meeting is to discuss upcoming employee evaluations.
此次會議的 purpose 是要討論即將來臨的員工評鑑。

423 **rearrange** [ˌriəˈrendʒ] *v.* 重新安排

例 Suzanne had to **rearrange** her schedule so she could attend the workshop.
蘇珊必須 rearrange 她的時間表,以便能參加研討會。

424 **reschedule** [riˈskɛdʒʊl] *v.* 重新安排(時間表)

例 I might have to **reschedule** our meeting on Friday to Monday.
我可能必須將我們這週五的會議 reschedule 到下週一。

Chapter 3 辦公室生活

85

研討會；研討班	425 **seminar** [ˈsɛməˌnɑr] *n.*
	例 The **seminar** may be of interest to employees who want a promotion.
	想升職的員工可能會對這 seminar 感興趣。

會議，集會	426 **session** [ˈsɛʃən] *n.*
	例 The **session** will last four to five hours.
	這個 session 將會持續四至五小時。

解決方法	427 **solution** [səˈluʃən] *n.*
	例 Let's have a quick meeting to think of some **solutions** to the problem.
	讓我們簡短開會一下，想想問題的 solutions。

演講者	428 **speaker** [ˈspikɚ] *n.*
	例 One of the **speakers** at the conference is an old classmate of mine.
	會議裡有個 speaker 是我的老同學。

演講	429 **speech** [spitʃ] *n.*
	例 The **speech** given by the speaker was boring.
	這演說者的 speech 著實無趣。

陳述，聲明	430 **statement** [ˈstetmənt] *n.*
	例 Our boss made some rude **statements** at our last meeting.
	我們老闆在上次會議裡說了些不禮貌的 statements。

431 **subject** [ˋsʌbdʒɪkt] *n.* 主題

例 What is the **subject** of debate between John and Maria?

約翰與瑪麗亞在辯論什麼 subject？

432 **subscribe** [səbˋskraɪb] *v.* 同意，認同

例 I don't **subscribe** to the same beliefs as the boss.

我不 subscribe 老闆的信念。

433 **summary** [ˋsʌmərɪ] *n.* 概要，概述

例 Could you please give me a **summary** of what happened at the meeting I missed yesterday?

能否麻煩您提供一份會議 summary，昨天的會議我沒出席。

434 **teleconference** [ˋtɛləˏkɑnfərəns] *n.* 遠距會議

例 I was asked to join the **teleconference** with our overseas clients this morning.

我們海外客戶要求我加入今早的 teleconference。

435 **topic** [ˋtɑpɪk] *n.* 主題

例 The main **topic** of the meeting was the new parking fees.

會議的首要 topic 是新的停車費率。

436 **videoconference** [ˋvɪdɪoˏkɑnfərəns] *n.* 視訊會議

例 We have regular **videoconferences** with our overseas clients.

我們與海外客戶定期會進行 videoconferences。

Chapter 3 辦公室生活

87

觀點，見解	437	**viewpoint** [`vju͵pɔɪnt] *n.*
		例 You have to see the details in the document from different **viewpoints**.
		你必須從不同的 viewpoints 看文件裡的細節。
研討會	438	**workshop** [`wɝk͵ʃɑp] *n.*
		例 Are you attending the **workshop** next week?
		你會參加下星期舉辦的 workshop 嗎？

4　Building　建築物 ⑩

建築	439	**architecture** [`ɑrkɪ͵tɛktʃɚ] *n.*
		例 The firm is looking to move to an office building with a more modern style of **architecture**.
		該公司打算搬到較現代 architecture 的辦公室。
檔案室	440	**archives** [`ɑrkaɪvz] *n.*
		例 All the old issues of our catalog are stored in the **archives**.
		所有過季的目錄都存放在 archives 裡。
街區	441	**block** [blɑk] *n.*
		例 The company headquarters is only two **blocks** from the train station.
		公司總部離火車站只有兩個 blocks。
建築（業）者，營造商	442	**builder** [`bɪldɚ] *n.*
		例 Our boss is disappointed with the **builder** because the project is two months behind schedule.
		我們老闆對 builder 不滿，因為工程落後兩個月。

443 **capacity** [kəˋpæsətɪ] *n.*　　容量
　　例 Please do not exceed the elevator **capacity**.
　　　　請勿超過電梯所能負載的 capacity。

444 **centimeter** [ˋsɛntə͵mitɚ] *n.*　　公分，厘米
　　例 The doorways were built two **centimeters** lower than the original plans.
　　　　這門口做得比原施工圖低了兩 centimeters。

445 **chamber** [ˋtʃembɚ] *n.*　　室，房間
　　例 The formula for our company's best selling product is stored in a secret **chamber** in the office.
　　　　我們公司最暢銷產品的配方就放在公司某個祕密的 chamber 裡。

446 **construction** [kənˋstrʌkʃən] *n.*　　建築，建造，工程
　　例 If the **construction** on the new building doesn't speed up, we won't be able to move until the spring.
　　　　假如新大樓的 construction 速度再不加快些，我們將無法在來年春天前搬遷。

447 **contractor** [ˋkɑntræktɚ] *n.*　　（工程）承包人
　　例 The **contractor** told us the job would be done ahead of schedule.
　　　　Contractor 告訴我們工程將會提前完工。

448 **corridor** [ˋkɔrɪdɚ] *n.*　　走廊，迴廊
　　例 We decided on an open-concept office space, and eliminated the need for **corridors**.
　　　　我們決定採用開放的辦公空間，省去需留給 corridors 的空間。

Chapter 3 辦公室生活

89

窗簾　　449　**curtain** [ˋkɝtn̩] *n.*

　　　　　　例　Employees were asked to close the **curtains** in the summer to keep the office space cool.
　　　　　　　　夏季時，公司要求員工緊閉 curtains，以便維持涼爽的辦公空間。

訂金　　450　**deposit** [dɪˋpɑzɪt] *n.*

　　　　　　例　The real estate agent advised us to enclose a ten percent **deposit** with our offer.
　　　　　　　　房仲建議我們在開價外附上百分之十的 deposit。

拆毀　　451　**destroy** [dɪˋstrɔɪ] *v.*

　　　　　　例　The company plans to **destroy** the building that is currently on the property they purchased.
　　　　　　　　公司計畫 destroy 所購入土地上的現存建物。

不利，缺點　452　**disadvantage** [͵dɪsədˋvæntɪdʒ] *n.*

　　　　　　例　It would be a huge **disadvantage** to our clients if we cannot find a more convenient location.
　　　　　　　　如我們無法找到更便利的地點，將會對我們的客戶非常 disadvantage。

電扶梯　453　**escalator** [ˋɛskə͵letɚ] *n.*

　　　　　　例　The **escalator** must be in good working order when the property is sold.
　　　　　　　　出售該房產時，escalator 必須運作良好。

出口　　454　**exit** [ˋɛgzɪt] *n.*

　　　　　　例　The **exits** are located at the end of the hallway.
　　　　　　　　走道的盡頭就是 exits。

455 **expand** [ɪk`spænd] *v.*   擴展，擴充

例 The office space is large enough to allow us to **expand** over the next few years.

這辦公室大到能容納我們往後數年 expand 之用。

456 **floor plan** [`flɔr ˌplæn] *n. phr.*   樓層平面圖

例 The **floor plan** will allow for every employee to have a view of the city from their desk.

Floor plan 將顧及到每位員工，從他們的位子就能看到外面市區的景色。

457 **flooring** [`flɔrɪŋ] *n.*   （總稱）室內地面／地板

例 Replacing the carpet **flooring** will be a big expense.

換掉鋪地毯的 flooring 將會是一大筆開銷。

458 **furnish** [`fɝnɪʃ] *v.*   給（房間）配置（家具等）

例 How much do you think it will cost to **furnish** the staff room with a sofa and table?

你覺得買張沙發跟桌子來 furnish 員工休息室要花多少錢？

459 **gas** [gæs] *n.*   瓦斯

例 The heating system of this building was recently changed from electric to **gas**.

這棟大樓最近才從電力暖氣換成 gas 暖氣。

460 **heater** [`hitɚ] *n.*   暖氣

例 There are **heaters** in every room of the office.

公司裡的每間辦公室都有 heaters。

Chapter 3 辦公室生活

91

高度	461	**height** [haɪt] *n.*
		例 The **height** of the storage area is perfect for tall shelving units.
		儲藏室的 height 正適合放高的層架。
高樓	462	**high-rise** [ˋhaɪ͵raɪz] *n.*
		例 The top floor of the **high-rise** went on the market today.
		這棟 high-rise 的頂樓樓層於今日公開銷售。
室內	463	**interior** [ɪnˋtɪrɪɚ] *n.*
		例 The outside of the building is in great condition, but the **interior** needs some work.
		大樓的外觀狀況絕佳，但 interior 則需要整修。
室內設計	464	**interior design** [ɪnˋtɪrɪɚ dɪ͵zaɪn] *n.*
		例 I got some great ideas for our new office color scheme in an **interior design** magazine.
		我從 interior design 雜誌中找新辦公室配色的靈感。
照明	465	**lighting** [ˋlaɪtɪŋ] *n.*
		例 The **lighting** fixtures in the staff washroom will need to be replaced before this place is put on the market.
		在公開銷售此房產前，得先更換員工專用洗手間裡的 lighting 設備。
地段，地點	466	**location** [loˋkeʃən] *n.*
		例 If the **location** were more convenient, we would be interested in purchasing the property.
		如果 location 可以更便利些，我們就會有意願購買這件房產。

467 **measurement** [ˋmɛʒɚmənt] *n.*　尺寸，大小

例　The total **measurement** of the floor space is 2000 square feet.

總樓層的 measurement 為 2000 平方英尺。

468 **neighborhood** [ˋnebɚˏhʊd] *n.*　附近，鄰近地區

例　There are five comparable properties available in the same **neighborhood**.

在這 neighborhood 擁有相似條件的待售房產就有五件。

469 **next door** [ˋnɛkst ˋdɔr] *adv. phr.*　隔壁

例　There is a great hotel right **next door** for clients visiting from out of town.

Next door 就有一家大飯店可供外地客戶拜訪時住宿。

470 **plumber** [ˋplʌmɚ] *n.*　水管工

例　I would like to have a qualified **plumber** do an inspection of the plumbing as a condition of the offer.

我想找位擁有專業證照的 plumber，請他就檢查房屋的水管報價。

471 **quality** [ˋkwɑlətɪ] *n.*　品質

例　The construction materials were all top **quality**.

用於工程的建材全都是頂級 quality 的建材。

472 **relocate** [riˋloket] *v.*　重新安置

例　Our office is **relocating** at the end of the month.

我們辦公室月底即將要 relocating。

樓梯 | 473 **staircase** [ˈstɛrˌkes] *n.*

例 We should take the **staircase** instead of the elevator.
我們應該走 staircase 上樓，而不是搭電梯。

（房屋的）樓層 | 474 **story** [ˈstɔrɪ] *n.*

例 Our new client is looking for a two-**story** office space.
我們新客戶正在尋找兩層 story 的辦公室。

結構 | 475 **structure** [ˈstrʌktʃɚ] *n.*

例 The property inspector informed us that the **structure** of the building was weak.
房產的建築檢查員告知我們房子的 structure 有些脆弱。

環境 | 476 **surroundings** [səˈraʊndɪŋz] *n.*

例 Mr. Henderson wants to move the office to a building with greener **surroundings**.
韓德森先生想將辦公室搬到 surroundings 更為綠化的大樓裡。

地下的 | 477 **underground** [ˈʌndɚˈgraʊnd] *adj.*

例 The building offers **underground** parking.
本大樓附設 underground 停車場。

（電力、瓦斯等）公用事業設施 | 478 **utility** [juˈtɪlətɪ] *n.*

例 The fee includes all **utilities**.
本費用已包含所有的 utilities。

94

Exercises

請從選項中，選出最適當的答案完成句子。

1. The new regulation took effect after all the members _____. From then on , all the company employees had to observe it.

    (A) condensed (B) contended (C) concerned (D) concurred

2. This trail is the only _____ to the remote village in the mountains.

    (A) method (B) access (C) solution (D) outcome

3. That man must be from Georgia; he speaks with a heavy southern _____.

    (A) pronunciation (B) tone (C) accent (D) sound

4. Taiwan lacks natural _____; all the gasoline is imported.

    (A) coals (B) surroundings (C) resources (D) sources

5. I'm not _____ with the man; he is a stranger to me.

    (A) accustomed (B) acquainted (C) acquired (D) acknowledged

6. If I don't take the chance, what _____ do I have?

    (A) alternatives (B) possibilities (C) probabilities (D) opportunities

7. When the performance was over, the dancers received loud _____ from the audience.

    (A) approval (B) annoyance (C) disturbance (D) applause

8. After a lengthy discussion, they still couldn't reach a _____ whether to increase their investment or not.

    (A) notion (B) destination (C) conclusion (D) portion

9. When I met my cousin at the airport, I could hardly _____ her because I hadn't seen her for years.

    (A) recognize (B) distinguish (C) paralyze (D) analyze

10. The committee members were given a(n) _____ regarding the financial status of the company.

    (A) abstract (B) realization (C) procrastination (D) briefing

11. Give me some _____. Tell me what you think about my presentation.

    (A) establishments (B) comments (C) remarks (D) reminders

12. There was a message on my _____ telling me my rent was due in two days.

    (A) voicemail (B) vent (C) space (D) trade

13. There will be three candidates _____ for the presidency this time.

    (A) accounting (B) campaigning (C) activating (D) stimulating

14. Please fill the tank to _____; we have a long way to go.

    (A) density (B) necessity (C) capacity (D) ability

15. If you deposit or withdraw money from a bank, you have a _____ with the bank.

    (A) transparency (B) transaction (C) transportation (D) interaction

16. Jason's hobby is music. He has _____ over ten thousand music CDs.

    (A) suspected (B) applied (C) assumed (D) collected

17. The roads are slippery due to the rain. Please drive with _____.

    (A) caution (B) tension (C) sensation (D) pretension

18. To use this computer, you have to enter a _____.

    (A) passport (B) password (C) puzzle (D) riddle

19. Just follow the _____ described in the manual, and you will be able to assemble the machine.

    (A) proposals (B) productions (C) procedures (D) purposes

20. In writing an essay, a(n) _____ is needed. But, make it brief, and present your main points right after that.

    (A) proportion (B) introduction (C) summarization (D) development

Chapter 4
Sales & Marketing
業務行銷

Sales and marketing create value by attracting and retaining customers. A successful marketing strategy relies on an understanding of customer needs and current market trends. Companies launch marketing campaigns to boost sales or promote new products. Advertisers utilize tools such as social media, posters, and flyers to help their clients effectively reach their target audience. Together, these strategies enhance the visibility of the merchandise and attract a larger customer base.

Chapter 4 Sales & Marketing
業務行銷

New TOEIC 1200

1 Advertising 廣告 ⑪

消耗，耗費
479 absorb [əb`sɔrb] v.
例 Advertising will **absorb** a huge amount of the budget.
打廣告會 absorb 大筆預算。

登廣告
480 advertise [`ædvɚˌtaɪz] v.
例 Available properties are **advertised** in the classified section of the newspaper.
待售的房地產會 advertised 在報紙的分類廣告上。

廣告
481 advertisement [ˌædvɚ`taɪzmənt] n.
例 We should put an **advertisement** in the newspaper.
我們應該在報紙上登 advertisement。

廣告商
482 advertiser [`ædvɚˌtaɪzɚ] n.
例 We hired an **advertiser** to promote our services.
公司聘請了 advertiser 來宣傳我們的服務。

分配額；配置
483 allocation [ˌælə`keʃən] n.
例 We only have an **allocation** of ten thousand dollars to spend on advertising.
我們只有十萬元的 allocation 可用在廣告上。

484 **ambassador** [æm`bæsədɚ] *n.* 代表；大使

例 The company hired a celebrity to be an **ambassador** for their new line of make-up.

該公司聘請名人當 ambassador，為他們的新化妝品系列代言。

485 **anticipate** [æn`tɪsəˌpet] *v.* 預測；預料

例 The team can **anticipate** sales projections for next year based on this year's sales.

業務團隊能依據今年的銷售額 anticipate 明年度的銷售金額。

486 **booklet** [`bʊkˌlɪt] *n.* 小冊子

例 People are handing out **booklets** about flu prevention on the street.

有人在街上發送預防流感的 booklets。

487 **boost** [bust] *v.* 提高；促進

例 We may be able to **boost** sales if we put more money into advertising.

如果我們刊登更多廣告，或許可以 boost 銷售額。

488 **brand** [brænd] *n.* 品牌，牌子

例 This **brand** is not as popular as it used to be.

這 brand 現在沒有以前那麼受歡迎了。

489 **brochure** [bro`ʃʊr] *n.* 小冊子

例 We recently created a **brochure** to explain the benefits of this skin cream.

我們最近做了一本 brochure 說明這款潤膚霜的好處。

預算	490 **budget** [ˋbʌdʒɪt] *n.*
	例 The marketing team was given a strict **budget** for the promotion of the new clothing line.
	行銷團隊在促銷服飾新品上有嚴格的 budget 限制。

活動	491 **campaign** [kæmˋpen] *n.*
	例 Our new **campaign** will attract more clients.
	我們的新 campaign 將會吸引更多的客戶。

個案，案例	492 **case** [kes] *n.*
	例 That marketing firm has some high-profile **cases**.
	該行銷公司有一些高知名度的 cases。

名人	493 **celebrity** [səˋlɛbrətɪ] *n.*
	例 We need to get a **celebrity** to be the face of our new product.
	我們需要請 celebrity 來代言我們的新產品。

（報紙、雜誌的）專欄	494 **column** [ˋkaləm] *n.*
	例 Our product was mentioned in a newspaper **column**.
	報紙上的 column 裡有提到我們的產品。

專欄作家	495 **columnist** [ˋkaləmnɪst] *n.*
	例 The **columnist** gave our product a great review.
	Columnist 為我們的產品做了個很棒的評論。

496 **commentary** [ˋkɑmən͵tɛrɪ] n.　評論；實況報導

例　The media **commentary** about our new perfume is very positive.

媒體對我們新款香水的 commentary 非常正面。

497 **commercial** [kəˋmɝʃəl] n.　（電視、廣播中的）商業廣告

例　We finished filming the **commercial** yesterday.

我們昨天才剛拍完 commercial。

498 **compose** [kəmˋpoz] v.　創作（詩、樂曲等）

例　We need to hire someone to **compose** a jingle for our new commercial.

我們需要聘人來為新廣告 compose 押韻動聽的廣告詞。

499 **conduct** [kənˋdʌkt] v.　實施

例　After **conducting** the survey we realized there was no market for the product.

在 conducting 市調後，我們才發現這產品根本就沒有市場。

500 **coordinator** [koˋɔrdn͵etɚ] n.　協調員，企劃人員

例　The marketing **coordinator** said we should launch the product before our competitors.

行銷 coordinator 說我們應該搶在對手之前讓產品上市。

501 **develop** [dɪˋvɛləp] v.　發展，開發

例　We need to **develop** a new marketing strategy.

我們需要 develop 新的行銷策略。

101

有效的	502 **effective** [əˋfɛktɪv] *adj.*
	例 We have to come up with an **effective** strategy to promote the product.
	我們必須想個 effective 策略來推銷產品。

藝人，表演者	503 **entertainer** [͵ɛntɚˋtenɚ] *n.*
	例 It is important to secure a popular **entertainer** to help promote our product.
	找到受歡迎的 entertainer 來幫忙促銷我們的產品很重要。

執行，實施	504 **execute** [ˋɛksɪ͵kjut] *v.*
	例 The sales team is **executing** their plan to attract more customers.
	業務團隊正 executing 他們的計畫以求吸引更多的客戶。

（廣告）傳單	505 **flyer** [ˋflaɪɚ] *n.*
	例 The advertisement is being printed on **flyers** and distributed this week.
	廣告已印成 flyers，本週就會發送

募款者；募款活動	506 **fundraiser** [ˋfʌnd͵rezɚ] *n.*
	例 The company donated some merchandise for the **fundraiser**.
	公司為支持 fundraiser 而捐出一些商品。

募款的	507 **fundraising** [ˋfʌnd͵rezɪŋ] *adj.*
	例 The **fundraising** committee asked us for donations.
	Fundraising 委員會要求我們捐款。

508 **influential** [ˌɪnfluˈɛnʃəl] *adj.* 發揮影響

例 The marketing strategy must be **influential** enough to attract new customers.

行銷策略必須能夠 influential 才能吸引新顧客。

509 **invest** [ɪnˈvɛst] *v.* 投資

例 Many people have **invested** in our new business.

許多人已經 invested 我們的新生意。

510 **investigate** [ɪnˈvɛstəˌget] *v.* 調查；研究

例 We need to **investigate** why sales have suddenly dropped.

我們必須 investigate 為什麼銷售額突然下降。

511 **investment** [ɪnˈvɛstmənt] *n.* 投資

例 Our **investment** in the new product has certainly paid off.

我們在新產品上的 investment 確實得到回報。

512 **investor** [ɪnˈvɛstɚ] *n.* 投資人

例 We will have a meeting with **investors** tomorrow afternoon.

我們明天下午將與 investors 一起開會。

513 **layout** [ˈleˌaʊt] *n.* 版面設計，版面編排

例 The **layout** for the new advertisement looks great.

新廣告的 layout 看起來很棒。

傳單	514 **leaflet** [ˋlɪflɪt] *n.*
	例 This **leaflet** explains the benefits of using the product.
	這份 leaflet 說明了使用本產品的好處。

連結	515 **link** [lɪŋk] *n.*
	例 Click on the **link** in this email to visit our website.
	點擊此電子郵件中的 link 便可連結至本公司的網站。

登入	516 **login** [ˋlɑɡ͵ɪn] *v.*
	例 I forgot to **login** to the website.
	我忘記 login 此網站。

媒體	517 **media** [ˋmidɪə] *n.*
	例 We need to get the attention of the **media** to help boost sales.
	我們需要得到 media 的關注，才能增加產品的銷售。

商品，貨品	518 **merchandise** [ˋmɝtʃən͵daɪz] *n.*
	例 The **merchandise** will be shipped from the factory in the morning.
	該 merchandise 上午會從工廠出貨。

新聞播報員	519 **newscaster** [ˋnjuz͵kæstɚ] *n.*
	例 The **newscaster** reported bad news for the economy.
	Newscaster 報導了不利於經濟的壞消息。

520 **newsletter** [ˋnjuz͵lɛtɚ] *n.* （定期發給客戶/員工）簡報，通訊

例 Our sales team was highlighted in the company **newsletter**.
我們的銷售團隊在公司的 newsletter 上成為焦點。

521 **outlet** [ˋaʊt͵lɛt] *n.* 暢貨中心；特賣會

例 Overstock of last year's merchandise is sold at factory **outlets**.
去年過剩的庫存商品在 outlets 販售。

522 **perspective** [pɚˋspɛktɪv] *n.* 看法，觀點

例 The graphic designers had different **perspectives** on the layout for the book.
平面造型設計者對書的版面設計有不同的 perspectives。

523 **poll** [pol] *n.* 民調，民意測驗

例 **Polls** show that most women prefer fruity to floral scents.
Polls 顯示出大多數的女性比較喜歡水果香味，而不是花香。

524 **possibility** [͵pɑsəˋbɪlətɪ] *n.* 可能性

例 There is a **possibility** that I may be promoted if this product line is successful.
如果此系列產品大賣，或許有 possibility 我會升職。

525 **potential** [pəˋtɛnʃəl] *n.* 潛力，潛能

例 I don't believe sales have reached their full **potential**.
我不認為銷售員已經完全發揮他們的 potential。

Chapter 4 業務行銷

105

初步的	526	**preliminary** [prɪˋlɪməˌnɛrɪ] *adj.*
	例	The **preliminary** feedback from clients suggests that we should offer a broader range of services.
		客戶 preliminary 意見反映建議我們應該提供更加寬廣的服務範圍。
報刊	527	**press** [prɛs] *n.*
	例	There hasn't been any mention of our new campaign in the **press**.
		Press 上尚未有任何關於我們新活動的報導。
產品	528	**product** [ˋprɑdʌkt] *n.*
	例	The **product** is sold at numerous locations across the city.
		這款 product 的販售地點遍及本市。
問卷	529	**questionnaire** [ˌkwɛstʃənˋɛr] *n.*
	例	In order to understand customer preferences, we should ask them to fill out a **questionnaire**.
		為了解客戶的喜好，我們應該請客戶填寫 questionnaire。
代言人；發言人	530	**spokesperson** [ˋspoksˌpɝsn̩] *n.*
	例	We need to find a celebrity to be a **spokesperson** for our new product.
		我們需要找個名人來擔任 spokesperson，為我們的新產品代言。
資助，贊助	531	**sponsor** [ˋspɑnsɚ] *v.*
	例	Our company **sponsors** two professional athletes.
		我們公司 sponsors 兩名職業運動選手。

532 **strategy** [ˋstrætədʒɪ] *n.* — 策略

例 The marketing team came up with a brilliant **strategy**.

行銷團隊想到了一個高明的 strategy。

533 **suggest** [səˋdʒɛst] *v.* — 建議，提議

例 Our team leader **suggested** we start targeting a younger clientele.

我們團隊的領導者 suggested 我們開始把目標放在較年輕的顧客群。

534 **survey** [ˋsɝve] *n.* — 調查

例 The customer **survey** showed that most women are willing to pay more for a high-quality product.

顧客 survey 顯示出，大多數的女性願意多付錢買高品質的產品。

535 **target** [ˋtɑrgɪt] *v.* — 把…作為目標

例 We need to **target** single men in this campaign.

此次活動裡我們要 target 單身男人。

536 **trend** [trɛnd] *n.* — 趨勢

例 It is important that all clothing manufactured is in line with current **trends**.

不論製作什麼樣的衣服，符合流行 trends 很重要。

107

2 Marketing 行銷 ⑫

積極的，果敢的

537 **aggressive** [əˋgrɛsɪv] *adj.*

例 You need to be more **aggressive** with your sales strategy.

你的銷售策略需更加 aggressive 一些。

大概的，大約的

538 **approximate** [əˋprɑksəmɪt] *adj.*

例 We need an **approximate** arrival date for the delivery.

我們需要到貨的 approximate 日期。

文章

539 **article** [ˋɑrtɪkl] *n.*

例 One of our products was mentioned in this magazine **article**.

這雜誌裡有篇 article 提到我們其中的一個產品。

評估

540 **assessment** [əˋsɛsmənt] *n.*

例 Following our **assessment**, we decided to double the production.

根據我們的 assessment，我們決定加倍生產。

作者

541 **author** [ˋɔθɚ] *n.*

例 The **author** will be signing copies of her newest book this weekend.

這位 author 將在本周末舉辦新書發表簽名會。

平均

542 **average** [ˋævərɪdʒ] *n.*

例 We sell an **average** of five hundred bottles of shampoo a month at that store.

我們在那間商店 average 一個月賣出五百瓶洗髮精。

543 **circumstance** [ˋsɝ·kəmˌstæns] *n.*   情況，情勢，環境

> 例 Under different **circumstances**, I think the product would have had better success.
>
> 在不同的 circumstances 下，我認為這項產品會更成功。

544 **close down** [ˋkloz ˋdaʊn] *v. phr.*   停業

> 例 If this product is not successful, we will have to **close down** the business.
>
> 如果這產品賣不好，我們公司將必須 close down。

545 **collaborate** [kəˋlæbəˌret] *v.*   合作；共同工作

> 例 The two teams stayed at the office until 10 pm **collaborating** on the new project.
>
> 直到晚上十點，兩團隊都還留在辦公室 collaborating 新的企劃案。

546 **commerce** [ˋkɑmɝs] *n.*   商業；貿易

> 例 International **commerce** is unstable at the moment.
>
> 國際 commerce 目前很不穩定。

547 **compete** [kəmˋpit] *v.*   競爭

> 例 Our new product will have to **compete** with many other similar products.
>
> 我們的新產品將必須與許多其他類似的產品 compete。

Chapter 4 業務行銷

109

競爭；比賽	548 **competition** [ˌkɑmpəˈtɪʃən] *n.*
	例 Our product is in direct **competition** with a product from another company.
	我們的產品與另一家公司所生產的產品面臨直接的 competition。

結果，因此	549 **consequently** [ˈkɑnsəˌkwɛntlɪ] *adv.*
	例 The product was defective, and **consequently**, all boxes were removed from the shelves.
	由於產品有瑕疵，consequently 全部產品都下架了。

相當大的；相當多的	550 **considerable** [kənˈsɪdərəbl] *adj.*
	例 A **considerable** amount of money was spent on advertizing the product.
	他們花了一筆 considerable 錢在產品廣告上。

消費者	551 **consumer** [kənˈsumɚ] *n.*
	例 **Consumers** will appreciate the low cost of the merchandise.
	Consumers 會喜歡低價的商品。

與…相比	552 **in contrast to** [ɪnˈkɑntræst tu] *phr.*
	例 **In contrast to** our competitor's product, our product comes with a five-year warranty.
	In contrast to 競爭對手的產品，我們的產品多加上五年的保固。

十年	553 **decade** [ˈdɛked] *n.*
	例 Over the past **decade**, we have sold over a million units of this product.
	過去 decade 來，這產品我們賣了超過上百萬組。

554 **decline** [dɪˋklaɪn] *v.*　　　　　　　下降，減少，衰退

　例　Sales have **declined** since last quarter.
　　　銷售額自上一季以來已經 declined。

555 **devise** [dɪˋvaɪz] *v.*　　　　　　　想出；設計

　例　The sales team **devised** a new plan for the product.
　　　銷售團隊為產品 devised 了一個新計畫。

556 **double** [ˋdʌbl] *adv.*　　　　　　　兩倍（地）

　例　We have sold **double** the number of products this month.
　　　我們這個月就已經賣了 double 多的產品。

557 **drop off** [ˋdrɑp ˋɔf] *v. phr.*　　　把⋯順便送過來

　例　They said they would **drop off** the samples in the morning.
　　　他們說早上會把樣品 drop off。

558 **enlarge** [ɪnˋlɑrdʒ] *v.*　　　　　　擴大，擴展

　例　If we **enlarge** the area of the promotion, we will be able to get more customers.
　　　假如我們 enlarge 宣傳區域，就能夠招來更多顧客。

559 **estimate** [ˋɛstəˋmet] *v.*　　　　　估計

　例　The manufacturer **estimated** it would take three days before they would be ready to ship the product.
　　　廠商 estimated 他們需要三天的時間才能把貨備好。

發展；進化	560	**evolve** [ɪ`valv] *v.*
		例 The product has **evolved** a lot over the past two years.
		該產品兩年來已歷經不少 evolved。
獨家（地）	561	**exclusively** [ɪk`sklusɪvlɪ] *adv.*
		例 For the first two months, the product will be sold **exclusively** on-line.
		這產品頭兩個月會在線上 exclusively 販售。
解釋；說明	562	**explain** [ɪk`splen] *v.*
		例 The instructions **explain** how to use the product.
		說明書 explain 如何使用本產品。
爆炸	563	**explode** [ɪk`splod] *v.*
		例 The product cannot be used close to open flames or it will **explode**.
		請勿在靠近開放式火焰處使用本產品，以免發生 explode。
補救；修理	564	**fix** [fɪks] *v.*
		例 If we don't **fix** this error, we may lose clients.
		如果我們不 fix 錯誤，我們可能會失去客戶。
預測，預報	565	**forecast** [`for͵kæst] *n.*
		例 Our financial **forecast** doesn't look very good.
		我們的財務 forecast 看起來不太樂觀。

566 **goal** [gol] *n.* 目標

例 We haven't met our sales **goals** for this quarter.
我們尚未達到本季的銷售 goals。

567 **guidance** [ˋgaɪdn̩s] *n.* 指導，引導

例 I look forward to your **guidance** on how to proceed with the project.
我期待接受您針對本企劃案如何進行的 guidance。

568 **handle** [ˋhændl̩] *v.* 負責，處理

例 Jim is currently **handling** our most important clients.
吉姆目前 handle 我們最重要的客戶群。

569 **implement** [ˋɪmpləˏmɛnt] *v.* 實施；執行

例 We need to **implement** more effective sales strategies for this product.
我們需要 implement 更有效率的銷售策略來銷售產品。

570 **improve** [ɪmˋpruv] *v.* 改善，改進

例 If the sales don't **improve**, we will have to discontinue the product.
假如銷售額沒有 improve，我們將得中斷本產品的銷售。

571 **initial** [ɪˋnɪʃəl] *adj.* 初始的，最初的

例 The **initial** costs to manufacture the product are too high.
製造該產品的 initial 費用太高了。

創新的	572 **innovative** [ˈɪnəˌvetɪv] *adj.*
	例 Our sales team has come up with an **innovative** idea to promote our products.
	我們的銷售團隊想出一個 innovative 的點子來促銷產品。

新聞記者	573 **journalist** [ˈdʒɝnl̩ɪst] *n.*
	例 The **journalist** wanted to do an article on our company.
	Journalist 想要寫篇文章報導我們公司。

把（商品）投入市場；上市	574 **launch** [lɔntʃ] *v.*
	例 The product will be **launched** in the fall.
	產品將於秋季 launched。

當地的，本地的	575 **local** [ˈlokl̩] *adj.*
	例 Our company is being featured on the **local** news tonight.
	今晚 local 新聞將會特別報導我們公司。

損失；虧損	576 **loss** [lɔs] *n.*
	例 We cannot afford to take any **losses** in sales.
	我們無法承擔任何銷售上的 losses。

管理階層，資方	577 **management** [ˈmænɪdʒmənt] *n.*
	例 **Management** will be meeting today to discuss productivity in the office.
	Management 今天將要開會討論辦公室裡的生產力。

578 **market** [ˋmɑrkɪt] *n.* 市場

例 If we want to sell more merchandise, we need to target a younger **market**.
如果我們想要銷售更多的商品，就必須針對年輕族群的 market。

579 **marketing** [ˋmɑrkɪtɪŋ] *n.* 行銷

例 The **marketing** plan is going to cost the company a lot of money.
Marketing 計畫將會讓公司花掉一大筆錢。

580 **merger** [ˋmɝdʒɚ] *n.* （公司等的）合併

例 News of the company **merger** has already hit the media.
公司 merger 的消息已經在媒體上披露。

581 **objective** [əbˋdʒɛktɪv] *n.* 目標；目的

例 Our main **objective** is to promote our services throughout a broader area.
我們的主要 objective 是將服務推廣至更為廣大的地區。

582 **opportunity** [ˌɑpɚˋtjunətɪ] *n.* 機會

例 James was offered an **opportunity** to join the marketing department.
詹姆士得到一個能加入行銷部門的 opportunity。

583 **outline** [ˋaʊtˌlaɪn] *n.* 綱要，概要

例 The **outline** of the project was missing some important details.
計畫的 outline 遺漏了一些重要的細節。

115

概觀；概要	584 **overview** [ˈovɚˌvju] *n.*
	例 An **overview** of our new sales strategy will be presented at the next meeting.
	我們新銷售策略的 overview 將會在下次的會議中呈現。

懸而未決	585 **pending** [ˈpɛndɪŋ] *adj.*
	例 The agreement made with the company is still **pending**.
	與該公司訂下的協議仍然 pending。

百分比	586 **percentage** [pɚˈsɛntɪdʒ] *n.*
	例 The sales team was promised a **percentage** of the profits.
	銷售團隊承諾得到一定 percentage 的獲利。

計畫	587 **plan** [plæn] *n.*
	例 The sales manager said he has a new **plan** for marketing the product.
	業務經理說他有個行銷此產品的新 plan。

主要的	588 **primary** [ˈpraɪˌmɛrɪ] *adj.*
	例 The **primary** reason we haven't sold much product is poor marketing.
	我們產品銷售不佳的 primary 原因是行銷不力。

印刷字體	589 **print** [prɪnt] *n.*
	例 The **print** on the back of the product is too small to read.
	產品後面的 print 太小，看不清楚。

590 **prior to** [ˋpraɪɚ tu] *prep.* 在⋯之前

例 We haven't had overseas clients **prior to** this year.

Prior to 今年，我們從未有過海外客戶。

591 **progression** [prəˋgrɛʃən] *n.* 進程

例 The **progression** of the marketing campaign is slow.

行銷活動的 progression 發展緩慢。

592 **project** [ˋprɑdʒɛkt] *n.* 計畫

例 The **project** is due by the end of the week.

該 project 在這星期結束前就應完成。

593 **promote** [prəˋmot] *v.* 促銷；推廣

例 We need to **promote** our services in a variety of places.

我們需要在各種場合 promote 我們的服務。

594 **proposal** [prəˋpozl] *n.* 建議；方案

例 Our boss didn't like our **proposal** for the sales strategy.

我們老闆並不喜歡我們針對銷售策略所提出的 proposal。

595 **profit** [ˋprɑfɪt] *n.* 利潤

例 If we don't keep our costs down, we won't make a **profit**.

如果我們不繼續維持低成本，我們就無法創造 profit。

Chapter 4 業務行銷

117

有利潤的	596 **profitable** [ˋprɑfɪtabl̩] *adj.*
	例 Online sales can be very **profitable**.
	網路銷售能夠很 profitable。

節目單； 程序表	597 **program** [ˋprogræm] *n.*
	例 Please print a lot of **programs** so we won't run out at the event.
	請大量印製 programs，以免活動中會不夠用。

期望，希望	598 **prospect** [ˋprɑspɛkt] *n.*
	例 The **prospect** of us making a profit on the sale of this merchandise is slim.
	我們對這項商品能獲利的 prospect 是很渺茫的。

說明書， 簡章	599 **prospectus** [prəˋspɛktəs] *n.*
	例 It took the team over three days to prepare a **prospectus**.
	團隊花了三天的時間準備一份 prospectus。

繁榮，昌盛	600 **prosper** [ˋprɑspɚ] *v.*
	例 We hope that our company will continue to **prosper**, even during difficult financial times.
	我們希望公司能繼續 prosper，即使在金融艱困的年代。

季度	601 **quarter** [ˋkwɔrtɚ] *n.*
	例 Sales for the new product rose during the first **quarter**.
	新產品的銷售在第一 quarter 上揚。

602 **quarterly** [ˋkwɔrtɚlɪ] *adv.* 　　　　　　　　　每季

　　例 Overseas sales brings in over two million dollars **quarterly**.
　　Quarterly 海外銷售賺進兩百萬元以上。

603 **reach** [ritʃ] *v.* 　　　　　　　　　　　　　　抵達；達到

　　例 If we want to **reach** a broader clientele, we need to advertise more.
　　如果我們想要 reach 更廣大的客戶群，我們需要更多的廣告宣傳。

604 **remark** [rɪˋmɑrk] *n.* 　　　　　　　　　　　言論，評論

　　例 Customers have made a lot of negative **remarks** about the quality of the product.
　　客戶說了許多有關產品品質方面的負面 remarks。

605 **representative** [͵rɛprɪˋzɛntətɪv] *n.* 　　　　代表

　　例 We should send a senior **representative** from the company to the meeting.
　　我們應該從公司派個資深 representative 去開會。

606 **sale** [sel] *n.* 　　　　　　　　　　　　　　　低價拍賣

　　例 If the products are not selling, perhaps we should have a **sale**.
　　假如產品不暢銷，或許我們應該辦個 sale。

607 **scale** [skel] *n.* 　　　　　　　　　　　　　　規模

　　例 We need to promote the product on a much larger **scale**.
　　我們需要更大 scale 的產品促銷。

刺激，激勵	608	**stimulate** [ˋstɪmjəˌlet] *v.*
		例 The new business policy **stimulated** sales.
		新的經營策略 stimulated 銷售量。
技巧，技術	609	**technique** [tɛkˋnik] *n.*
		例 You will have to teach me your **technique** for getting what you want from the boss!
		你一定要教我你從老闆那予取予求的 technique！
營業額	610	**turnover** [ˋtɝnˌovɚ] *n.*
		例 That store has a high **turnover** of our product.
		我們產品在那家店的 turnover 很高。
（有利可圖/新）風險事業	611	**venture** [ˋvɛntʃɚ] *n.*
		例 The company's new investment is an exciting **venture** for all employees.
		公司的新投資對所有的員工來說是令人興奮的 venture。
富有，有錢	612	**wealthy** [ˋwɛlθɪ] *adj.*
		例 Online sales have made many people **wealthy**.
		網路銷售讓許多人變得 wealthy。

Exercises

請從選項中，選出最適當的答案完成句子。

1. When the army landed on the beaches, they met less resistance than originally _____.
   (A) anticipated   (B) participated   (C) restricted   (D) prepared

2. There is an _____ in the paper about the popularity of Korean soap operas.
   (A) item   (B) article   (C) itinerary   (D) isolation

3. My dad told me that under no _____ should I tell lies.
   (A) elements   (B) surroundings   (C) environment   (D) circumstances

4. While a century is 100 years, a _____ is ten years.
   (A) decade   (B) decay   (C) cavity   (D) décor

5. The method is _____, as can be proven by the progress the students have made.
   (A) affective   (B) effective   (C) influential   (D) infectious

6. Larry's _____ is to be an entertainer—he loves singing, dancing, and acting.
   (A) suspicion   (B) ambition   (C) retention   (D) attention

7. I don't know the theory very well; I can't _____ it to you.
   (A) reason   (B) identify   (C) explain   (D) extend

8. The new system of a 12-year compulsory education will eventually be _____ in Taiwan.
   (A) implanted   (B) substituted   (C) implemented   (D) transplanted

9. Nowadays an _____ person can live to be 70 years old.
   (A) curious   (B) common   (C) average   (D) mean

10. Ann Lee is now a _____ in the movie industry.
    (A) dispute   (B) celebrity   (C) reputation   (D) fame

11. An ad on TV or on the radio is called a _____.

    (A) commercial (B) commencement (C) graduation (D) interruption

12. Rachael _____ a scheme to promote the company's new product.

    (A) projected (B) devised (C) suspected (D) disguised

13. Candidates for the vacancy will be _____ for three months before they are officially hired.

    (A) estimated (B) predicted (C) evaluated (D) calculated

14. The club is _____ for members.

    (A) selectively (B) exclusively (C) extremely (D) intensively

15. The news that Japan was hit by both earthquakes and tsunamis made the _____.

    (A) markets (B) media (C) headlines (D) commerce

16. The police are _____ who committed the murder.

    (A) suspecting (B) detecting (C) surviving (D) investigating

17. Scientists have been _____ experiments to find a cure for cancer.

    (A) conducting (B) surveying (C) seeking (D) searching

18. As we have a very limited _____, we have to spend our money wisely.

    (A) economy (B) budget (C) project (D) scheme

19. Because our products are cheaper and last longer, they have an edge over other _____.

    (A) supervisors (B) clients (C) consumers (D) competitors

20. People who write for newspapers or magazines are called _____.

    (A) journalists (B) manufacturers (C) industrialists (D) tourists

Review 2

I Photographs (33)

Look at the pictures below and listen to the statements. Then choose the statement that best describes what you see in the picture.

1. (A) (B) (C) (D)

2. (A) (B) (C) (D)

II Conversations (34)

You will hear some conversations between two people. Listen to the conversations and answer the questions below.

Questions 3-4

3. How does the woman feel about Claire?
   (A) She is kind.
   (B) She is polite.
   (C) She works very hard.
   (D) She talks too much.

4. What does the woman say she will do?
   (A) Laugh at Claire.
   (B) Apologize to the man.
   (C) Say sorry to Claire.
   (D) Try really hard.

Questions 5-6

5. Why does the man look uneasy?
   - (A) He has caught a cold.
   - (B) He has lost his job.
   - (C) He has an important presentation to make.
   - (D) He has been promoted.

6. Where are the people likely to be?
   - (A) In a banker's office.
   - (B) At a telephone booth.
   - (C) At a police station.
   - (D) On a ferry.

III Short Talks (35)

You will hear some short talks given by a single speaker. Listen to the short talks and answer the questions below.

Questions 7-8

7. What is the main cause of the problem?
   - (A) The office is being repaired.
   - (B) People listen to music at work.
   - (C) Employees talk loudly.
   - (D) The boss yells at his employees.

8. What suggestion has been made?
   - (A) Keep the office tidy.
   - (B) Make more phone calls.
   - (C) Lower the volume on the radio.
   - (D) Walk across the room to talk to people.

Questions 9-10

9. What percentage of lost customers came from the top 25 accounts?
   - (A) 7.5   (B) 15   (C) 25   (D) 50

10. What will they discuss at the meeting?
    (A) A letter from a customer.
    (B) The increasing number of customers.
    (C) How to improve their customer service.
    (D) A birthday party.

IV Incomplete Sentences

A word or phrase is missing in each of the sentences below. Four answer choices are given below each sentence. Select the best answer to complete the sentence.

11. We tried every possible way to _____ you this morning.
    (A) communicate (B) generate   (C) set up   (D) contact
12. Now let's move to the next item on the _____.
    (A) agenda   (B) participant (C) outcome   (D) impact
13. The students worked together to produce a one-act play and performed before a live _____.
    (A) consumer   (B) audience   (C) assignment (D) auditorium
14. Holly is considering _____ her restaurant on the Internet.
    (A) transferring (B) generating (C) advertising (D) delivering
15. Eric _____ in Bangkok from 2003 to 2006.
    (A) lives   (B) lived   (C) living   (D) is living
16. David _____ the sales manager of Sunray Industry for three years.
    (A) is   (B) are   (C) has been   (D) have been
17. Millions of toys are _____ from China every year.
    (A) export   (B) exported   (C) exporting   (D) exports
18. "_____ do you go to the cinema?" "About twice a month."
    (A) How   (B) How many   (C) How much   (D) How often

V Reading Comprehension

In this part, you will read a selection of texts. Each text is followed by several questions. Select the best answer for each question and circle the letter (A), (B), (C), or (D).

Questions 19-21 refer to the following email.

To: MelissaM@hyperark.com

From: Lewislevee@cintron.net

Dear Melissa:
To answer your questions about our cell phone service plans:

— There are no "roaming" charges. Calls made from anywhere in the country are charged at the same rate.
— There is no limit on minutes during weekends. On weekdays, the limit is 300 minutes.
— Call forwarding and voice mail are provided to all customers.

This program is available to you and all your employees when you choose Cintron as your cell phone service provider.
Thank you.
Lewis Levee

19. Where can Cintron customers make cell phone calls?
    (A) Only from home.
    (B) Only within the state.
    (C) Anywhere nationwide.
    (D) On weekdays and weekends.

21. Who can buy the service plan?
    (A) Melissa and her family.
    (B) All customers.
    (C) Melissa and all her employees.
    (D) All of Melissa's employees.

20. How many minutes can a customer use on a Friday?
    (A) There is no limit on Friday.
    (B) Up to 300.
    (C) Up to 250.
    (D) It depends on where the calls are made.

Questions 22-23 refer to the following notice.

What Is Happening In The IT Industry?
A presentation by
Tobias W. Wilson
CEO of Luna Corp.
December 13, 2009
The Hilton Ballroom

Mr. Wilson will talk about the recent developments in the IT industry. He will also discuss the future impact on investors and employees of the IT industry.

The presentation will include:
What do the recent job cuts mean for the future of the IT industry?
How will the job cuts affect other industries?
What are the risks for investors?

We invite business people, investors, or anyone with an interest in the IT industry to attend this event.

22. What will be discussed at this event?
    (A) The risk of investing in the IT industry.
    (B) The increase in employment in the IT industry.
    (C) How to make job cuts.
    (D) The overall history of the IT industry.

23. Who should attend this event?
    (A) IT industry workers who have lost their jobs.
    (B) IT industry employers looking to hire new workers.
    (C) Anyone with an interest in the IT industry.
    (D) People who have invested more than $100,000.

VI Text Completion

Read the text that follows. A word or phrase is missing in some of the sentences. For each blank, four answer choices are given. Select the best answer to complete the text.

Cyril is nervous every time he has to give a presentation. But presentations are an important part of his job. Therefore, Cyril (24)_____ to manage his fear. He always arrives early on the day of a presentation. He checks the (25)_____ , the lights, and the (26)_____. When he is sure that everything is working, he starts to relax.

Cyril is always well-prepared. He prints handouts for the audience. He also uses (27)_____ and pictures to keep his listeners' attention during his presentation. For these reasons, the audience always gives him good (28)_____. Although Cyril is still nervous before a presentation, he has learned to control his fear.

24. (A) has learned (B) have learned (C) learn (D) learns
25. (A) trust (B) tip (C) visual (D) microphone
26. (A) research (B) projector (C) competitor (D) budget
27. (A) windows (B) investment (C) graphs (D) chairperson
28. (A) divided (B) feedback (C) brochure (D) stressful

Chapter 5
Business Trip 商務旅行/出差

Business trips frequently involve air travel. Salespeople often take domestic or international flights to reach their destinations. Upon landing at the airport, the passengers retrieve their luggage from a carousel before proceeding through customs. They may then head to their accommodations to settle in before meeting with their business partners or clients. The fees incurred during these trips are often reimbursed, as they are necessary expenses to secure profitable deals.

Chapter 5　Business Trip
商務旅行/出差

New TOEIC 1200

1　Air Travel 搭飛機 ⑬

午夜至正午，上午
613 **am** [`e`ɛm] *adv.*
　　例　My flight leaves at 1:30 **am**.
　　　　我的班機在 am 一點半起飛。
　　　　• 為拉丁語 ante meridiem 縮寫

在國外
614 **abroad** [ə`brɔd] *adv.*
　　例　We have many clients **abroad**.
　　　　我們 abroad 有許多客戶。

飛機票價
615 **airfare** [`ɛr͵fɛr] *n.*
　　例　How much is the **airfare** to the conference?
　　　　參加那場研討會的 airfare 是多少呢？

航空公司
616 **airline** [`ɛr͵laɪn] *n.*
　　例　Which **airline** are you flying with?
　　　　你搭乘哪家 airline？

飛機
617 **airplane** [`ɛr͵plen] *n.*
　　例　The **airplane** must be inspected before take-off.
　　　　Airplane 必須在起飛前做好檢查。

機場
618 **airport** [`ɛr͵pɔrt] *n.*
　　例　The **airport** is located about 20 minutes from the capital.
　　　　該 airport 距離首都約二十分鐘路程。

619 **aisle seat** [`aɪlˌsit] *n. phr.*　　靠走道的座位

例 I prefer sitting in an **aisle seat**.

坐飛機時，我喜歡坐在 aisle seat。

620 **alert** [ə`lɝt] *v.*　　提醒，警惕

例 The captain **alerted** the passengers that he must make an emergency landing.

機長 alerted 乘客，他必須迫降飛機。

621 **altitude** [`æltəˌtjud] *n.*　　海拔高度

例 Please leave your seat belts on until we reach full **altitude**.

在飛機上升到充分的 altitude 前，請繫好安全帶。

622 **apologize** [ə`pɑləˌdʒaɪz] *v.*　　道歉

例 The flight attendant **apologized** for spilling coffee on the passenger's lap.

空服員因為把咖啡濺到乘客腿上，向對方 apologized。

623 **approximate** [ə`prɑksəmɪt] *adj.*　　大約

例 The captain announced that the **approximate** time to landing was one hour.

機長廣播離降落時間 approximate 還有一小時。

624 **baggage** [`bægɪdʒ] *n.*　　行李

例 We need to pick up our **baggage** after we land.

飛機降落後，我們得去領取 baggage。

行李領取處　625 **baggage claim area** *n. phr.*

例 I think I forgot one of my suitcases in the **baggage claim area**.
我有個手提箱好像在 baggage claim area 忘了拿。

財產，　626 **belongings** [bɪˋlɔŋɪŋz] *n.*
攜帶物品

例 Please be sure not to leave any personal **belongings** on the plane.
請注意別將個人的 belongings 遺留在飛機上。

上，登　627 **board** [bɔrd] *v.*
（船、飛機
等）　　例 The flight will start **boarding** in about ten minutes.
飛機即將在十分鐘內開始 boarding。

登機　　628 **boarding** [ˋbɔrdɪŋ] *n.*

例 The **boarding** process for the flight is very slow.
Boarding 的過程很緩慢。

登機證　629 **boarding pass** [ˋbɔrdɪŋ͵pæs] *n. phr.*

例 Please have your **boarding pass** ready to show the flight attendant.
請將您的 boarding pass 準備好讓空服員檢查。

預約，預訂　630 **book** [bʊk] *v.*

例 I **booked** my flight to Chicago last week.
我上週 booked 去芝加哥的班機。

631 **broadcast** [ˈbrɔdˌkæst] *v.* 播送，廣播

例 Images of the airplane crash were **broadcasted** all over the world.

那場墜機空難的畫面在世界各地 broadcasted。

632 **business trip** [ˈbɪznɪsˌtrɪp] *n.* 出差

例 There are currently five employees away on **business trips**.

目前有五位員工在 business trips 中。

633 **captain** [ˈkæptən] *n.* 機長，船長

例 The **captain** asked passengers to fasten their seat belts.

Captain 要求乘客繫上安全帶。

634 **carousel** [ˌkɛrəˈsɛl] *n.* 行李轉盤，行李輸送帶

例 Did you see my suitcase come around on the **carousel**?

你有看見我的手提箱在 carousel 上嗎？

635 **chain** [tʃen] *n.* 鏈條

例 The **chain** on the carousel is broken.

行李輸送帶上的 chain 壞了。

636 **cheap** [tʃip] *adj.* 便宜的，廉價的

例 We were able to get **cheap** flights by booking last minute.

我們成功訂到了 cheap 的機票，因為是在截止前訂到的。

Chapter 5 商務旅行

結帳櫃台 | 637 **checkout** [ˋtʃɛk͵aʊt] *n.*

例 John was waiting at the **checkout** when he heard his flight number called.

約翰聽到他的班機號碼時,他正在 checkout 前。

淨空 | 638 **clearance** [ˋklɪrəns] *n.*

例 The flight cannot take off until the captain has received **clearance** from the control tower.

在機長接到塔台通知已 clearance 前,飛機無法起飛。

上升,爬升 | 639 **climb** [klaɪm] *v.*

例 The plane began to **climb** higher and higher.

這架飛機開始逐漸越 climb 越高。

記錄(時間) | 640 **clock** [klɑk] *v.*

例 I'm going to **clock** the amount of time it takes to get from my hotel to the airport.

我要 clock 從飯店到機場要多久時間。

陰天,多雲 | 641 **cloudy** [ˋklaʊdɪ] *adj.*

例 The captain said that although the sky was **cloudy**, it was safe to fly.

機長說雖然天氣 cloudy,但不影響飛行安全。

轉接班機 | 642 **connecting flight** [kəˋnɛktɪŋ ˋflaɪt] *n. phr.*

例 Gina was able to get a good deal on her ticket, because she has two **connecting** flights.

吉娜買到便宜的機票,因為她得轉兩次 connecting flights。

643 **crew** [kru] *n.* 機組人員

例 The flight **crew** was exhausted after the long flight.
在長途飛行之後，整個 crew 都疲憊不堪。

644 **cruise** [kruz] *n.* 巡航

例 Our company will be attending a conference on a **cruise** ship.
我們公司將參加一場在 cruise 輪船上舉辦的會議。

645 **customs** [`kʌstəmz] *n.* 海關

例 We have to go through **customs** before we can exit the airport.
出機場前，我們需先經過 customs。

646 **delay** [dɪ`le] *v.* 延遲，延期

例 Heather's flight was **delayed** by three hours.
海瑟的班機 delayed 了三個多小時。

647 **departure** [dɪ`pɑrtʃɚ] *n.* （人、飛機等）離開，起程

例 What time is your **departure**?
你的 departure 時間是幾點？

648 **destination** [ˌdɛstə`neʃən] *n.* 目的地；終點

例 We will reach our **destination** in twenty minutes.
我們將在二十分鐘內抵達 destination。

國內航班　649　**domestic flight** [dəˋmɛstɪk ˏflaɪt] *n. phr.*

　　☐　例　You don't need your passport for **domestic flights**.
　　☐　　　搭乘 domestic flights 不需要護照。

經濟艙　650　**economy class** [ɪˋkɑnəmɪ ˏklæs] *n. phr.*

　　☐　例　It is more affordable to go **economy class**.
　　☐　　　搭 economy class 比較負擔得起。

引擎　　651　**engine** [ˋɛndʒən] *n.*

　　☐　例　When the **engine** started, I knew it wouldn't be long before take-off.
　　☐　　　Engine 一啟動，我知道飛機很快就要起飛。

昂貴　　652　**expensive** [ɪkˋspɛnsɪv] *adj.*

　　☐　例　First class tickets are much more **expensive** than I thought they would be.
　　☐　　　頭等艙機票比我想像中的還要 expensive。

班機　　653　**flight** [flaɪt] *n.*

　　☐　例　The **flight** will be departing in five minutes.
　　☐　　　五分鐘內 flight 即將起飛。

空服員　654　**flight attendant** [ˋflaɪt əˏtɛndənt] *n. phr.*

　　☐　例　The **flight attendant** asked passengers if they wanted chicken or beef for dinner.
　　☐　　　Flight attendant 詢問乘客晚餐要吃雞肉餐還是牛肉餐。

655 **fuel** [`fjuəl] *n.*　　　　　　　　　　　燃料

例 The rising cost of **fuel** has affected the price of airplane tickets.

Fuel 的價格上漲已經影響了機票的價格。

656 **gate** [get] *n.*　　　　　　　　　　　登機門

例 Only passengers are allowed behind the **gate**.

只有旅客才能進 gate。

657 **highway** [`haɪ͵we] *n.*　　　　　　　公路

例 You have to take the **highway** to get to the airport.

您必須走 highway 才能到機場。

658 **inexpensive** [͵ɪnɪk`spɛnsɪv] *adj.*　　便宜

例 Domestic flights are very **inexpensive** in this country.

該國的國內班機票價很 inexpensive。

659 **insurance** [ɪn`ʃʊrəns] *n.*　　　　　　保險

例 Be sure to buy **insurance** for your flight.

搭飛機前請務必要買 insurance。

660 **landing** [`lændɪŋ] *n.*　　　　　　　降落

例 Please fasten your seat belts during take-off and **landing**.

請在起飛與 landing 時繫緊安全帶。

失物招領處	661	**Lost and Found** [ˋlɔst and ˋfaʊnd] *n. phr.*
		例 Someone turned in my sunglasses to the **Lost and Found**.
		有人把我的太陽眼鏡送到 Lost and Found。
超額預定	662	**overbook** [͵ovɚˋbʊk] *v.*
		例 The flight was **overbooked** so we had to catch a later flight.
		這班機 overbook，所以我們得搭乘之後的班機。
下午，午後	663	**pm** (post meridiem) [ˋpi ˋɛm] *adv.*
		例 The meeting will begin at 7 **pm**.
		會議將於 pm 七點開始。
乘客，旅客	664	**passenger** [ˋpæsn̩dʒɚ] *n.*
		例 The **passengers** were asked to prepare for landing.
		Passengers 被通知要準備降落。
護照	665	**passport** [ˋpæs͵pɔrt] *n.*
		例 I missed my flight because I left my **passport** at home.
		因為我把 passport 忘在家裡，所以錯過了班機。
飛行員，機師	666	**pilot** [ˋpaɪlət] *n.*
		例 The **pilot** asked passengers to turn off all electronic devices.
		Pilot 要求旅客關掉所有的電子用品。

667 **platform** [ˈplæt͵fɔrm] *n.*   平臺

☐ 例 The helicopter landed on the company rooftop
☐   **platform** helipad.
       直升機降落在公司屋頂上的 platform。

668 **price** [praɪs] *n.*   價格

☐ 例 International flight **prices** have gone up over the
☐   last few years.
       國際機票的 prices 在最近幾年來上揚。

669 **procrastinate** [proˈkræstə͵net] *v.*   延遲，拖拖拉拉

☐ 例 Please don't **procrastinate** on booking your
☐   flight, or there may not be any seats left.
       請勿 procrastinate 預定您的班機，否則可能沒有機位。

670 **queue** [kju] *n.*   排隊

☐ 例 If you don't arrive at the airport early enough
☐   you will have to wait in a **queue** for a long time.
       如果沒有早點到機場，您將需 queue 等很久。

671 **seat belt** [ˈsit ͵bɛlt] *n. phr.*   安全帶

☐ 例 The flight attendant informed passengers that it
☐   was okay to unfasten their **seat belts**.
       空服員通知旅客可以鬆開他們的 seat belts 了。

672 **signal** [ˈsɪgn!] *v.*   （以動作）示意

☐ 例 The flight attendants **signaled** the way to the
☐   emergency exits.
       空服員 signaled 到緊急出口的方式。

航空站　　673 **terminal** [`tɝmənl] *n.*

　　　　　　例 Charlotte went to the wrong **terminal** for her flight.
　　　　　　夏綠蒂搭飛機時跑錯 terminal。

轉換　　　674 **transfer** [træns`fɝ] *v.*

　　　　　　例 I have to **transfer** airlines when I get to Chicago.
　　　　　　我抵達芝加哥後還得要再 transfer 飛機。

運輸，運送 675 **transit** [`trænsɪt] *n.*

　　　　　　例 The high-speed train is the most efficient means of **transit** in this country.
　　　　　　這國家最有效率的 transit 方式是高鐵。

亂流　　　676 **turbulence** [`tɝbjələns] *n.*

　　　　　　例 The captain warned the passengers that they would be experiencing some **turbulence**.
　　　　　　機長警告旅客可能會遇到 turbulence。

2　Accommodation 膳宿 ⑭

住宿，膳宿 677 **accommodation** [ə͵kɑmə`deʃən] *n.*

　　　　　　例 Does the conference fee include **accommodations**?
　　　　　　會務費有包含 accommodations 嗎？

指控；指責 678 **accuse** [ə`kjuz] *v.*

　　　　　　例 The man **accused** the airline of losing his luggage.
　　　　　　那位男子 accused 該家航空公司遺失他的行李。

140

679 **arrive** [əˋraɪv] v. 抵達，到達

例 I hope we don't **arrive** at the hotel too late.
我希望我們不會太晚 arrive 飯店。

680 **ballroom** [ˋbɔl͵rum] n. 大舞廳

例 The **ballroom** is the perfect size to host our office Christmas party.
這間 ballroom 的大小很適合用來辦公司的聖誕節派對。

681 **bathroom** [ˋbæθ͵rum] n. 浴室，洗手間

例 I forgot to go to the **bathroom** before I got on the bus.
上巴士前，我忘了去 bathroom。

682 **bedroom** [ˋbɛd͵rum] n. 臥室

例 The company paid for a two-**bedroom** suite for me.
公司幫我出錢，訂了一間雙 bedroom 的套房。

683 **bellhop** [ˋbɛl͵hɑp] n. 侍者，行李員

例 The **bellhop** helped me carry my bags to my room.
飯店的 bellhop 幫我把行李提進房間。

684 **booking** [ˋbʊkɪŋ] n. 預訂

例 More and more people are using the Internet for **bookings**.
越來越多的人使用網路 bookings。

Chapter 5 商務旅行

141

煞車，制動器

685 **brake** [brek] *n.*

　例 The plane has faulty **brakes**.
　　這架飛機的 brakes 出了問題。

表達；傳達

686 **convey** [kən`ve] *v.*

　例 The passenger **conveyed** disappointment with the service provided by the flight attendants.
　　該名乘客 conveyed 不滿空服員的服務品質。

信用卡

687 **credit card** [`krɛdɪt ˌkard] *n. phr.*

　例 The server told me my **credit card** was declined.
　　服務生說我的 credit card 不能刷了。

顧客，客戶

688 **customer** [`kʌstəmɚ] *n.*

　例 Many of our **customers** are overseas.
　　我們有許多海外 customers。

方向，方位

689 **direction** [də`rɛkʃən] *n.*

　例 The taxi driver didn't understand the **directions** to my hotel.
　　計程車司機不清楚我下榻飯店的 directions。

距離

690 **distance** [`dɪstəns] *n.*

　例 What is the **distance** from my hotel to the conference center?
　　從我住的飯店到會議中心的 distance 有多遠？

691 **entrance** [ˈɛntrəns] *n.* — 門口，入口

例 The **entrance** of the hotel was blocked by two tour buses.

旅館的 entrance 被兩輛觀光巴士堵住了。

692 **expense** [ɪkˈspɛns] *n.* — 費用，支出

例 My company told me to charge all **expenses** to my hotel room.

我的公司說所有的 expenses 都記在我旅館房間的帳上。

693 **fee** [fi] *n.* — 費用

例 Are there any additional **fees** that I should know about before I book the flight?

在預訂機票前，有沒有什麼額外 fees 是我該知道的呢？

694 **fill out** [ˈfɪl ˈaʊt] *v. phr.* — 填寫

例 Please **fill out** the form with your personal information.

請在這張表格 fill out 您的個人資料。

695 **front desk** [ˈfrʌnt ˌdɛsk] *n. phr.* — 服務台

例 Jake called the **front desk** to request more towels.

傑克打電話到 front desk 要求更多的毛巾。

696 **hostel** [ˈhɑstl̩] *n.* — 旅舍（尤指青年旅舍）

例 We would never arrange for overseas clients to stay at a **hostel**.

我們決不會安排海外客戶住 hostel。

143

旅館	697 **hotel** [hoˋtɛl] *n.*
	例 The **hotel** is in walking distance from our office.
	從 hotel 到本公司的距離很近。

旅館大廳	698 **lobby** [ˋlɑbɪ] *n.*
	例 There is information about local attractions in the **lobby**.
	Lobby 裡有當地旅遊景點的資訊。

住宿，寓所	699 **lodging** [ˋlɑdʒɪŋ] *n.*
	例 The company provided **lodging** for the entire group of guests.
	公司提供 lodging 給整團的賓客。

行李	700 **luggage** [ˋlʌgɪdʒ] *n.*
	例 I will need some assistance with my **luggage**.
	我需要人幫忙提我的 luggage。

英里，哩	701 **mile** [maɪl] *n.*
	例 The hotel is twenty **miles** from the office.
	該旅館距離本公司二十 miles 遠。

選擇	702 **option** [ˋɑpʃən] *n.*
	例 There aren't very many **options** on the take-out menu.
	外帶餐點的菜單上沒有太多的 options。

停放（車輛）	703 **park** [pɑrk] *v.*
	例 Visitors are asked to **park** behind the building.
	遊客需將車輛 park 在建物後面。

704 **parking lot** [ˈpɑrkɪŋ ˌlɑt] *n. phr.* 停車場
　　例 There are no more spots left in the **parking lot**.
　　　Parking lot 裡已經沒有停車位了。

705 **reservation** [ˌrɛzəˈveʃən] *n.* 預訂
　　例 Jim made **reservations** for us at the restaurant downstairs.
　　　吉姆為我們在樓下餐廳 reservations 位子。

706 **room service** [ˈrum ˌsɝvɪs] *n. phr.* 客房餐飲服務
　　例 It is more expensive to order food through **room service** than it is to eat in the hotel restaurant.
　　　透過 room service 點餐比在飯店附設的餐廳吃還要貴。

707 **suitcase** [ˈsut ˌkes] *n.* 行李箱
　　例 I bought a red **suitcase** so it would be easy to identify in baggage claim.
　　　我買了一個紅色的 suitcase，在領取行李時就很容易分辨出來。

708 **suite** [swit] *n.* 套房
　　例 The company paid for me to stay in a **suite** during my business trip.
　　　出差時，公司會付我住 suite 的費用。

709 **voucher** [ˈvaʊtʃɚ] *n.* 抵用券，票券
　　例 The hotel gave me a **voucher** for breakfast.
　　　飯店給了我一張早餐 voucher。

Chapter 5 商務旅行

145

3 Schedule Arrangement 行程規劃 (15)

加速，加快   710 **accelerate** [æk`sɛlə‚ret] *v.*

☐ 例 Peter asked the taxi driver to **accelerate** so he
☐ wouldn't miss his flight.
彼得請計程車司機 accelerate，免得他錯過班機。

意外，   711 **accident** [`æksədənt] *n.*
偶然的事
☐ 例 My meeting was delayed by the **accident**.
☐ 我因為那場 accident 而延誤會議。

抵達時間   712 **arrival time** [ə`raɪvḷ ‚taɪm] *n. phr.*

☐ 例 What is your **arrival time**?
☐ 你的 arrival time 是幾點？

汽車   713 **automobile** [`ɔtəmə‚bil] *n.*

☐ 例 The company I am visiting said they would lend
☐ me an **automobile** to drive while I am in town.
我將去拜訪的公司會在我停留的那段時間借我一部 automobile。

有空   714 **available** [ə`veləbḷ] *adj.*

☐ 例 I'm not **available** to travel during the first two
☐ weeks of June.
六月的頭兩週要出差的話，我無法 available。

取消   715 **cancel** [`kænsḷ] *v.*

☐ 例 We may have to **cancel** our trip in August if we
☐ do not meet the project deadline.
要是無法準時完成專案，我們可能得 cancel 八月的旅行。

716 **choice** [tʃɔɪs] *n.*   選擇，決定

例 I think it was a good **choice** to upgrade to first class.

我認為升等到頭等艙是個好 choice。

717 **clear** [klɪr] *adj.*   空出來

例 Please keep your schedule **clear** during the first week of May.

請你將五月第一週的時間 clear。

718 **confirm** [kən`fɝm] *v.*   確認，證實

例 Jim asked his secretary to **confirm** his flight.

吉姆要他的秘書 confirm 他的班機。

719 **confirmation** [ˌkɑnfɚ`meʃən] *n.*   確認；確實

例 I am waiting for **confirmation** from the travel agency that our flights have been booked.

我正等旅行社的 confirmation 以確定我們的機票已訂好。

720 **early** [`ɝlɪ] *adv.*   早，提早

例 It looks like our flight will arrive **early**.

看來我們的班機將會 early 抵達。

721 **exchange rate** [ɪks`tʃendʒ ˌret] *n. phr.*   匯率

例 What is the **exchange rate** for American dollars?

美元的 exchange rate 是多少？

導遊；
旅遊指南

722 **guide** [gaɪd] *n.*

例 A **guide** will be available to show you around the city.

將會有 guide 帶您看看這個城市。

國際航班

723 **international flight** [ˌɪntɚˋnæʃənḷ ˋflaɪt] *n. phr.*

例 You need to arrive at the airport at least two hours prior to **international flights**.

搭乘 international flights，您需提早至少兩小時到達機場。

行程，
旅遊計畫

724 **itinerary** [aɪˋtɪnəˌrɛrɪ] *n.*

例 If you check your **itinerary**, you will see that the conference begins at 8 am.

如果您查看您的 itinerary，將會看到會議在八點鐘開始。

路程，旅程

725 **journey** [ˋdʒɝnɪ] *n.*

例 It is a two-hour **journey** from company headquarters to the factory.

從公司總部到工廠得花兩小時的 journey。

公斤

726 **kilogram** [ˋkɪləˌgræm] *n.*

例 The airline will not allow passengers to check luggage weighing over 20 **kilograms**.

航空公司將不會許可旅客托運超過二十 kilograms 的行李。

公里

727 **kilometer** [ˋkɪləˌmitɚ] *n.*

例 The hotel is about ten **kilometers** from company headquarters.

從本公司總部到該旅館的距離大約是十 kilometers。

148

728 **late** [let] *adj.* 遲到

　　例 If we don't leave now, we are going to be **late** for the meeting.
　　　如果我們現在不走，開會就會 late。

729 **leave for** [ˋliv ˋfɔr] *v. phr.* 前往

　　例 When are you **leaving for** California?
　　　您何時要 leave for 加州？

730 **o'clock** [əˋklɑk] *adv.* …點鐘

　　例 We need to wake up at five **o'clock** if we want to get to the airport on time.
　　　如果我們想要準時抵達機場，就需要在五 o'clock 起床。

731 **on holiday** [an ˋhɑləˏde] *adv. phr.* 在休假中

　　例 Our entire staff goes **on holiday** for the month of July.
　　　七月整個月我們全部的員工都 on holiday。

732 **punctual** [ˋpʌŋktʃʊəl] *adj.* 準時的

　　例 It is important to be **punctual** for all your meetings.
　　　要 punctual 出席您所有的會議是很重要的。

733 **reception** [rɪˋsɛpʃən] *n.* 接待

　　例 Please sign in at the **reception** desk when you arrive.
　　　請您抵達後到 reception 處簽名。

149

接待員	734 **receptionist** [rɪˋsɛpʃənɪst] *n.*
	例 The **receptionist** said Mr. Johnston was unavailable.
	receptionist 說詹斯頓先生沒有時間見面。

路線	735 **route** [rut] *n.*
	例 Can you tell me the fastest **route** to get to the airport?
	你可以告訴我到機場最快的 route 嗎？

時間表；計畫表	736 **schedule** [ˋskɛdʒʊl] *n.*
	例 My **schedule** is full until next week.
	我的 schedule 滿到下星期。

逗留，停留	737 **stay** [ste] *n.*
	例 Wanda requested to extend her **stay** at the hotel.
	汪達要求延長在旅館 stay 的時間。

時刻表	738 **timetable** [ˋtaɪm͵tebl] *n.*
	例 My **timetable** indicates that the conference starts at nine in the morning.
	我的 timetable 顯示會議在早上九點鐘舉行。

遊覽，旅行	739 **tour** [tʊr] *n.*
	例 One of the employees offered to take me on a **tour** of the city after the meeting.
	有個員工提議在會議後帶我來場城市 tour 。

740 **tourism** [ˋtʊrɪzəm] *n.* 觀光業

例 **Tourism** is one of the biggest industries in this city.

Tourism 是本市最重要的產業之一。

741 **tourist** [ˋtʊrɪst] *n.* 觀光客

例 There were many **tourists** on my flight to Los Angeles.

我這班機上有許多到洛杉磯旅遊的 tourists。

742 **transit visa** [ˋtrænsɪt ˏvizə] *n. phr.* 過境簽證

例 I forgot to apply for a **transit visa** before I left.

出國前我忘記要申請 transit visa。

743 **travel** [ˋtrævl̩] *v.* 旅行

例 Bob is used to **traveling** three to four months of the year for business.

鮑伯習慣一年中總有三、四個月要商務 traveling。

744 **travel agency** [ˋtrævl̩ ˏedʒənsɪ] *n. phr.* 旅行社

例 The **travel agency** was able to get our employees a great deal on flights to the conference in the spring.

Travel agency 能幫我們員工拿到飛往春季會議的優惠機票。

745 **trip** [trɪp] *n.* 旅行

例 I haven't taken a **trip** for pleasure in years.

我已經好幾年沒有為了消遣而 trip。

| 參觀，拜訪 | 746 **visit** [ˋvɪzɪt] *v.*
| | 例 I hope that I will be able to **visit** some historical sites on my business trip.
| | 我希望這次出差我能夠 visit 一些歷史景點。

4 Transportation 交通運輸 ⑯

| 大道，大街 | 747 **avenue** [ˋævə͵nu] *n.*
| | 例 I don't even want to think about going down that **avenue** unless we are desperate.
| | 除非真的沒辦法，不然我絕不考慮走那條 avenue。

| 街區 | 748 **block** [blɑk] *n.*
| | 例 Our new office is only one **block** from the river.
| | 我們新的辦公室離這條河只有一個 block 遠。

| 通勤 | 749 **commute** [kəˋmjut] *v.*
| | 例 I wish I lived in the city so I didn't have to spend so much time **commuting** every day.
| | 我真希望住在城裡，這樣就不用每天 commuting。

| 通勤者 | 750 **commuter** [kəˋmjutɚ] *n.*
| | 例 The heavy traffic in the morning is caused by all the **commuters**.
| | 早晨繁忙的交通是所有 commuters 造成的。

| 壅塞，擁擠 | 751 **congestion** [kənˋdʒɛstʃən] *n.*
| | 例 I would prefer to stay at a hotel outside the city because there is too much **congestion** downtown.
| | 我寧願住在城外的旅館，因為城裡實在太 congestion。

152

752 **dangerous** [ˈdendʒrəs] *adj.* 　　　　　　有危險的

　　例 It is much more **dangerous** to travel by car than it is by plane.
　　搭乘汽車比搭乘飛機 dangerous 多了。

753 **driver** [ˈdraɪvɚ] *n.* 　　　　　　司機

　　例 The company paid for a **driver** to pick me up at the airport.
　　公司付費讓 driver 到機場接我。

754 **fare** [fɛr] *n.* 　　　　　　車資，票價

　　例 How much is the bus **fare** in this city?
　　這城市的公車 fare 是多少？

755 **ferry** [ˈfɛrɪ] *n.* 　　　　　　渡輪

　　例 You will have to take a **ferry** from your hotel to the office.
　　從你下榻的旅館到公司需搭乘 ferry。

756 **gasoline** [ˈɡæslˌin] *n.* 　　　　　　汽油

　　例 The bus smelled like **gasoline**.
　　公車上有 gasoline 味。

757 **harbor** [ˈhɑrbɚ] *n.* 　　　　　　港口

　　例 Our main office has a view of the **harbor**.
　　我們總公司能看到 harbor 的景色。

758 **minute** [ˈmɪnɪt] *n.* 　　　　　　分鐘

　　例 The train will be arriving in five **minutes**.
　　火車將於五 minutes 內抵達。

Chapter 5 商務旅行

大眾捷運系統	759	**MRT** (mass rapid transit) *n.*
		例 The **MRT** is the fastest way to travel in the city.
		在城市裡往返最快速的方式就是搭 MRT。
上船；登機	760	**on board** [ɑn `bɔrd] *adv. phr.*
		例 Welcome **on board**!
		歡迎 on board！
準時	761	**on time** [an `taɪm] *adv. phr.*
		例 The train will be arriving **on time**.
		火車將 on time 抵達。
允許，准許	762	**permit** [pɚ`mɪt] *v.*
		例 Smoking is not **permitted** on the flight.
		飛機上不 permitted 抽菸。
港口	763	**port** [pɔrt] *n.*
		例 The ferry will be arriving at the **port** in ten minutes.
		渡輪將於十分鐘內抵達 port。
鐵路	764	**railroad** [`rel͵rod] *n.*
		例 The **railroad** was closed after the train accident.
		在火車發生意外事故後，railroad 就遭到關閉。
可退費的	765	**refundable** [rɪ`fʌndəbl̩] *adj.*
		例 Is your train ticket **refundable** if you decide to leave later?
		如果你決定晚點離開，你的火車票是 refundable 嗎？

766 **rush hour** [ˋrʌʃ ˌaʊr] *n. phr.*　　尖峰時間

例 We should leave for the train station early if we want to avoid **rush hour**.

若要避開 rush hour，我們就應該要早點到火車站。

767 **shuttle bus** [ˋʃʌtḷ ˌbʌs] *n. phr.*　　接駁車

例 The **shuttle bus** leaves for the airport every half-hour.

Shuttle bus 每半小時開往機場。

768 **station** [ˋsteʃən] *n.*　　車站，站

例 The closest bus **station** is a five-minute walk from here.

最近的公車 station 距離此處五分鐘的路程。

769 **steer** [stɪr] *v.*　　駕駛

例 The driver **steered** the bus to the side of the road because he felt sleepy.

司機因為想睡而把公車 steered 到路邊。

770 **traffic jam** [ˋtræfɪk ˌdʒæm] *n. phr.*　　塞車，交通壅塞

例 If this **traffic jam** doesn't clear up soon, I'm going to miss my flight.

假如 traffic jam 沒有快點清除的話，我就會錯過班機了。

771 **transportation** [ˌtrænspɚˋteʃən] *n.*　　運輸；交通工具

例 The public **transportation** in this city is much better than I thought it would be.

這城市的大眾 transportation 比我想像中的好很多。

Chapter 5 商務旅行

155

隧道　　　772 **tunnel** [ˋtʌnḷ] *n.*

　　　　　☐　例 We can either take the ferry or the **tunnel** to get
　　　　　☐　　 to the hotel.
　　　　　　　 我們可以搭渡輪或者是通過 tunnel 到旅館。

車輛　　　773 **vehicle** [ˋvihɪkḷ] *n.*

　　　　　☐　例 I would give your entire team a ride to the office,
　　　　　☐　　 but my **vehicle** only seats five.
　　　　　　　 我很想載你們全體到公司，但是我的 vehicle 只有
　　　　　　　 五人座。

方向盤；　774 **wheel** [hwil] *n.*
輪子
　　　　　☐　例 Could you please take the **wheel** while I take off
　　　　　☐　　 my jacket?
　　　　　　　 你可以幫我握一下 wheel 嗎？我要把夾克脫下。

Exercises

請從選項中，選出最適當的答案完成句子。

1. Airplane passengers must check in at least two hours before _____.

    (A) accomplishment   (B) appointment   (C) arrival   (D) departure

2. Jack _____ to work every day; he takes the train.

    (A) composes   (B) commutes   (C) communicates   (D) contends

3. The news that the minister resigned has been _____. A new minister has been appointed.

    (A) assured   (B) affirmed   (C) confirmed   (D) decided

4. Life is often compared to a _____; it is the process that is important, not the destination.

    (A) flight   (B) trap   (C) errand   (D) journey

5. In order to work in Taiwan, foreigners must have a work _____.

    (A) permit   (B) allowance   (C) agreement   (D) consent

6. As more mainlanders are visiting Taiwan, _____ is booming.

    (A) cynicism   (B) tourism   (C) enthusiasm   (D) criticism

7. If you are not satisfied with the merchandise, you can return it and we will _____ you.

    (A) retain   (B) refund   (C) repay   (D) return

8. People are _____ outside the hall for tickets to the concert featuring a famous pianist.

    (A) increasing   (B) adding   (C) accumulating   (D) queuing

9. Currently there are two _____ at the CKS International Airport.

    (A) terminals   (B) organs   (C) organisms   (D) destinations

10. I called several hotels before I was finally able to make a _____.

    (A) determination   (B) reservation   (C) conservation   (D) prevention

11. Passengers were asked not to leave their seats when the plane was flying through _____.

    (A) nuisance   (B) turbulence   (C) annoyance   (D) disturbance

12. Tim loves flying; he is training to be a(n) _____.

    (A) aircraft   (B) stewardess   (C) technician   (D) pilot

13. You should be _____ for your interview. You will leave a very bad impression if you are late.

    (A) punctual   (B) permanent   (C) eternal   (D) casual

14. Because of bad weather and poor visibility, there were many car _____ yesterday.

    (A) bumpers   (B) accidents   (C) incidents   (D) events

15. Jason received a full scholarship last year; it was enough to cover all his _____ at college.

    (A) pills   (B) expenses   (C) skills   (D) costs

16. Our National Health _____ is a very good welfare program admired by many other nations.

    (A) Insurance   (B) Assurance   (C) Confidence   (D) Indication

17. Carry-on _____ can be stored in the overhead compartment.

    (A) luggage   (B) briefcase   (C) suitcase   (D) staircase

18. Your _____ is your ID when you travel abroad. You should carry it with you all the time.

    (A) support   (B) passport   (C) visa   (D) signature

19. A bus is a _____ that can take you almost anywhere in the city.

    (A) vehicle   (B) measurement   (C) instrument   (D) tool

20. My cousin is visiting Taipei, so I suggested that he put the National Palace Museum on his _____.

    (A) proposal   (B) scheme   (C) itinerary   (D) project

Chapter 6
Social Events 社交活動

Social events fulfill two essential purposes: networking and relationship building. A company may cater a banquet to celebrate achievements with its investors or to show appreciation to its employees. Similarly, a company may host or sponsor an opera or orchestra performance to demonstrate its commitment to support cultural activities. These events not only offer relaxation and recreation but also help business professionals strengthen relationships with co-workers or clients on a more personal level.

Chapter 6 Social Events 社交活動

New TOEIC 1200

1   Dining 用餐 ⑰

出席，參加 | 775 **attend** [əˋtɛnd] *v.*
例 Are you going to **attend** Bob's retirement party?
你會去 attend 鮑伯的退休派對嗎？

食慾，胃口 | 776 **appetite** [ˋæpəˌtaɪt] *n.*
例 Alisa hasn't had an **appetite** since she got sick.
愛莉莎自從生病之後，就一直沒有 appetite。

開胃菜 | 777 **appetizer** [ˋæpəˌtaɪzɚ] *n.*
例 What would you like to order as an **appetizer**?
你想點什麼 appetizer？

宴會 | 778 **banquet** [ˋbæŋkwɪt] *n.*
例 Gina and I went to a friend's wedding **banquet** last night.
吉娜和我昨晚參加一個朋友的結婚 banquet。

酒吧 | 779 **bar** [bɑr] *n.*
例 Jerry likes to hit the **bar** after a long day at work.
傑瑞喜歡在辛苦工作一天後到 bar 去。

飲料 | 780 **beverage** [ˋbɛvərɪdʒ] *n.*
例 This restaurant doesn't serve alcoholic **beverages**.
這家餐廳不供應含酒精的 beverages。

781 **brunch** [brʌntʃ] *n.*　早午餐

例 I usually have **brunch** with my friends on Saturdays.
我通常會跟朋友在星期六的時候去吃 brunch。

782 **buffet** [bʊˋfe] *n.*　自助餐廳

例 There are many dishes to choose from at all-you-can-eat **buffets**.
在吃到飽的 buffets 有很多可以選擇的菜餚。

783 **cafeteria** [ˌkæfəˋtɪrɪə] *n.*　（學校內的）自助餐廳

例 The students don't like the food in their school **cafeteria**.
學生們不喜歡學校 cafeteria 提供的菜色。

784 **cater** [ˋketɚ] *v.*　提供飲食，承辦宴席

例 That world famous chef is going to **cater** the royal wedding.
那位世界級的主廚將為皇家婚禮 cater。

785 **check** [tʃɛk] *v.*　檢查

例 Before the food was served at the annual banquet, the manager **checked** every dish himself.
尾牙的每道菜端上桌前，經理都會親自 checked。

786 **chef** [ʃɛf] *n.*　主廚

例 My colleagues and I go to that restaurant so often that we have become friends with the **chef**.
我和同事太常到那家餐廳，跟 chef 都變成朋友了。

筷子	787 **chopstick** [ˋtʃɑpˏstɪk] *n.*
	例 Our foreign customers are always interested in learning how to use **chopsticks**.
	我們的外國客戶總是對學習使用 chopsticks 很有興趣。

雞尾酒	788 **cocktail** [ˋkɑkˏtel] *n.*
	例 A bar near our office has the best **cocktails** in the world.
	在我們公司附近的一間酒吧有全天下最棒的 cocktails。

甜點	789 **dessert** [dɪˋzɝt] *n.*
	例 The bakery around the corner has the best **desserts** in the city.
	轉角那間麵包店的 cesserts 是城裡最好吃的。

消化；了解	790 **digest** [daɪˋdʒɛst] *v.*
	例 The information I just got from the meeting is too much for me to **digest** right now.
	剛在會議室裡的事讓我現在一時還無法 digest。

用餐	791 **dining** [ˋdaɪnɪŋ] *n.*
	例 Before we get a table in the **dining** room, we have to wait at the bar.
	在 dining 區有位置前，我們得在吧台等。

飲料	792 **drinks** [ˋdrɪŋks] *n.*
	例 Our Japanese customers had too many **drinks** at the bar last night.
	我們的日本客戶昨晚在酒吧喝了太多 drinks。

793 **drunk** [drʌŋk] *adj.* 酒醉

例 Cocktails are easy to drink, but can also get you **drunk** very easily!

雞尾酒很容易入口卻也很容易讓你 drunk。

794 **entrée** [ˋɑntre] *n.* 主菜

例 What would you like for your **entrée**?

你的 entrée 想點什麼？

795 **etiquette** [ˋɛtɪˌkɛt] *n.* 禮節，禮儀

例 According to business **etiquette**, you should present your name card when introducing yourself.

根據商業 etiquette，介紹自己的時候要遞出名片。

796 **guest** [gɛst] *n.* 賓客

例 Our **guests** will be arriving for dinner at 6:00.

我們晚宴的 guests 將於六點鐘抵達。

797 **gourmet** [ˋgʊrme] *adj.* 美味的

例 Nothing beats having a **gourmet** meal with good friends.

沒什麼比跟好友一同享受 gourmet 餐點更好的了。

798 **host** [host] *v.* 主辦；主持

例 Our company is **hosting** the annual business dinner for offices in our building.

我們公司為我們這棟大樓的各家公司行號 hosting 年度商業晚宴。

Chapter 6 社交活動

番茄醬　799 **ketchup** [ˋkɛtʃəp] *n.*

例　Could you please ask the waiter for more **ketchup**?
你可以跟服務生多要些 ketchup 嗎？

酒；烈酒　800 **liquor** [ˋlɪkɚ] *n.*

例　Lisa can really hold her **liquor**. No matter how much she drinks, she just won't get drunk.
莉莎很會喝 liquor，不管她喝多少都不會醉。

午餐會　801 **luncheon** [ˋlʌntʃən] *n.*

例　The executive manager told everyone we will be going to a fancy restaurant for the staff **luncheon**.
總經理告訴大家，我們要到一家豪華餐廳舉行員工 luncheon。

禮貌，規矩　802 **manners** [ˋmænɚz] *n.*

例　The boss's kids all have very good table **manners**.
我們老闆的小孩餐桌 manners 非常好。

（一頓）飯　803 **meal** [mil] *n.*

例　You've been working all day. When was your last **meal**?
你已經工作一整天了。你上一頓 meal 是什麼時候？

菜單　804 **menu** [ˋmɛnju] *n.*

例　May I have the **menu**, please?
請給我 menu 好嗎？

805 **preparation** [ˌprɛpəˈreʃən] n. 準備

例 In **preparation** for this evening's gala, we hired an event coordinator.

為了為今天的晚會做好 preparation，我們請了個活動企劃。

806 **sauce** [sɔs] n. 醬汁

例 What kind of **sauce** would you like for your steak?

你的牛排需要何種 sauce？

807 **seafood** [ˈsiˌfud] n. 海鮮

例 My friend is allergic to **seafood**, so please tell the kitchen.

請告訴廚房我朋友對 seafood 過敏。

808 **server** [ˈsɝvɚ] n. （餐館）服務生

例 The **server** spilled coffee on my lap by accident.

這 server 不小心把咖啡灑到我的腿上。

809 **serving** [ˈsɝvɪŋ] n. 一份（食物）

例 The bag contains five **servings** of cookies.

這包裡頭有五 servings 餅乾。

810 **spicy** [ˈspaɪsɪ] adj. 辛辣的

例 Not everyone can handle **spicy** food.

不是所有人都能吃 spicy 食物。

Chapter 6 社交活動

165

拿走 | 811 **take away** [`tek ə`we] *v. phr.*
- 例 The waiter **took away** my plate before I even finished.
- 我還沒吃完，服務生就把我的盤子 took away 了。

給…小費 | 812 **tip** [tɪp] *v.*
- 例 It is not customary to **tip** servers in Taiwan.
- 在台灣並沒有 tip 服務生的習慣。

紙巾 | 813 **tissue** [`tɪʃʊ] *n.*
- 例 I need some **tissue** to blow my nose.
- 我需要一些 tissue 擤鼻涕。

托盤 | 814 **tray** [tre] *n.*
- 例 Servers carry dishes on a **tray**.
- 服務生用 tray 端送菜餚。

2 Art & Music 藝術與音樂 (18)

古董 | 815 **antique** [æn`tik] *n.*
- 例 Helen loves to collect **antiques**.
- 海倫很愛收集 antiques。

祖先，祖宗 | 816 **ancestor** [`ænsɛstɚ] *n.*
- 例 My **ancestors** can be traced back to the Ching Dynasty.
- 我的 ancestors 可以追溯到清朝年間。

166

817 **ancient** [ˈenʃənt] *adj.*   古老的

例 Tomb sweeping is an **ancient** custom passed on through generations.

掃墓是歷代傳承下來的 ancient 習俗。

818 **appreciation** [ˌəpriʃɪˈeʃən] *n.*   欣賞；感謝

例 The audience showed their **appreciation** for the singer by standing up and applauding.

觀眾們起立鼓掌以表達對該歌手的 appreciation。

819 **artist** [ˈɑrtɪst] *n.*   藝術家；畫家

例 Marc Chagall is one of my favorite **artists**.

馬克‧夏卡爾是我最欣賞的 artists 之一。

820 **artistic** [ɑrˈtɪstɪk] *adj.*   有藝術天分的

例 Susan is a very **artistic** person.

蘇珊很 artistic。

821 **compose** [kəmˈpoz] *v.*   作曲，創作

例 This song was **composed** especially for the company party.

這首歌是專為公司派對所 composed 的。

822 **concert** [ˈkɑnsɝt] *n.*   音樂會，演唱會

例 That famous tenor is going to give a **concert** here next month.

這位男高音即將在下個月舉辦他的 concert。

Chapter 6 社交活動

音樂廳	823	**concert hall** [ˈkɑnsɝtˌhɔl] *n. phr.*
		例 Enjoying a performance at a **concert hall** is such a great way to spend an evening.
		到 concert hall 聆聽演奏真是消磨傍晚的最佳活動。
微妙的，敏感的	824	**delicate** [ˈdɛləkɪt] *adj.*
		例 It's important to not talk about **delicate** subjects, such as religion, with colleagues.
		千萬不要跟同事談論一些像是宗教之類的 delicate 話題。
設計師	825	**designer** [dɪˈzaɪnɚ] *n.*
		例 Tom said that if he were not a salesman, he would be a clothing **designer**.
		湯姆說他要不是業務員的話，他有可能是服裝 designer。
展覽	826	**exhibition** [ˌɛksəˈbɪʃən] *n.*
		例 The Picasso **exhibition** is something you don't want to miss.
		畢卡索的 exhibition 是絕不能錯過的。
美術館；畫廊	827	**gallery** [ˈgælərɪ] *n.*
		例 Cheryl spends a lot of time visiting **galleries** and museums.
		雪柔花很多時間參觀 galleries 與博物館。
耳機，耳麥	828	**headset** [ˈhɛdˌsɛt] *n.*
		例 A **headset** is convenient when you talk online.
		用 headset 在網路上聊天很方便。

829 **historian** [hɪsˋtorɪən] *n.*　歷史學家

　　例 Bob's son wants to be a **historian** when he grows up.
　　鮑伯的兒子長大後想當 historian。

830 **museum** [mjuˋzɪəm] *n.*　博物館

　　例 You can spend a whole day at the Metropolitan **Museum** of Art in New York and still not see everything.
　　你可以在紐約的大都會藝術 Museum 逛上一整天都還看不完。

831 **musician** [mjuˋzɪʃən] *n.*　音樂家

　　例 It takes talent and many years of training to be a good **musician**.
　　要成為一位傑出的 musician 得具有才華與多年的訓練。

832 **opera** [ˋɑpərə] *n.*　歌劇

　　例 Sitting in a theater enjoying an **opera** is not something that would interest my husband.
　　坐在劇院裡欣賞 opera 不是我丈夫會感興趣的事。

833 **orchestra** [ˋɔrkɪstrə] *n.*　管弦樂隊

　　例 When the **orchestra** started to play, the audience got quiet.
　　當 orchestra 開始演奏時，聽眾都安靜了下來。

834 **philosopher** [fəˋlɑsəfɚ] *n.*　哲學家

　　例 He thinks like a **philosopher** because he often says things that make people think.
　　他思考的方式像個 philosopher，常說出讓人沈思的話。

Chapter 6 社交活動

169

鋼琴家	835	**pianist** [pɪˋænɪst] *n.*
		例 James thinks he is a good **pianist** but he doesn't really play well.
		詹姆士認為他是個出色的 pianist，但他其實彈得並不好。

代表	836	**represent** [ˌrɛprɪˋzɛnt] *v.*
		例 The dove in this painting **represents** peace and love.
		這幅畫裡的鴿子 represents 和平與愛。

雕像，雕刻品	837	**sculpture** [ˋskʌlptʃɚ] *n.*
		例 The museum has both paintings and **sculptures**.
		博物館裡有畫作也有 sculptures。

陳列室	838	**showroom** [ˋʃoˌrum] *n.*
		例 All the exhibits are displayed in the **showroom**.
		所有的展出品都會在 showroom 裡展示。

雕像，塑像	839	**statue** [ˋstætʃʊ] *n.*
		例 You can see **statues** of great men in that park.
		在公園裡你會看到偉人的 statues。

工作室	840	**studio** [ˋstjudɪˌo] *n.*
		例 Amy owns a small art **studio**.
		艾咪有一間小型的藝術 studio。

小提琴手	841	**violinist** [ˌvaɪəˋlɪnɪst] *n.*
		例 Yo-Yo Ma's father was a **violinist**.
		馬友友的父親曾是一位 violinist。

3 Plays & Movies 戲劇與電影 (19)

842 **attractive** [əˋtræktɪv] *adj.*　　　　　　　　　　有吸引力的

例 John finds filmstars with curves more **attractive**.
約翰認為凹凸有致的影星更 attractive。

843 **audience** [ˋɔdɪəns] *n.*　　　　　　　　　　　　觀眾

例 The **audience** didn't really enjoy the show.
這些 audience 並不喜歡這場表演。

844 **audio** [ˋɔdɪ͵o] *adj.*　　　　　　　　　　　　　聽覺的，聲音的

例 Tim recorded himself reading and saved it as an **audio** file on his computer.
提姆錄下他讀書的聲音並將 audio 檔案存在電腦。

845 **audiovisual** [͵ɔdɪoˋvɪʒʊəl] *adj.*　　　　　　　視聽的

例 Ted rents **audiovisual** equipment.
泰德專門出租 audiovisual 器材。

846 **auditorium** [͵ɔdəˋtorɪəm] *n.*　　　　　　　　禮堂，會堂

例 The **auditorium** was packed with people who came to enjoy the show.
這座 auditorium 擠滿了來看表演的群眾。

847 **drama** [ˋdrɑmə] *n.*　　　　　　　　　　　　　戲劇

例 Nick studied **drama** in college and almost became an actor.
尼克在大學時修過 drama 課，還差點成為演員。

171

電影 848 **film** [fɪlm] *n.*

　　□ 例 What **film** genre do you prefer?
　　□ 　　你喜歡哪一種類型的 film？

導演 849 **filmmaker** [ˋfɪlmˌmekɚ] *n.*

　　□ 例 Ang Lee is my favorite **filmmaker**.
　　□ 　　李安是我最喜歡的 filmmaker。

原來的； 850 **original** [əˋrɪdʒənl̩] *adj.*
原創的
　　□ 例 The artist's performance was very **original**.
　　□ 　　這位藝術家的表演非常 original。

表演者 851 **performer** [pɚˋfɔrmɚ] *n.*

　　□ 例 The **performer** fell on stage.
　　□ 　　那位 performer 在舞台上摔倒。

攝影師 852 **photographer** [fəˋtɑgrəfɚ] *n.*

　　□ 例 Jacob is an excellent **photographer** because
　　□ 　　most of his shots turn out great.
　　　　雅各是一位傑出的 photographer，他總能拍出很棒
　　　　的作品。

海報 853 **poster** [ˋpostɚ] *n.*

　　□ 例 A huge **poster** of the popular singer is hanging
　　□ 　　outside the building.
　　　　那受歡迎的歌手大型 poster 正掛在大樓的外面。

172

854 **premiere** [prɪˋmɪr] *n.*　　　　　　　首映會

例 Not everyone can be invited to a movie **premiere**.

不是任何人都能受邀參加電影 premiere。

855 **present** [ˋprɛznt] *adj.*　　　　　　出席，在場

例 How many people will be **present** at the party?

這場派對會有多少人 present？

856 **preview** [ˋpri͵vju] *n.*　　　　　　　預映，預告片

例 You can watch the latest movie **previews** online.

你可以在網路上看到最新的電影 previews。

857 **rehearsal** [rɪˋhɝsl] *n.*　　　　　　排演，排練

例 Before officially going on the stage, all actors need to do a dress **rehearsal**.

在正式上台前，所有的演員都必須先著戲服 rehearsal。

858 **theater** [ˋθiətɚ] *n.*　　　　　　　　電影院

例 Would you like to go to the **theater** with me this Sunday?

這週日你願意跟我去 theater 看電影嗎？

Chapter 6 社交活動

173

4 Leisure & Hobbies 休閒與嗜好 ⑳

認識的人
859 acquaintance [əˋkwentəns] *n.*
例 He is just an **acquaintance**, not really a friend.
他只是一個 acquaintance，不是朋友。

娛樂活動，消遣
860 amusement [əˋmjuzmənt] *n.*
例 This park has many activities for **amusement**.
這個公園裡有許多 amusement。

烘烤，烘焙
861 bake [bek] *v.*
例 **Baking** cakes is something Sara loves to do in her spare time.
Baking 蛋糕是莎拉在閒暇之餘很愛做的事。

大舞廳
862 ballroom [ˋbɔl͵rum] *n.*
例 A **ballroom** is a dance hall.
Ballroom 就是讓人跳舞的廳堂。

炊具，烹調器具
863 cooker [ˋkʊkɚ] *n.*
例 We have a rice **cooker** in the office.
我們辦公室裡有一個煮飯的 cooker。

烹飪，烹調
864 cooking [ˋkʊkɪŋ] *n.*
例 I like to do my own **cooking** when I get home from work.
我喜歡下班回家後自己 cooking。

174

865 **ingredient** [ɪn`gridɪənt] *n.*　　　　　　原料，食材

☐ 例 There is a very special **ingredient** in this dish.
☐ 　　這道菜裡有一種很特別的 ingredient。

866 **inspire** [ɪn`spaɪr] *v.*　　　　　　　　鼓舞，激勵

☐ 例 Talking to you really **inspired** me to broaden
☐ 　　my horizons.
　　跟你談話 inspired 我拓廣視野。

867 **invitation** [ˏɪnvə`teʃən] *n.*　　　　　邀請

☐ 例 It was a pity that Sherry turned down the
☐ 　　**invitation** to the company party.
　　真可惜，雪莉回絕參加公司派對的 invitation。

868 **invite** [ɪn`vaɪt] *v.*　　　　　　　　　邀請

☐ 例 Thanks for **inviting** me for a drink, but I think I
☐ 　　am going to head home.
　　謝謝你 inviting 我去喝一杯，但我還是想先回家
　　了。

869 **juicy** [`dʒusɪ] *adj.*　　　　　　　　　多汁

☐ 例 The steak we had yesterday was tender and
☐ 　　**juicy**.
　　我們昨天吃的牛排真是又嫩又 juicy。

870 **leisure** [`liʒɚ] *adj.*　　　　　　　　　閒暇的

☐ 例 Michelle loves to read during her **leisure** time.
☐ 　　蜜雪兒喜歡在 leisure 時看書。

Chapter 6 社交活動

175

麥克風　　871 **microphone** [ˋmaɪkrəˌfon] n.

例 When some people sing karaoke, they just won't let go of the **microphone**!

有些人一唱卡拉 OK 就無法放下 microphone！

表演　　872 **perform** [pəˋfɔrm] v.

例 There will be a belly dancer **performing** tonight at the restaurant.

這家餐廳今晚將會有肚皮舞孃 perform。

照片　　873 **photo** (photograph) [ˋfoto] n.

例 Taking **photos** of wild birds is one of her hobbies.

拍攝野鳥的 photos 是她的嗜好之一。

食譜　　874 **recipe** [ˋrɛsəpɪ] n.

例 Can you share your pasta **recipe**? It is so delicious!

你可以給我你的義大利麵 recipe 嗎？這實在太好吃了！

娛樂，消遣　　875 **recreation** [ˌrɛkrɪˋeʃən] n.

例 Dancing is a form of **recreation** for Mary.

舞蹈對瑪麗來說是一種 recreation。

放鬆，休息　　876 **relax** [rɪˋlæks] v.

例 You always work so hard. You really need to **relax** more.

你老是拼命工作，你需要多 relax。

877 **release** [rɪˋlis] *v.*   釋放

☐ 例 Massages can help **release** the tension in your body.
☐
按摩可以幫你 release 身體的緊繃。

878 **roast** [rost] *v.*   烘，烤

☐ 例 At Chris's barbeque, he **roasted** a big chunk of beef.
☐
在克里斯的烤肉會上，他 roasted 一大塊的牛肉。

879 **rotten** [ˋratn̩] *adj.*   腐敗的

☐ 例 You should throw out the **rotten** food in your refrigerator.
☐
你該把你冰箱裡那些 rotten 食物丟掉。

880 **stadium** [ˋstedɪəm] *n.*   運動場

☐ 例 Yankee **Stadium** has a long history.
☐
洋基 Stadium 具有悠久的歷史。

881 **tablecloth** [ˋtebḷ͵klɔθ] *n.*   桌布

☐ 例 I can't believe you made this **tablecloth**. It is so beautiful.
☐
我真不敢相信你做了這件 tablecloth。它好漂亮。

882 **tasty** [ˋtestɪ] *adj.*   美味，可口

☐ 例 Whatever you are cooking, it must be **tasty**; it smells so good!
☐
不管你在煮什麼一定很 tasty，因為聞起來好香啊！

Chapter 6 社交活動

177

用具　　　883 **utensils** [ju`tɛns!z] *n.*

例 Helen bought her parents a set of stainless steel cooking **utensils**.

海倫買了一組不銹鋼的烹飪 utensils 給她父母。

素食者　　884 **vegetarian** [ˌvɛdʒə`tɛrɪən] *n.*

例 More and more people are becoming **vegetarians** for the sake of the environment.

為了地球環境，越來越多人成為 vegetarians。

Exercises

請從選項中,選出最適當的答案完成句子。

1. Jenny doesn't eat meat; she is a _____.
   (A) librarian (B) historian (C) vegetarian (D) politician

2. When Lily was told that snake meat was being served, she lost her _____ and left the table.
   (A) etiquette (B) stomach (C) appetite (D) attitude

3. A famous chef, Sam, will _____ my sister's wedding feast.
   (A) cook (B) attend (C) cater (D) prepare

4. They prepared _____ to entertain their guest, including a concert.
   (A) amusements (B) apartments (C) compartments (D) developments

5. Topics concerning religion and politics should be avoided because they are _____.
   (A) weak (B) delicate (C) tender (D) fragile

6. The _____ was amazed when the magician mysteriously made the elephant disappear.
   (A) congress (B) audience (C) congregation (D) assembly

7. Nick _____ a love song for his girlfriend, which she liked.
   (A) compiled (B) condensed (C) composed (D) adopted

8. The anniversary _____ was a success; many friends came and the food was good.
   (A) banquet (B) bouquet (C) bunch (D) handkerchief

9. Lily found Roy _____; he had a kind heart and was knowledgeable.
   (A) constructive (B) inactive (C) attractive (D) distractive

10. The twin brothers look so much alike that I often fail to _____ one from the other.
    (A) recognize (B) identify (C) extinguish (D) distinguish

11. Don't buy _____ CDs; it is against the law and it hurts the entertainment industry.

    (A) duplicated (B) imported (C) exported (D) pirated

12. The dance will be held at the school _____, the only place large enough for 500 students.

    (A) conference (B) library (C) laboratory (D) auditorium

13. I intend to sell my car, so I put an _____ in the paper.

    (A) suggestion (B) advertisement (C) commercial (D) advice

14. I like gardening; I weed the flower beds and water the plants in my _____ time.

    (A) leisure (B) lifetime (C) hobby (D) boredom

15. I've seen the _____ before, so I may not go to see the performance tomorrow.

    (A) operation (B) exercise (C) rehearsal (D) drill

16. Social _____ requires that men wear a tie on formal occasions.

    (A) etiquette (B) cigarette (C) eaglet (D) regulation

17. The elderly lady hugged the young man to show her _____ for his kindness in taking her across the busy street.

    (A) suspension (B) comprehension (C) apprehension (D) appreciation

18. After dinner, they had apple pie for _____.

    (A) assertion (B) concert (C) dessert (D) desert

19. Two presidential candidates attended the _____ of the movie.

    (A) prevention (B) premiere (C) primary (D) primitive

20. Many filmmakers were _____ by the writer; they based their stories on her novels.

    (A) inflicted (B) spurred (C) stimulated (D) inspired

Review 3

I Photographs (36)

Look at the pictures below and listen to the statements. Then choose the statement that best describes what you see in the picture.

1. (A) (B) (C) (D)   2. (A) (B) (C) (D)

II Conversations (37)

You will hear some conversations between two people. Listen to the conversations and answer the questions below.

Questions 3-4

3. Which location will the man choose?
    (A) Near the city center.
    (B) Near the airport.
    (C) By the beach.
    (D) He hasn't decided yet.

4. What does the woman say about the traffic?
    (A) It is bad downtown all day.
    (B) It is bad downtown early in the morning.
    (C) It is bad near the airport in the evening.
    (D) It is bad near the airport early in the morning.

Questions 5-6

5. What does the woman think about trains?
   (A) The price is reasonable.
   (B) It is a very fast method of travel.
   (C) The man has too many bags for a train.
   (D) The beautiful scenery is worthwhile.

6. What is the man's main reason for taking the train?
   (A) It is cheaper.
   (B) The scenery is beautiful.
   (C) He can take more luggage.
   (D) It helps protect the environment.

III Short Talks (38)

You will hear some short talks given by a single speaker. Listen to the short talks and answer the questions below.

Questions 7-8

7. What time is this information being given?
   (A) 7:15 am   (B) 8:00 am
   (C) 1:01 pm   (D) 7:45 pm

8. Who is this announcement for?
   (A) Truck drivers.   (B) Traffic policemen.
   (C) People driving to work. (D) Cleaning staff.

Questions 9-10

9. What does the speaker say about St. Monique?
   (A) There used to be more painters working there.
   (B) It is a business district.
   (C) It is famous for its cafés.
   (D) Many famous people live there.

10. Where are they going next?
    (A) To see a studio.   (B) To visit an art gallery.
    (C) To have a drink.   (D) To exchange money.

IV Incomplete Sentences

A word or phrase is missing in each of the sentences below. Four answer choices are given below each sentence. Select the best answer to complete the sentence.

11. I hope _____ you again soon.
    (A) see　　　(B) to see　　　C) seeing　　　(D) will see

12. Steven is planning _____ a long vacation at the end of this year.
    (A) to take　　　(B) taking　　　(C) take　　　(D) took

13. I'm thinking of _____ a day off on Monday.
    (A) to take　　　(B) taking　　　(C) take　　　(D) will take

14. The driver asked me how _____ to the airport.
    (A) getting　　　(B) he gets　　　(C) can get　　　(D) to get

15. I'm sorry, but I'm too busy _____ you right now.
    (A) seeing　　　(B) to see　　　(C) not see you　　　(D) see

16. Ben suggested _____ the event until after the national holiday.
    (A) postpone　　　(B) to postpone　　　(C) postponing　　　(D) to postponing

17. I remember nothing about the day of the accident, except _____ the house in the morning.
    (A) I left　　　(B) to leave　　　(C) leaving　　　(D) leave

18. We booked a _____ car when we traveled by overnight train to Madrid.
    (A) sleep　　　(B) slept　　　(C) to sleep　　　(D) sleeping

V Reading Comprehension

In this part, you will read a text. The text is followed by several questions. Select the best answer for each question and mark the letter (A), (B), (C), or (D).

Questions 19-20 refer to the following review.

> Stepping into Yanyan's cozy little restaurant, one first notices the pleasantly strong presence of authentic aromas. You will be greeted by Yanyan's wife as the two do all of the work at the restaurant themselves – Yanyan cooking and his wife taking care of the customers. Anything you order off the menu will be authentic and delicious, but the most famous are Yanyan's large prawn spring rolls and Shanghai-style noodles in sesame seed soup. Don't let the inexpensive prices fool you – everything on the menu tastes so good that you'd be willing to pay three times as much. So, for those of you who are big fans of good Chinese food, no place in the area could be more highly recommended than Yanyan's. Yanyan's is open every night except Tuesdays from 5 until midnight.

19. What might a customer at the restaurant think?
    (A) The food Yanyan serves is overpriced.
    (B) Yanyan uses a microwave oven.
    (C) The food may not taste good because of the low prices.
    (D) Yanyan does not pay his employees well.

20. What does the author recommend?
    (A) Leaving a tip.
    (B) Arriving early.
    (C) Looking for a different restaurant in the area.
    (D) Trying the prawn spring rolls.

VI Text Completion

Read the text that follows. A word or phrase is missing in some of the sentences. For each blank, four answer choices are given below. Select the best answer to complete the text.

Dear Clifford Hotel (21)_____,
(22)_____ is your hotel room card key. To use this card, simply slide the card into the slot on the door handle, then (23)_____ the card. The red light will turn green, and you just turn the handle to (24)_____ the room. If you lose this card key, please (25)_____ the front desk (26)_____; your old card will be (27)_____, and a new card will be issued to you. We thank you for your (28)_____ and wish you a very pleasant stay.

Yours sincerely,
Ronald Diego
Front Desk (29) _____

21. (A) customer   (B) consumer   (C) guest   (D) staff
22. (A) Enclosed   (B) Recommended   (C) Targeted   (D) Scheduled
23. (A) recommend (B) remove   (C) arrange   (D) slide
24. (A) enter   (B) entered   (C) entering   (D) have entered
25. (A) assume   (B) inform   (C) approve   (D) recognize
26. (A) immediate (B) immediately   (C) convenient   (D) conveniently
27. (A) canceled   (B) reduced   (C) removed   (D) contributed
28. (A) cooperation (B) information   (C) resignation   (D) arrangement
29. (A) Member   (B) Employer   (C) Supervisor   (D) Boss

Chapter 7
Finance 財務

Finance involves the management of a company's assets. The accounting department is tasked with recording transactions and producing financial reports. These reports provide analysis and insights into the company's finances and debts. They help the management make informed decisions based on identifying inflation and other factors that can cause costs to increase and profits to decrease. Furthermore, they serve as an essential indicator for investors and brokers to evaluate when considering investing.

Chapter 7 Finance 財務

1 Accounting 會計 ㉑

會計；
會計師

885 **accountant** [ə`kaʊntənt] *n.*

例 You need to be thorough to be a good **accountant**.

你需要非常仔細才能當一個好 accountant。

會計，
會計學

886 **accounting** [ə`kaʊntɪŋ] *n.*

例 The company just decided to switch to a new **accounting** system.

我們公司剛決定更換新的 accounting 系統。

分析

887 **analysis** [ə`næləsɪs] *n.*

例 After more **analysis**, Peter has decided the only way to reduce costs is to lay off two employees.

彼得在經過諸多 analysis 後，決定解雇兩名員工以降低成本。

申請；
申請書

888 **application** [ˌæplə`keʃən] *n.*

例 John's **application** for a bank loan was denied.

約翰向銀行貸款的 application 遭到拒絕。

債券，公債

889 **bond** [bɑnd] *n.*

例 During the economic recession, many people sold their **bonds**.

在經濟衰退時，許多人都將他們的 bonds 賣了。

890 **broker** [ˋbrokɚ] *n.*　（股票或證券）經紀人

例　Many people want to work on Wall Street as stock **brokers**.

有很多人想到華爾街當股票 brokers。

891 **check** [tʃɛk] *n.*　支票

例　The **check** you gave me bounced.

你給我的 check 跳票了。

892 **checkbook** [ˋtʃɛk͵bʊk] *n.*　支票簿

例　A **checkbook** comes in handy when you don't have cash.

手邊沒現金的時候，checkbook 就很方便了。

893 **controller** [kənˋtrolɚ] *n.*　主計員，查帳員

例　The accounting department error must be discussed with the financial **controller**.

會計部出的錯要會同財務 controller 一起討論。

894 **conversion** [kənˋvɝʃən] *n.*　折合，換算

例　What's the currency **conversion** between the US dollar and Euro today?

今天美元對歐元的貨幣 conversion 是多少？

895 **currency** [ˋkɝənsɪ] *n.*　貨幣，通貨

例　Most countries have their own **currencies**.

大部分的國家都有自己的 currencies。

Chapter 7 財務

189

削減，減少	896 **cut down** [ˋkʌtˋdaʊn] *v. phr.*
	例 Our company wants us to **cut down** on the amount of paper we use.
	公司希望大家 cut down 用紙量。

借款，債務	897 **debt** [tʃif] *adj.*
	例 The company went out of business because it ran up huge **debts**.
	這家公司因為巨額 debts 而關門大吉了。

減少，降低	898 **decrease** [dɪˋkris] *v.*
	例 In order to make more profit, the company has to **decrease** costs.
	為了要增加利潤，公司必須要 decrease 成本。

資產，財產	899 **estate** [əˋstet] *n.*
	例 The family **estate** was worth over five million dollars.
	這家人的 estate 價值五百萬美元以上。

位數	900 **figure** [ˋfɪgjɚ] *n.*
	例 If we can pull off the deal, there will be at least a seven **figure** profit for the company.
	如果我們能談成這個案子，公司將至少會有筆七 figure 的進帳。

財務狀況，資金	901 **finances** [ˋfaɪnænsɪz] *n. pl.*
	例 Before going to the bank for a loan, make sure your **finances** are in order.
	去銀行貸款前，請確定您的 finances 無虞。

902 **fluctuate** [ˋflʌktʃʊ͵et] v. 波動，變動

例 The stock market has **fluctuated** due to the recent earthquakes in Japan.

日本近日發生的地震造成股市 fluctuated。

903 **inflation** [ɪnˋfleʃən] n. 通貨膨脹

例 The **increase** in the cost of the product takes inflation rates into account.

產品成本增加的成因納入了 inflation 率。

904 **investor** [ɪnˋvɛstɚ] n. 投資者

例 The country tried to attract foreign **investors** by offering low interest rates.

這個國家希望藉由提供低率優惠吸引外來 investors。

905 **loan** [lon] n. 貸款

例 Lisa still owes the bank a hundred thousand dollars on her student **loan**.

莉莎還欠銀行十萬美元的學生 loan。

906 **maximum** [ˋmæksəməm] n. 最大值

例 Ten thousand NT dollars is the **maximum** we can spend on the company dinner.

我們能花在公司晚餐聚會的費用 maximum 為一萬元。

907 **mean** [min] n. 平均值

例 Could you get me the sales totals for each day of the month so I can calculate the daily **mean**?

可以給我當月每日的銷售金額，我好計算每日的 mean 嗎？

最小值；最低的，最少的	908	**minimum** [ˋmɪnəməm] *adj.*
		例 The **minimum** wage is 190 NT per hour.
		Minimum 時薪為 190 元。
欠	909	**owe** [o] *v.*
		例 The company still **owes** the supplier two thousand dollars.
		該公司還 owes 供應商兩千元。
預測，預言	910	**predict** [prɪˋdɪkt] *v.*
		例 Some financial experts **predict** the economy will stay the same as last year.
		有些金融專家 predict 經濟情況將和去年一樣。
壓力	911	**pressure** [ˋprɛʃɚ] *n.*
		例 Many households are feeling financial **pressure** due to the rise of living costs.
		許多家庭都因為物價上漲而有經濟 pressure。
不動產	912	**real estate** [ˋril əˌstet] *n.*
		例 **Real estate** in Shanghai is constantly going up.
		上海的 real estate 不斷地飆漲。
（經濟）衰退	913	**recession** [rɪˋsɛʃən] *n.*
		例 Everyone tightened their belts during the economic **recession**.
		經濟 recession 時，大家都會節省開銷。

914 **report** [rɪˋpɔrt] *n.* 報告

例 The annual fiscal **report** will be presented during the shareholders meeting.
年度會計 report 將會在股東大會上提出。

915 **risk** [rɪsk] *n.* 危險,風險

例 Your are taking a **risk** when you invest money in the stock market.
投資股市是有 risk 的。

916 **savings** [ˋsevɪŋz] *n.* 積蓄,存款

例 Danny has enough **savings** to put a down payment on a new home.
丹尼有足夠的 savings 來付新房子的頭期款。

917 **settlement** [ˋsɛt!mənt] *n.* 結算,(欠款的)償付

例 Your job is to handle the **settlement** of customer accounts.
你的工作是要處理顧客帳戶的 settlement。

918 **shares** [ʃɛrz] *n.* 股份,股票

例 He holds half of the **shares** in this company.
他擁有這家公司一半的 shares。

919 **slump** [slʌmp] *n.* 暴跌,衰退

例 There was a big **slump** in third-quarter revenues.
第三季的盈收慘遭重大 slump。

推測	920 **speculate** [ˈspɛkjəˌlet] *v.*
	例 Lola **speculates** there will be a drop in stock values.
	蘿拉 speculates 股市將會大跌。

穩定的	921 **stable** [ˈstebl̩] *adj.*
	例 We should make sure our finances are **stable** before we invest in that new idea.
	在將資金投入那新構想前，我們應該確保我們的財務狀況是 stable。

統計的，統計學的	922 **statistical** [stəˈtɪstɪkl̩] *adj.*
	例 Accounting is a **statistical** method of calculating numbers.
	會計是一種計算數字的 statistical 方法。

股票市場	923 **stock market** [ˈstɑkˌmɑrkɪt] *n.*
	例 The **stock market** in that country crashed during the war.
	在戰爭爆發期間，該國家的 stock market 崩盤了。

股東	924 **shareholder** [ˈʃɛrˌholdɚ] *n.*
	例 There are many **shareholders** involved in the project.
	有許多 shareholders 參與這項計畫。

小計	925 **subtotal** [ˈsʌbˌtotl̩] *n.*
	例 The **subtotal** for your purchase is twelve thousand NT (dollars).
	你所購物品的 subtotal 為一萬兩千元。

926 **transaction** [træn`zækʃən] n.   交易

例 How many **transactions** do you have with clients each day?

你每天與客戶有多少 transactions ？

927 **valuate** [`vælju‚et] v.   估計

例 The merchandise in stock was **valuated** at over one hundred thousand dollars.

商品存貨 valuated 有十萬美元以上的價值。

928 **yearly** [`jɪrlɪ] adj.   年度的

例 The **yearly** accounting report is confidential.

這份 yearly 會計報告屬機密文件。

2　Assets 資產 ㉒

929 **afford** [ə`fɔrd] v.   負擔得起

例 The company can't **afford** to lose profit on the sale of their downtown office building.

公司無法 afford 賣掉市區辦公大樓所造成的虧損。

930 **apartment** [ə`pɑrtmənt] n.   公寓

例 The **apartment** is only available to purchase as a residence, not as office space.

這 apartment 只能買來作為住家，不能作為辦公室。

195

估價，鑑定	931	**appraisal** [əˋprezl] *n.*
	例	Jack had someone do an **appraisal** on the house he inherited.
		傑克請人將他繼承的房子作個 appraisal。
資產	932	**asset** [ˋæsɛt] *n.*
	例	Patricia's downtown property is one of her more valuable **assets**.
		派翠西亞位於市區的房地產是她較有價值的 asset 之一。
拍賣	933	**auction** [ˋɔkʃən] *n.*
	例	The company is up for **auction**.
		那家公司將付之 auction。
證明書	934	**certificate** [səˋtɪfəkɪt] *n.*
	例	All employees were given a **certificate** that details their investment in company stocks.
		所有的員工都會有一份 certificate，詳註投資公司股票的細目。
耗盡	935	**drain** [dren] *v.*
	例	Mark and Judy **drained** their savings to purchase the small office space.
		馬克和茱蒂 drain 他們的積蓄，買了那間小小的辦公室。
估算，預估	936	**estimate** [ˋɛstəmet] *n.*
	例	Frank asked for an **estimate** on the cost of the repairs needed in the foyer.
		法蘭克要求提供維修玄關所需的費用 estimate。

937 **facilitate** [fə`sɪləˌtet] v.　　協助

例 Maria **facilitates** at least two open houses every weekend.

瑪麗亞每個週末至少 facilitates 兩間以上的待售屋看房。

938 **housing** [`haʊzɪŋ] n.　　（總稱）房屋，住宅

例 **Housing** downtown can be very expensive.

市區的 housing 可能非常昂貴。

939 **landmark** [`lændˌmɑrk] n.　　地標

例 The property is located next to one of the city's most famous **landmarks**.

該房產就座落在該市最富盛名的 landmark 旁。

940 **lend** [lɛnd] v.　　出借

例 Jake's parents offered to **lend** him enough money for a down payment on the property.

傑克的父母 lend 給他買房子的頭期款。

941 **ownership** [`onɚˌʃɪp] n.　　所有權

例 Please sign this agreement to indicate the date **ownership** takes effect.

請簽署這份合約，以表建物 ownership 移轉於簽署日期生效。

942 **period** [`pɪrɪəd] n.　　一段時間，時期

例 The property was on the market for a long **period** before any offers were made.

這房子公開銷售很長的 period 後才有人出價。

Chapter 7 財務

197

財產	943	**possession** [pəˋzɛʃən] *n.*
		例 They lost all of their **possessions**, including their house.
		他們失去了全部的 possessions，包括他們的房子。
重建	944	**rebuild** [riˋbɪld] *v.*
		例 It is going to take at least three months to **rebuild** the house that burned down.
		Rebuild 這間燒毀的房子少說也要三個月。
遷徙，重新安置	945	**relocate** [riˋloket] *v.*
		例 If we are going to **relocate** the business by the end of the month, we'd better start packing now!
		如果我們要在月底前 relocate 公司，那麼我們最好現在開始打包。
修繕，整修	946	**renovation** [ˌrɛnəˋveʃən] *n.*
		例 The estimated **renovation** cost exceeds our budget.
		預估的 renovation 費用超過我們的預算。
租	947	**rent** [rɛnt] *v.*
		例 It might be a good idea to **rent** a small retail space before purchasing one.
		在買之前先 rent 個小店面或許是個不錯的主意。
租賃的	948	**rental** [ˋrɛntl̩] *adj.*
		例 **Rental** spaces in this neighborhood are quite affordable.
		這附近 rental 物件價錢合適，租得起。

949 **residence** [ˋrɛzədəns] *n.*　　　　　　　　　住家

例 This office space used to be a **residence**.
這辦公室曾經是 residence。

950 **restructuring** [rɪˋstrʌktʃərɪŋ] *n.*　　　　　重組

例 The company is currently undergoing a troubled debt **restructuring**.
公司正在進行債務 restructuring。

951 **sale** [sel] *n.*　　　　　　　　　　　　　　買賣交易

例 The **sale** of the property was in the news.
該房產的 sale 上了新聞。

952 **tenant** [ˋtɛnənt] *n.*　　　　　　　　　　　房客

例 Rent from all **tenants** is due on the first of each month.
所有 tenants 的租金都是在每月的第一天到期。

Chapter 7 財務

Exercises

請從選項中,選出最適當的答案完成句子。

1. The _____ received a three-day notice from his landlord. If he didn't pay his rent then, he would have to move out.
   (A) tenant   (B) client   (C) guest   (D) customer

2. The ability to speak a foreign language is a great personal _____ .
   (A) property   (B) estate   (C) belonging   (D) asset

3. Your _____ of US$500 has been received; the balance of US$1500 is due in two months.
   (A) consumption   (B) investment   (C) deposit   (D) composite

4. The builder designer _____ that the remodeling cost would be around one hundred thousand.
   (A) investigated   (B) commented   (C) estimated   (D) surveyed

5. The government is issuing _____ to raise funds for the housing project.
   (A) bonds   (B) tickets   (C) coupons   (D) checks

6. Jane needs a _____ to expand her company.
   (A) loan   (B) load   (C) ladder   (D) lantern

7. Having made substantial profits, the investors had a difficult time trying to decide who should get the lion's _____ .
   (A) share   (B) sector   (C) part   (D) section

8. The _____ of 30 and 50 is 40.
   (A) mean   (B) addition   (C) division   (D) result

9. There is a certain _____ in going out with someone you don't know very well.
   (A) embarrassment   (B) risk   (C) reason   (D) anxiety

10. The _____ of your purchase is NT$ 3,458.
    (A) title   (B) subtotal   (C) measure   (D) amount

11. The dollar has been a strong _____ for quite some time, but the Euro seems to be catching up.
    (A) efficiency (B) currency (C) tendency (D) fluency

12. We benefit from the _____ wisdom of our elders if we listen to them.
    (A) concerned (B) related (C) assembled (D) accumulated

13. The _____ in the finance department said she could advance my payment if necessary.
    (A) salesman (B) attendant (C) waiter (D) accountant

14. The country is gradually recovering from a _____. The unemployment rate is dropping.
    (A) recession (B) detention (C) frustration (D) discussion

15. Because competition is intense, children are under a lot of _____ to do well in school.
    (A) pressure (B) treasure (C) leisure (D) pleasure

16. I'd rather not invest my money in the stock market; it _____ and makes me full of uncertainty.
    (A) violates (B) vibrates (C) fluctuates (D) drops

17. The company has gone bankrupt; it is up for _____.
    (A) auction (B) action (C) reduction (D) induction

18. I prefer to pay by _____ rather than by credit card.
    (A) note (B) cash (C) sum (D) unit

19. The _____ discount we can offer is 20 percent.
    (A) highest (B) minimum (C) maximum (D) largest

20. The figure doesn't look right. Please do the _____ again.
    (A) speculation (B) calculation (C) circulation (D) ventilation

Chapter 8
Purchasing & Logistics
採購與後勤

A strong purchasing and logistics department is essential for the effective operation of a company. A purchasing department's role is to select high-quality products, negotiate prices, and place orders with suppliers. Certain shippers may require clients to prepay for their orders before being shipped. The shipments are then delivered to the warehouse, where the logistics department is responsible for the proper storage of the items and their subsequent distribution to vendors and customers.

Chapter 8 Purchasing & Logistics 採購與後勤

New TOEIC 1200

1 Purchasing 採購 ㉓

贊成；同意

953 **approve** [əˋpruv] *v.*

例 The accounting department doesn't **approve** of the stationery purchase.

會計部不 approve 購買文具。

討價還價

954 **bargain** [ˋbɑrgɪn] *v.*

例 Always **bargain** before you agree to the final price.

在同意最後的價錢之前一定要 bargain。

出價；喊價

955 **bid** [bɪd] *v.*

例 The two companies are **bidding** to be the sole agent for a famous brand.

這兩家公司在競爭 bidding 知名品牌的獨家代理權。

提貨單

956 **bill of lading** [ˋbɪl əv ˋledɪŋ] *n.*

例 A **bill of lading** usually contains the shipping company name, shipper's name and description of goods.

Bill of lading 上通常會有海運公司、托運人的名稱以及貨名。

957 **brand-new** [ˋbrænd ˋnju] *adj.* 全新的，嶄新的

例 A **brand-new** machine has been set up in the factory.

工廠裡裝設了一架 brand-new 機器。

958 **buyer** [ˋbaɪɚ] *n.* 採購員；買主

例 Tom works at that company as a **buyer**.

湯姆在該公司擔任 buyer 的職位。

959 **carriage** [ˋkærɪdʒ] *n.* 運輸；運費

例 That airline charges a lot for **carriage**.

這家航空公司收取高額 carriage 費用。

960 **cash** [kæʃ] *n.* 現金

例 If you pay the bill in **cash**, the owner might not charge you tax.

如果你以 cash 交易，賣家可能不會加收稅金。

961 **catalog** [ˋkætəlɔg] *n.* 目錄

例 **Catalogs** were mailed to customers in the mail.

Catalogs 經電子郵件傳給客戶。

962 **charge** [tʃɑrdʒ] *v.* 要價

例 That company is **charging** way too much for photocopy paper.

那家公司的影印紙 charging 太高了。

商品；貨物　　963　**commodity** [kə`mɑdətɪ] *n.*

例　Coffee is one of South America's biggest **commodities**.
咖啡是南非最大宗的 commodities。

優惠券　　964　**coupon** [`kupɑn] *n.*

例　If you have a **coupon**, you can save ten percent on your purchase.
如果你有 coupon 的話，購買的商品可以打九折。

貿易商　　965　**dealer** [`dilɚ] *n.*

例　The computer **dealer** visits the office once a year to sell us updates.
電腦 dealer 每年都會來我們公司拜訪，兜售最新的產品。

折扣　　966　**discount** [`dɪskaʊnt] *n.*

例　We received a **discount** on the office furniture.
我們收到了辦公室家具的 discount。

免（稅）　　967　**exemption** [ɪg`zɛmpʃən] *n.*

例　The government offered a tax **exemption** on the purchase of wheelchair ramps for businesses.
政府提供企業 exemption 的條件設置無障礙坡道。

出口產品，輸出品　　968　**export** [`ɛkspɔrt] *n.*

例　Sugar cane is one of the major **exports** of the Philippines.
甘蔗是菲律賓主要 exports 之一。

969 **import** [ɪmˋpɔrt] v. 進口

☐ 例 The coffee in Canada is **imported** from countries with warmer climates.
☐ 加拿大的咖啡是從較暖和氣候的國家 imported 而來的。

970 **invoice** [ˋɪnvɔɪs] n. 發票

☐ 例 The shipping department forgot to put the **invoice** in the box.
☐ 裝運部門忘了將 invoice 放入箱中。

971 **negotiate** [nɪˋgoʃɪ͵et] v. 談判；商議

☐ 例 We will need to **negotiate** the price when purchasing new computers for the office.
☐ 我們為公司購買新電腦時將需要 negotiate 價格。

972 **on sale** [ɑnˋsel] phr. （廉價）出售，特價

☐ 例 The secretary said there are desks **on sale** at the furniture store down the street.
☐ 秘書說沿這條街往下走有間家具行，他們的書桌正在 on sale。

973 **order** [ˋɔrdɚ] v. 訂購

☐ 例 We usually order enough pens and pencils to last an entire year.
☐ 我們平常會 order 足夠一年份使用的筆和鉛筆。

974 **payable** [ˋpeəbl̩] adj. 支付給⋯

☐ 例 Please make your check **payable** to the owner.
☐ 請將支票上寫明憑票 payable 給該業主。

207

款項 | 975 **payment** [ˋpemənt] *n.*

例 **Payment** is due upon arrival of the order.

貨物送達後即需支付 payment。

預付 | 976 **prepay** [priˋpe] *v.*

例 We prefer for our customers to **prepay**, but you can also wait until delivery.

我們比較希望客戶能夠 prepay，但是您也可以等貨到了再付款。

價格 | 977 **price** [praɪs] *n.*

例 The **price** of mailing labels has gone up.

地址標籤的 price 已調漲。

（尤指為政府或機構）採購；收購 | 978 **procurement** [proˋkjʊrmənt] *n.*

例 When purchasing the company, the organization used a number of **procurement** strategies to lower costs and risks.

該機構採用一些 procurement 策略，以為了在收購該公司時能降低成本與風險。

採購；購買 | 979 **purchase** [ˋpɝtʃəs] *v.*

例 We have **purchased** enough staples for the entire year.

我們已經 purchased 一整年用量的釘書針。

折抵 | 980 **rebate** [ˋribet] *n.*

例 If we purchase five laptops for the office, we can receive a two-hundred dollar **rebate**.

如果我們辦公室買五部筆電，我們就能得到兩百元的 rebate。

981 **receipt** [rɪ`sit] *n.* 　　　　　　　　　收據

例 I can't find the **receipt** for the new fax machine.
我找不到新傳真機的 receipt。

982 **refuse** [rɪ`fjuz] *v.* 　　　　　　　　　拒絕

例 The salesperson **refused** to give us a lower price.
銷售員 refused 降價賣我們。

983 **reimbursement** [ˌriɪm`bɝsmənt] *n.* 　　償還；退款

例 If this coffee maker doesn't work, I will want a full **reimbursement**.
如果咖啡機無法運作，我要求全額 reimbursement。

984 **second-hand** [`sɛkənd`hænd] *adj.* 　　　二手的

例 If we cannot afford new office furniture, we may be able to find some **second-hand** furniture in good condition.
如果我們買不起新的辦公家具，也許可以買一些狀況不錯的 second-hand 家具。

985 **secure** [sɪ`kjʊr] *adj.* 　　　　　　　　安全的

例 Don't pay with a credit card online unless you are sure it is **secure**.
別在網路上使用信用卡付款，除非你確信它很 secure。

986 **seller** [`sɛlɚ] *n.* 　　　　　　　　　　賣方

例 The **seller** requested that payment be made upfront.
Seller 要求當面付款。

Chapter 8 採購與後勤

209

買東西，購物	987 **shop** [ʃɑp] *v.*
	例 The only way we can compare prices is if we **shop** around.
	我們唯一可以比價的方式就是到處去 shop。

商人，交易商	988 **trader** [ˈtredɚ] *n.*
	例 Mark has been a **trader** in the industry for over ten years.
	馬克在業界當 trader 已超過十年了。

緊急的	989 **urgent** [ˈɝdʒənt] *adj.*
	例 The manager of the purchasing department has an **urgent** call on line one.
	採購經理在一線有一通 urgent 電話。

多樣化；種類	990 **variety** [vəˈraɪətɪ] *n.*
	例 When selecting the products for the spring line, make sure there is a lot of **variety**.
	在選擇春季產品時，要確定有許多 variety。

販賣	991 **vend** [vɛnd] *v.*
	例 Before becoming a salesperson in the company, Maria used to **vend** clothing at night markets.
	瑪麗亞在成為公司的業務員之前，她曾經在夜市 vend 衣服。

2 Logistics 後勤 ㉔

992 **airmail** [ˋɛrˌmel] *n.*   航空郵件

例 Please send the invoice by **airmail**.
請將發票以 airmail 寄出。

993 **by sea** [baɪˋsi] *adv. phr.*   經由海運地

例 Sending products **by sea** takes a long time.
以 by sea 寄送貨物需要很長的時間。

994 **cargo** [ˋkɑrgo] *n.*   船貨，貨物

例 The **cargo** was delivered to the warehouse in poor condition.
Cargo 送到倉庫時已經破損。

995 **courier** [ˋkʊrɪɚ] *n.*   快遞員

例 The **courier** was supposed to drop off the package before noon.
Courier 應該在中午之前將包裹送達。

996 **coverage** [ˋkʌvərɪdʒ] *n.*   保固，擔保

例 The warranty for the fax machine gives us **coverage**.
這張保證書給予這台傳真機 coverage。

997 **damage** [ˋdæmɪdʒ] *v.*   損害

例 The gifts I packed were **damaged** during the flight.
我包好的禮物在飛機運送過程中 damaged 了。

遞送 | 998 **deliver** [dɪ`lɪvɚ] v.

例 If the package isn't **delivered** on time, it will delay our work.

如果那件包裹沒有準時 delivered，那將會延宕我們的工作。

經銷 | 999 **distribution** [ˌdɪstrə`bjuʃən] n.

例 **Distribution** of the product across the country is our number one goal.

我們的首要目標是將產品 distribution 到全國各地。

快捷 | 1000 **express** [ɪk`sprɛs] adj.

例 It costs extra to ship the product via **express** mail.

用 express 郵件寄出這產品得支付額外的費用。

運輸的貨物 | 1001 **freight** [fret] n.

例 The **freight** was damaged in the accident.

Freight 不小心損毀了。

檢查，檢驗 | 1002 **inspection** [ɪn`spɛkʃən] n.

例 All merchandise must go through a careful **inspection** process before being shipped to buyers.

所有的商品在出貨給買方之前，必須經過仔細的 inspection 流程。

有存貨／庫存 | 1003 **in stock** [ɪn`stak] phr.

例 Unfortunately, we don't have any more colored paper **in stock**.

很遺憾，我們並沒有任何的色紙 in stock。

1004 **merchandise** [ˈmɝtʃənˌdaɪz] *n.* 商品；貨物

　　例　All **merchandise** must be inspected when it arrives.
　　　　所有的 merchandise 到貨時皆須經過檢驗。

1005 **origin** [ˈɔrədʒɪn] *n.* 由來；起源

　　例　Does anyone know the **origin** of this coffee?
　　　　有人知道這咖啡的 origin 嗎？

1006 **out of stock** [ˈaʊt əvˈstɑk] *phr.* 售完，沒有庫存

　　例　When I called to place an order, the supplier said they were currently **out of stock**.
　　　　我打電話給供應商下訂單時，他們說現已 out of stock。

1007 **overweight** [ˈovɚˈwet] *adj.* 超重

　　例　You are going to have to remove some merchandise from the box because it is **overweight**.
　　　　因為箱子 overweight，你必須把一些貨物移出來。

1008 **package** [ˈpækɪdʒ] *n.* 包裝

　　例　The **package** got wet during shipment.
　　　　在運送過程中，外 package 潮濕了。

1009 **parcel** [ˈpɑrsl̩] *n.* 包裹

　　例　Jane sent the **parcel** by airmail.
　　　　珍以航空郵件寄這 parcel。

Chapter 8　採購與後勤

213

郵資

1010 **postage** [ˋpostɪdʒ] *n.*

例 How much is the **postage** for an over-sized envelope?

特大信封的 postage 是多少錢？

郵務的，
郵遞的

1011 **postal** [ˋpostl] *adj.*

例 The **postal** service is expensive in this country.

該國的 postal 服務是昂貴的。

明信片

1012 **postcard** [ˋpost͵kɑrd] *n.*

例 Many people enjoy collecting **postcards** and sending them to their homes or friends while they travel.

許多人喜歡收集明信片，並在旅行途中寄明信片回家或給朋友。

郵戳

1013 **postmark** [ˋpost͵mɑrk] *n.*

例 The **postmark** indicates the package was sent last Monday.

Postmark 顯示，這包裹是上星期一寄出的。

收件者

1014 **recipient** [rɪˋsɪpɪənt] *n.*

例 The **recipient** should check the contents of the package carefully.

Recipient 應該小心檢查包裹的內容物。

零售

1015 **retail** [ˋritel] *n.*

例 Most **retail** stores are open from 9 am to 9 pm.

大多數的 retail 商店營業時間為早上九點到晚上九點。

1016 **retailer** [ˋritelɚ] *n.* 零售商

例 Bob Hendry is one of the biggest **retailers** in the city.

鮑伯・亨德利是本市最大的 retailers 之一。

1017 **return** [rɪˋtɝn] *n.* 退貨

例 We only accept **returns** up to thirty days after purchase.

我們只接受購買後三十天內的 returns。

1018 **review** [rɪˋvju] *n.* 檢查，複查

例 The packaging process is under **review**.

包裝流程正在 review 當中。

1019 **ship** [ʃɪp] *v.* 運送

例 Your products will be **shipped** within the next two weeks.

您的產品將於兩星期內 shipped。

1020 **shipment** [ˋʃɪpmənt] *n.* （裝運的）貨物；貨運

例 Your **shipment** has been delayed due to availability issues.

您的 shipment 因產品缺貨而延遲出貨。

1021 **shipper** [ˋʃɪpɚ] *n.* 承運商，運貨商

例 The **shipper** misplaced your package.

Shipper 出錯貨了。

Chapter 8 採購與後勤

215

商店經理；店主	1022 **shopkeeper** [ˋʃɑpˌkipɚ] *n.*
	例 If the **shopkeeper** is not in, ask to speak to the assistant manager.
	如果 shopkeeper 不在，那就找副理。

存貨；庫存品	1023 **stock** [stɑk] *n.*
	例 We need to place a new order because our **stock** is getting low.
	我們需要下新的訂單，因為我們的 stock 快沒了。

貯藏；倉庫	1024 **storage** [ˋstorɪdʒ] *n.*
	例 The **storage** shelves are full of office supplies.
	Storage 架上放滿了辦公用品。

供應商	1025 **supplier** [səˋplaɪɚ] *n.*
	例 Our **supplier** contacts us regularly to see if we need to place an order.
	我們的 supplier 會定期聯絡，看看我們是否有需要下單。

庫存；供應	1026 **supply** [səˋplaɪ] *n.*
	例 The **supply** closet is too small for all our supplies.
	Supply 櫃太小了，放不下我們所有的存貨。

（貨運）追蹤編號	1027 **tracking number** [ˋtrækɪŋ ˌnʌmbɚ] *n. phr.*
	例 Make sure you keep the **tracking** number, just in case the parcel goes missing.
	一定要保留貨運的 tracking number，以防包裹遺失。

1028 **transport** [træns`pɔrt] v.　　　　運送，運輸

- 例 How will the product be **transported**?
  產品將要怎麼 transported 呢？

1029 **trunk** [trʌŋk] n.　　　　汽車車尾的行李箱

- 例 You will have to ship the order to my office because it won't fit in my **trunk**.
  因為訂貨無法放進我車子的 trunk，你必須要用貨運寄出。

1030 **unload** [ʌn`lod] v.　　　　卸貨

- 例 I will need some help to **unload** the product from my car.
  我需要人幫忙從我的車子 unload 產品。

1031 **unpack** [ʌn`pæk] v.　　　　打開包裹

- 例 Employees in the shipping and receiving department are asked to **unpack** merchandise carefully.
  貨物收發部門的職員須要小心翼翼地 unpack 商品。

1032 **unsecured** [ˌʌnsɪ`kjʊrd] adj.　　　　無擔保的

- 例 The boxes were **unsecured** during shipment.
  貨箱在托運過程中是 unsecured。

1033 **via** [`vaɪə] prep.　　　　經由

- 例 Your package will be shipped **via** express mail.
  你的包裹將會 via 快捷郵遞運送。

倉庫 | 1034 **warehouse** [ˋwɛrˏhaʊs] *n.*

例 Please drop off the merchandise at the **warehouse**, not our office.

請到 warehouse 卸貨，而不是在我們的辦公室。

在世界各地 | 1035 **worldwide** [ˋwɝˋlˋwaɪd] *adv.*

例 The cost of shipping product **worldwide** is very high.

將產品運送 worldwide 的費用非常高。

包裹 | 1036 **wrap** [ræp] *v.*

例 Be sure to **wrap** the breakable items with newspaper to prevent damage.

要用報紙 wrap 易碎的物品來避免毀壞。

X光，X射線 | 1037 **X-ray** [ˋɛksˋre] *n.*

例 Products that are shipped by air will need to go through **X-ray**.

用空運寄送的貨品需要通過 X-ray 檢查。

Exercises

請從選項中，選出最適當的答案完成句子。

1. There was a communication _____ when the customer ordered a snake instead of a snack.

   (A) breakdown   (B) shutdown   (C) breakup   (D) destruction

2. You need a birth _____ to provide information regarding your birthplace.

   (A) declaration   (B) degree   (C) certificate   (D) diploma

3. A(n) _____ of food can be found at the night market.

   (A) odd   (B) variety   (C) obstacle   (D) structure

4. The manager told the secretary to order more _____ for the office.

   (A) resources   (B) supplies   (C) services   (D) attendants

5. Jack has a part time job _____ pizza.

   (A) providing   (B) delivering   (C) offering   (D) sending

6. The man is very sick; it is _____ that he be sent to a hospital.

   (A) desirable   (B) urgent   (C) unavoidable   (D) inevitable

7. Some parents don't _____ of their children staying overnight at a friend's place.

   (A) approve   (B) agree   (C) consent   (D) allow

8. The _____ of the word datum is Latin, while the _____ of kung fu is Chinese.

   (A) benchmark   (B) milestone   (C) origin   (D) source

9. Bicycles are one of the products that are _____ from Taiwan.

   (A) extended   (B) exposed   (C) escorted   (D) exported

10. We put all the fishing gear in the _____ of the car and headed for the sea.

    (A) cabinet   (B) trunk   (C) closet   (D) case

11. You can return any defective _____ and we will refund your money or give you a replacement.
    (A) commodity (B) supply (C) amount (D) catalog

12. My dealer said I could delay the _____ until I was satisfied with his product.
    (A) total (B) payment (C) debt (D) sum

13. I think you are being unreasonably _____—this used car isn't worth that much.
    (A) confined (B) chained (C) charged (D) changed

14. When you buy anything, be sure to keep the _____; you might win some big prize money.
    (A) attention (B) reception (C) receipt (D) deception

15. The _____ let me test drive the new car, and I bought it as a result.
    (A) leader (B) dealer (C) healer (D) jumper

16. Remember you have the right to _____ to be questioned by the police without the presence of your lawyer.
    (A) cancel (B) refuse (C) deject (D) project

17. I was hesitant about the party, but my sister _____ me to go and I had a good time.
    (A) pretended (B) intended (C) dissuaded (D) persuaded

18. The kidnappers didn't want to _____; the only thing they would accept was the full ransom, not a penny less.
    (A) communicate (B) negotiate (C) associate (D) depreciate

19. A(n) _____ is a very useful guide when you go shopping.
    (A) catalog (B) index (C) appendix (D) summary

20. Troops were _____ to the battlefield by plane and ship.
    (A) delivered (B) mailed (C) assigned (D) transported

Review 4

I Photographs (39)

Look at the pictures below and listen to the statements. Then choose the statement that best describes what you see in the picture.

1. (A) (B) (C) (D)

2. (A) (B) (C) (D)

II Conversations (40)

You will hear some conversations between two people. Listen to the conversations and answer the questions below.

Questions 3-4

3. What is the problem?
   (A) A customer made a complaint.
   (B) The phone isn't working.
   (C) A client hasn't paid his bill.
   (D) The notice didn't arrive.

4. What does the man suggest?
   (A) Calling the customer.
   (B) Notifying the police.
   (C) Sending a notice.
   (D) Paying the bill.

Questions 5-6

5. Which statement is true?

    (A) They made fewer long-distance phone calls this month.

    (B) Their phone bill is less expensive than last month's.

    (C) The company informed them in advance.

    (D) They recently found a new provider.

6. What does the woman suggest?

    (A) Informing the bank.

    (B) Complaining about the fees.

    (C) Making fewer phone calls.

    (D) Changing to a different company.

III Short Talks (41)

You will hear a short talk given by a single speaker. Listen to the short talk and answer the questions below.

Questions 7-8

7. What is the purpose of this meeting?

    (A) To discuss last year's financial statement.

    (B) To talk about the economic crisis.

    (C) To collect suggestions for cutting expenses.

    (D) To propose ideas for a new product.

8. What does the financial statement show?

    (A) The accounting department did a good job.

    (B) The company is in a state of emergency.

    (C) The economy is finally picking up again.

    (D) The company's revenue has gone down.

IV Incomplete Sentences

A word or phrase is missing in each of the sentences below. Four answer choices are given below each sentence. Select the best answer to complete the sentence.

9. I'm very _____ about my job interview tomorrow.
   (A) excite (B) excited (C) exciting (D) excitement

10. The manager's office is _____ on the second floor.
    (A) locate (B) located (C) locating (D) location

11. I will collect all the suggestions _____ in today's meeting.
    (A) make (B) made (C) were made (D) making

12. The _____ team will receive $1000 in cash.
    (A) win (B) won (C) winning (D) winner

13. To get to the marketing department, go _____ those stairs and turn right.
    (A) along (B) down (C) over (D) through

14. She left school and started working _____ the age of sixteen.
    (A) at (B) when (C) on (D) in

15. Emily is the girl standing _____ the man in the blue suit.
    (A) at (B) around (C) besides (D) next to

16. I'll grab some lunch _____ the two meetings..
    (A) in between (B) out of (C) during (D) over

223

V Reading Comprehension

In this part, you will read a selection of texts. Each text is followed by several questions. Select the best answer for each question and mark the letter (A), (B), (C), or (D).

Questions 17-19 refer to the following notice.

> Wiring money overseas is not a difficult thing. In fact, it can be quite easy if we have the correct information. First, we will need the bank's name, branch, address, telephone number, and bank code. We also need the recipient's account name and number. And finally, we will need your signature on the wire registration form. After all of this has been completed, you will be able to request a wire transfer of funds via our 24-hour customer service line.

17. What is being discussed?
    (A) Opening a bank account.
    (B) Applying for a credit card.
    (C) Sending money.
    (D) Finding a good bank.

18. What is needed for this process?
    (A) A deposit.
    (B) A check.
    (C) A signature.
    (D) An email address.

19. What is the advantage of this process?
    (A) You can do it by phone.
    (B) You can get a gift.
    (C) You can travel overseas.
    (D) You don't have to sign anything.

Questions 20-21 refer to the following letter.

June 4, 2010
Ms. Isabel Tan
3419 Green Street
Singapore

Dear Ms. Tan,
Our accounting department has noted a serious error in the billing of your recent order for carpeting. In computing the total amount, Sales Representative Alan Lim failed to include the estimates given to you for two of the bedrooms. The true cost of the carpeting is in fact SGD 3,605, not SGD 2,495. A new invoice is attached.
We sincerely regret any inconvenience our error has caused you.
We appreciate your down payment of SGD 1,500 and request that the new balance due of SGD 2,105 be paid within thirty days. Again, we apologize for the confusion and appreciate your business.
Sincerely,
Mark Chua
Owner
Carpets Plus

20. What did the Carpets Plus sales representative do wrong?

(A) He undercharged a customer.

(B) He told the customer that the carpet would cost SGD 2,105.

(C) He did not apologize for raising the price of the carpet.

(D) He forgot to send the bill.

21. How much does Ms. Tan still owe?

(A) SGD 1,500.

(B) SGD 2,105.

(C) SGD 2,495.

(D) SGD 3,605.

VI Text Completion

Read the text that follows. A word or phrase is missing in some of the sentences. For each blank, four answer choices are given below. Select the best answer to complete the text.

Dear New Subscriber,
We thank you for your (22)_____ order for Sport Times Magazine – the best, most exciting magazine in sports. We would like to (23)_____ you that your subscription (24)_____ is overdue. If you would like to continue (25)_____ issues, please send in your payment no later than January 10.

If you have already (26)_____ your payment, kindly disregard this letter and we thank you in (27)_____ . If you have any questions or comments, please call our tollfree (28)_____ service center at 1-800-788-4637.

Thank you very much.
ALF Distribution Services

22. (A) payment (B) questionnaire (C) invoice (D) subscription
23. (A) maintain (B) remind (C) appreciate (D) ship
24. (A) purchase (B) payment (C) survey (D) package
25. (A) receive (B) received (C) receiving (D) will receive
26. (A) make (B) made (C) have made (D) had made
27. (A) exchange (B) purchase (C) refund (D) advance
28. (A) employee (B) consumer (C) customer (D) staff

Chapter 9
Production 生產

Production refers to the process of manufacturing goods in large quantities, typically within a factory setting. Many factories utilize assembly lines, where a series of machines or workers assemble products step by step as the products move along the line. If the assembly line stops, even only for a moment, it can lead to substantial losses for the factory. Consequently, technicians are required to adhere to routine procedures for daily inspections and maintenance to prevent malfunctions, and operators are instructed to secure their long hair for safety reasons.

Chapter 9 Production 生產

New TOEIC 1200

1　Equipment 設備 ㉕

先進的，
進階的
1038 **advanced** [əd`vænst] *adj.*

　例　Our company has an **advanced** assembly line to reduce the number of defects in our products.
　　　本公司有 advanced 生產線可減少產品的不良數。

器具，器械
1039 **appliance** [ə`plaɪəns] *n.*

　例　The **appliances** made at our factory are energy efficient.
　　　本工廠所製造的 appliances 都是節能的。

自動的
1040 **automatic** [ˌɔtə`mætɪk] *adj.*

　例　Jim created an **automatic** machine that replaces the need for employees to seal packages manually.
　　　吉姆製造出一台 automatic 機器，可取代以人工封袋的人員需求。

停電
1041 **blackout** [`blæk͵aʊt] *n.*

　例　The factory is equipped with emergency lights in case of a **blackout**.
　　　工廠裝置了緊急照明燈，以防發生 blackout。

攪拌，混合
1042 **blend** [blɛnd] *v.*

　例　It is important to **blend** the mixture thoroughly before putting it in the machine.
　　　在投入機器前先將混合物徹底 blend 是至關重要的。

1043 **bulb** [bʌlb] *n.* 電燈泡

例 The headlights in the new car model have faulty **bulbs**.
新車款的前大燈 bulbs 有瑕疵。

1044 **chip** [tʃɪp] *v.* 碰出缺口

例 We can't sell any merchandise that has been **chipped**.
我們不能將已經 chipped 的商品賣出去。

1045 **device** [dɪˋvaɪs] *n.* 裝置

例 The company is designing a new **device** that will decrease the number of people needed on the assembly line.
公司正在研發一款新 device，能減少生產線上所需的人力。

1046 **electric** [ɪˋlɛktrɪk] *adj.* 電動的，電的

例 Due to the poor economy, production of the newest model of **electric** cars has slowed down.
由於經濟不景氣，最新款 electric 車的生產已趨減緩。

1047 **factory** [ˋfæktərɪ] *n.* 工廠

例 Production was delayed because of a fire at the **factory**.
因 factory 發生火災造成生產的延誤。

1048 **fridge** [frɪdʒ] *n.* 電冰箱

例 If you are looking for a new **fridge**, be sure to purchase one that is energy efficient.
假如我們要買新的 fridge，一定要買節能的。

運轉，作用 | 1049 **function** [ˈfʌŋkʃən] *v.*

例 The machine isn't **functioning** properly today.
今天機器有些 functioning 不良。

齒輪組 | 1050 **gear** [gɪr] *n.*

例 The **gears** in the machine are jammed.
機器的 gears 卡住了。

失準，錯誤 | 1051 **inaccuracy** [ɪnˈækjərəsɪ] *n.*

例 The **inaccuracy** of the new machine has created many production errors.
新機器的 inaccuracy 造成諸多生產錯誤。

結合，合併 | 1052 **incorporation** [ɪnˌkɔrpəˈreʃən] *n.*

例 The **incorporation** of this new technology will help us work faster.
這項新科技的 incorporation 將有助我們加速作業。

器具，儀器 | 1053 **instrument** [ˈɪnstrəmənt] *n.*

例 All **instruments** used in the manufacturing process need to be inspected on a daily basis.
製造過程中所使用的一切 instrument，每天都要檢測。

介紹 | 1054 **introduce** [ˌɪntrəˈdjus] *v.*

例 The new equipment will be **introduced** to the staff at the next meeting.
下次會議將會把新設備 introduce 給員工。

1055 **laboratory** [ˋlæbrə͵tɔrɪ] *n.*　　　　　　實驗室

例 The chemists are testing the quality of the new product in the **laboratory**.

化學家正在 laboratory 裡測試新產品的品質。

1056 **machine** [məˋʃin] *n.*　　　　　　機器，機械

例 The **machines** in the factory often break down.

工廠裡的 machines 時常故障。

1057 **machinery** [məˋʃinərɪ] *n.*　　　　　　（總稱）機器，機械

例 Jacob's company is purchasing new **machinery** for the factory.

雅各的公司將買進新 machinery。

1058 **maintenance** [ˋmentənəns] *n.*　　　　　　保養，維修

例 It is important that regular **maintenance** is performed on the assembly line equipment.

生產設備的定期 maintenance 是很重要的。

1059 **malfunction** [mælˋfʌŋkʃən] *v.*　　　　　　故障，失靈

例 When the equipment **malfunctions**, production (of the product) slows down.

當設備 malfunctions 時，產品製造的速度就會減慢。

1060 **mechanic** [məˋkænɪk] *n.*　　　　　　機械工，修理工

例 The **mechanic** said he wouldn't be able to fix the machine until tomorrow afternoon.

Mechanic 說他沒辦法在明天下午前修好這台機器。

Chapter 9 生產

231

機械的　1061 **mechanical** [mə`kænɪkl] *adj.*

- 例 There is no one on staff that knows how to fix the **mechanical** issues with the photocopier.
  員工裡無人知曉如何修理影印機 mechanical 方面的問題。

操作　1062 **operate** [`ɑpə͵ret] *v.*

- 例 Frank is training new employees on how to **operate** the machinery.
  法蘭克正訓練新員工如何 operate 機器。

操作人員　1063 **operator** [`ɑpə͵retɚ] *n.*

- 例 The **operator** reported a problem with the old equipment in the factory.
  Operator 報告工廠的老舊設備所衍生出的問題。

復原，恢復　1064 **recovery** [rɪ`kʌvərɪ] *n.*

- 例 The computer has gone into **recovery** mode because it was not shut down properly.
  由於未正常關機，電腦進入了 recovery 模式。

調整，校準　1065 **regulate** [`rɛgjə͵let] *v.*

- 例 Michael **regulated** the machinery so it would work properly again.
  麥可 regulated 機器，以便能再度正常運轉。

調整，校準　1066 **regulation** [͵rɛgjə`leʃən] *n.*

- 例 It is important to ensure machine **regulation** at all times.
  隨時確保機器 regulation 是很重要的。

1067 **repair** [rɪˋpɛr] *v.* 　　　　　　　　　　修理，修補

　例 If we aren't able to **repair** the equipment by this afternoon, we won't be able to meet our daily quota.
　　 如果我們在今天下午前沒辦法 repair 設備，我們將無法達到每日配額。

1068 **revolution** [ˌrɛvəˋluʃən] *n.* 　　　　變革，革命

　例 This equipment is the latest **revolution** in the manufacturing industry.
　　 這個設備可說是製造業最新的 revolution。

1069 **software** [ˋsɔftˌwɛr] *n.* 　　　　　　軟體

　例 Could you help me install this **software** on my computer?
　　 能麻煩您幫我把這 software 安裝到我的電腦嗎？

1070 **standard** [ˋstændɚd] *n.* 　　　　　　標準

　例 The equipment in the factory does not meet industry **standards**.
　　 工廠設備無法達到產業 standards。

1071 **steel** [stil] *n.* 　　　　　　　　　　鋼鐵

　例 The support beams in the warehouse are **steel**.
　　 倉庫裡的支撐梁是 steel 做的。

1072 **tool** [tul] *n.* 　　　　　　　　　　　工具

　例 This software program is an excellent **tool** for employees.
　　 這套軟體程式對員工來說是很棒的 tool。

233

關閉　　　1073 **turn off** [`tɝn `ɔf] *v. phr.*

例 Employees are asked to **turn off** all equipment before leaving the office.
員工要在離開辦公室時 turn off 所有的設備。

開啟　　　1074 **turn on** [`tɝn `ɑn] *v. phr.*

例 The machine must be **turned on** at least one hour before production begins.
該機器在開始製造前得至少先行 turn on 一小時。

升級　　　1075 **upgrade** [`ʌp`gred] *v.*

例 The boss is paying for all the computers in the office to be **upgraded**.
我們老闆付錢讓公司裡所有的電腦都能 upgraded。

保固　　　1076 **warranty** [`wɔrəntɪ] *n.*

例 The photocopier came with a five year **warranty**.
影印機有五年的 warranty。

線路　　　1077 **wire** [waɪr] *n.*

例 If the **wires** are not connected properly, the machine won't work.
如果 wire 沒有接對，機器就無法運轉。

2 Production 生產 (26)

1078 **amazing** [əˋmezɪŋ] *adj.* 令人驚訝的

☐ 例 Jane has an **amazing** idea to reduce production costs.
☐ 珍有個降低生產成本的 amazing 構想。

1079 **analyze** [ˋænəlaɪz] *v.* 分析

☐ 例 The accountants **analyzed** the sales data from last year to estimate this year's production costs.
☐ 會計師 analyzed 去年的銷貨數據來預估今年的生產成本。

1080 **approach** [əˋprotʃ] *n.* 方法，方式

☐ 例 We need to take a creative **approach** in promoting our new software.
☐ 我們需採取創意的 approach 來推廣新軟體。

1081 **artificial** [͵ɑrtəˋfɪʃəl] *adj.* 人工的

☐ 例 None of the products made in our factory contain **artificial** ingredients.
☐ 本工廠生產製造的產品都不含 artificial 成分。

1082 **assemble** [əˋsɛmbl] *v.* 裝配，組裝

☐ 例 All of our office furniture comes with instructions on how to **assemble** the pieces.
☐ 本公司所有的辦公家具皆附上如何 assemble 的說明書。

Chapter 9 生產

235

生產線　　1083 **assembly line** [əˋsɛmblɪˏlaɪn] *n. phr.*

例 It is important that employees working on the **assembly line** wear a hair net.

Assembly line 上的作業員戴髮網這件事很重要。

滲開，散開　1084 **bleed** [blid] *v.*

例 The dye used on this garment **bleeds** when wet.

染在這衣服上的顏色一碰到水就 bleeds 了。

品種　　1085 **breed** [brid] *n.*

例 In our body lotions we use extracts from rare plant **breeds** found only in the Amazon.

我們在身體乳液產品中所使用的濃縮精華，來自亞馬遜河地區才有的稀有植物 breeds。

分門別類　1086 **categorize** [ˋkætəgəˏraɪz] *v.*

例 They should **categorize** the products by weight, not size.

他們應以產品的重量，而非大小來 categorize。

化學物質　1087 **chemical** [ˋkɛmɪkl] *n.*

例 All factory employees must wear protective goggles when handling **chemicals**.

工廠所有的員工在處理 chemicals 時，皆需戴上護目鏡。

化學家；藥劑師　1088 **chemist** [ˋkɛmɪst] *n.*

例 The **chemist** will be sharing the results from the product trials at the meeting this morning.

Chemist 將在今早的會議上告訴大家產品測試的結果。

1089 **chemistry** [ˋkɛmɪstrɪ] *n.* 化學

例 We will need to hire someone with qualifications in **chemistry** for the design of the new dish washing liquid.

我們需要聘雇具 chemistry 專長的人研發新洗碗精。

1090 **competitive** [kəmˋpɛtətɪv] *adj.* 有競爭力的

例 Even though our sales are up, we have to remain **competitive** by trying to speed up production.

儘管我們的銷售量成長，仍須設法加速生產以維持 competitive。

1091 **consist** [kənˋsɪst] *v.* 組成，構成

例 Our factory staff **consists** of twenty full-time and ten part-time workers.

本工廠的員工是由二十名全職與十名兼職員工所 consists。

1092 **convenient** [kənˋvinɪənt] *adj.* 便利，方便

例 It would be more **convenient** if the warehouse was closer to the factory.

如果倉庫能更靠近工廠，那就會更加 convenient。

1093 **discover** [dɪˋskʌvɚ] *v.* 發現

例 It is important for us to **discover** a better way to package our product to ensure it is not damaged.

對我們來說，discover 更有效率的方式包裝商品，確保商品完好無缺是至關重要的。

Chapter 9 生產

237

劑量	1094 **dose** [dos] *n.*
	☐ 例 The instructions included on the back of the vitamin bottle indicate the recommended **dose** for adults.
	維他命瓶身上的使用說明指示了成人建議攝取的 dose。

電氣技師，電氣工	1095 **electrician** [ɪˌlɛkˋtrɪʃən] *n.*
	☐ 例 We have to wait until the **electrician** inspects the building before we can continue working safely.
	我們得等到 electrician 檢驗過大樓後才能繼續安全地施工。

發現，調查結果	1096 **finding** [ˋfaɪndɪŋ] *n.*
	☐ 例 The research conducted by the production team made some very important **findings**.
	生產團隊所進行的研究有非常重要的 findings。

指導原則，準則	1097 **guideline** [ˋgaɪdˌlaɪn] *n.*
	☐ 例 There are many safety **guidelines** to follow when working in a factory.
	在工廠工作有許多安全 guidelines 需要遵循。

產業	1098 **industry** [ˋɪndəstrɪ] *n.*
	☐ 例 The automotive **industry** is on a decline.
	汽車 industry 在衰退中。

產業的；工業的	1099 **industrial** [ɪnˋdʌstrɪəl] *adj.*
	☐ 例 Our office is located in an **industrial** area of the city.
	我們公司位於本市的 industrial 區。

1100 **invention** [ɪn`vɛnʃən] *n.* 發明

例 One of our employees came up with an **invention** to save time and money on the production of our best selling product.

有個職員提出一項 invention，能讓公司的暢銷產品製程省時又省錢。

1101 **journal** [`dʒɝnl] *n.* 日誌

例 Employees are asked to keep a **journal** of the number of product defects found each day.

員工必須寫 journal 以記錄每日發現的產品瑕疵數量。

1102 **manufacture** [ˌmænjə`fæktʃɚ] *v.* 生產，製造

例 The factory **manufactures** affordable vehicles.

這家工廠 manufactures 價格實惠的車輛。

1103 **measure** [`mɛʒɚ] *v.* 估量，斟酌

例 To avoid problems it is important to carefully **measure** the amount of material put into the machine.

為避免任何問題發生，精細 measure 放進機器裡的原料量是很重要的。

1104 **organic** [ɔr`gænɪk] *adj.* 有機的

例 Mary's company only uses **organic** ingredients in their food products.

瑪莉的公司只使用 organic 食材製造食品。

Chapter 9 生產

239

組織；規劃　1105 **organize** [ˋɔrgənˌaɪz] *v.*

例 This software program allows managers to easily **organize** deadlines and delivery dates.

軟體程式可讓經理人員輕而易舉 organize 完工日與出貨日。

產量；輸出　1106 **output** [ˋaʊtˌpʊt] *n.*

例 If we don't increase the amount of product **output**, we will not be able to keep up with demand.

假如我們不增加產品的 output，將無法趕上需求。

全面的，全體的　1107 **overall** [ˋovɚˌɔl] *adj.*

例 Our newest mini-van has the best **overall** rating in the industry.

在業界，我們最新款迷你廂型車的 overall 評比都是最佳的。

（製造）工廠　1108 **plant** [plænt] *n.*

例 The **plant** was closed for two weeks after the explosion.

該 Plant 在爆炸事件後關廠二個星期。

移動式的　1109 **portable** [ˋpɔrtəbl] *adj.*

例 Staff members had to use **portable** toilets while the bathrooms were undergoing maintenance.

員工在洗手間維修期間得改用 portable 廁所。

1110 **power failure** [ˋpaʊɚ ͵feljɚ] *n. phr.* 停電

例 Production stopped for two days when the city experienced a **power failure** last year.

去年該市 power failure，工廠還因此停工了二天。

1111 **power plant** [ˋpaʊɚ ͵plænt] *n. phr.* 發電廠

例 Many people protested against the construction of a **power plant** so close to a residential neighborhood.

許多人示威抗議緊鄰住宅區興建 power plant。

1112 **practical** [ˋpræktɪkl] *adj.* 實用的，有用的

例 At present, hybrid electric vehicles seem to be a more **practical** solution to the problem of greenhouse gas emissions.

如今，油電混合車似乎是減少溫室氣體排放問題較 practical 解決辦法。

1113 **prevent** [prɪˋvɛnt] *v.* 防止；避免

例 To **prevent** injury, please tie long hair back when using machinery.

為了 prevent 受傷，操作機械時請將長髮束起。

1114 **prevention** [prɪˋvɛnʃən] *n.* 預防措施

例 Employees wear goggles while operating the equipment as an injury **prevention** measure.

工作人員在操作設備時戴護目鏡，是為了避免受傷而採取的 prevention。

Chapter 9 生產

繼續進行　1115 **proceed** [prəˋsid] *v.*

例 The workers were told to **proceed** with production of the new product.
工人得知要 proceed 生產新產品。

程序，步驟　1116 **procedure** [prəˋsidʒɚ] *n.*

例 Please follow the **procedure** accurately.
請準確地遵循 procedure。

過程，程序　1117 **process** [ˋprɑsɛs] *n.*

例 This **process** is very similar to the one at my previous company.
這 process 與我先前待過的公司的程序很類似。

生產，製造　1118 **produce** [prəˋdjus] *v.*

例 Our company has been **producing** high quality products for the past thirty years.
本公司三十年來均 producing 高品質的產品。

有生產力的　1119 **productive** [prəˋdʌktɪv] *adj.*

例 The manager said that the assembly line workers were not **productive** enough.
經理說生產線上的工人不夠 productive。

職業的，專業的　1120 **professional** [prəˋfɛʃənl] *adj.*

例 Employees have to dress appropriately in a **professional** environment.
員工在 professional 場合必須穿戴合宜。

1121 **prohibit** [proˋhɪbɪt] *v.*　　　　　　　　　禁止

　　例 Jewelry is **prohibited** in the factory.
　　　在廠內 prohibit 戴珠寶飾物。

1122 **proof** [pruf] *n.*　　　　　　　　　證明，證據

　　例 Our research demonstrates **proof** of the quality of the product.
　　　我們的研究結果提供了本產品品質的 proof。

1123 **quality control** [ˋkwɑlətɪ ˏkəntrol] *n. phr.*　　品管

　　例 The company has an excellent reputation for **quality control**.
　　　該公司享有優良 quality control 的聲譽。

1124 **quantity** [ˋkwɑntətɪ] *n.*　　　　　　數量

　　例 Employees in the packaging department are asked to indicate the **quantity** of products in each box.
　　　包裝部門的員工得標示出每箱產品的 quantity。

1125 **quota** [ˋkwotə] *n.*　　　　　　　　　配額

　　例 It is only Thursday and we have already met our weekly **quota**.
　　　今天才星期四，我們就已經達到每週的 quota。

1126 **rapidly** [ˋræpɪdlɪ] *adv.*　　　　　　迅速地，很快地

　　例 If we cannot manufacture the product **rapidly**, our boss will be disappointed.
　　　如果我們無法 rapidly 生產，我們老闆會很失望。

Chapter **9** 生產

243

改良，改革	1127 **reform** [rɪˋfɔrm] *v.*
	例 We need to **reform** the manufacturing process to improve the quality of the product.
	為改善產品的品質，我們需要 reform 製程。

補救（辦法）	1128 **remedy** [ˋrɛmədɪ] *n.*
	例 Trina found a **remedy** for the issue with the computer system.
	崔娜找到電腦系統問題的 remedy。

更新	1129 **renewal** [rɪˋnjuəl] *n.*
	例 The clients asked for a **renewal** of the contract.
	客戶要求合約的 renewal。

整頓，重組	1130 **reorganization** [͵riɔrgənaɪˋzeʃən] *n.*
	例 The entire company is undergoing **reorganization** under new management.
	整個公司在新管理團隊下接受 reorganization。

重複，一成不變	1131 **repetition** [͵rɛpɪˋtɪʃən] *n.*
	例 Assembly line workers must get used to the **repetition** involved in their position.
	生產線上的員工必須習慣工作上的 repetition。

要求	1132 **request** [rɪˋkwɛst] *v.*
	例 The clients **requested** that one of their staff members be at the factory during production.
	客戶 requested 讓他們的一名員工在產品生產時留在工廠。

1133 **research** [rɪˋsɝtʃ] *n.* 研究

例 A lot of **research** went into the development of the product.

許多 research 進入了產品的研發。

1134 **researcher** [rɪˋsɝtʃɚ] *n.* 研究員

例 We need to hire a team of **researchers** to investigate the problem.

我們需聘雇一團隊的 researchers 來調查問題。

1135 **resolution** [ˌrɛzəˋluʃən] *n.* 解決，解答

例 The production team is meeting to find a **resolution** to the problems in the factory.

為了找出在工廠中發生的問題的 resolution，生產組正開會討論。

1136 **routine** [ruˋtin] *adj.* 常規的，例行公事的

例 Daily inspection of the machinery is a **routine** procedure.

每日檢查機器是 routine 程序。

1137 **safety** [ˋseftɪ] *n.* 安全

例 **Safety** in the factory is a very important issue.

工廠 safety 是非常重要的議題。

1138 **scheme** [skim] *n.* 計畫，方案

例 Our manager is working on a new **scheme** for the maintenance of machinery.

經理正在研議機器維修的新 scheme。

科學家　　1139 **scientist** [ˋsaɪəntɪst] *n.*

☐　例 Our research team consists of five **scientists**.
☐　　　本公司的研究團隊是由五名 scientist 組成的。

篩選　　　1140 **screening** [ˋskrinɪŋ] *n.*

☐　例 All products made in the factory go through
☐　　　careful **screening** before being sent to clients.
　　　　工廠生產的所有產品在送到客戶手上前，都會經
　　　　過仔細的 screening。

簡化　　　1141 **simplify** [ˋsɪmpləˏfaɪ] *v.*

☐　例 The assembly process must be **simplified** to save
☐　　　time.
　　　　裝配程序必須 simplified，以節省時間。

步驟　　　1142 **step** [stɛp] *n.*

☐　例 Please follow all the **steps** carefully.
☐　　　請小心遵循所有的 step。

監督，管理　1143 **supervise** [ˋsupɚˏvaɪz] *v.*

☐　例 There must be someone in the factory at all times
☐　　　to **supervise** production.
　　　　工廠裡必定有人隨時 supervise 產品的生產。

有系統的，　1144 **systematic** [ˏsɪstəˋmætɪk] *adj.*
有條理的
☐　例 Manufacturing follows a very **systematic**
☐　　　process.
　　　　生產製造依循非常 systematic 流程。

1145 **target** [ˋtɑrgɪt] v.　　　　　　　　　　挑出

　　□　例　The computer technician **targeted** the problem.
　　□　　　電腦維修技術員 targeted 問題。

1146 **technical** [ˋtɛknɪkl] adj.　　　　　　　技術上的

　　□　例　We are experiencing **technical** difficulties with
　　□　　　our equipment.
　　　　　　我們的設備現正遭遇 technical 的困難。

1147 **technician** [tɛkˋnɪʃən] n.　　　　　　　技師，
　　　　　　　　　　　　　　　　　　　　　　技術員
　　□　例　The **technician** isn't able to repair the machine.
　　□　　　Technician 無法維修這台機器。

Exercises

請從選項中，選出最適當的答案完成句子。

1. The cell phone is an ingenious _____ that has made a great difference in our everyday life.
   (A) trap　(B) deceit　(C) device　(D) gadget

2. It is _____ to keep my hair short; I don't have much time to take care of it.
   (A) amazing　(B) convenient　(C) satisfying　(D) exciting

3. All sports are _____; runners, for example, try to improve their skill by tenths of a second.
   (A) competitive　(B) reluctant　(C) memorable　(D) indecisive

4. The guitar and the harp are both string _____.
   (A) movements　(B) actions　(C) instruments　(D) organs

5. Students need to learn how to _____ their thoughts.
   (A) organize　(B) dispute　(C) rationalize　(D) realize

6. As an old saying goes, _____ is better than cure.
   (A) intervention　(B) industrialization　(C) automation　(D) prevention

7. The author made a detailed _____ regarding the cause and effect of the event.
   (A) conviction　(B) persuasion　(C) analysis　(D) narration

8. Although I am independent now, my parents' views still _____ mine.
   (A) contain　(B) contact　(C) affect　(D) infect

9. The bicycle can easily be _____ if you follow the instructions.
   (A) assembled　(B) organized　(C) departed　(D) assured

10. Automatic cars are the _____, but I prefer a manual.
    (A) trend　(B) fashion　(C) tendency　(D) indication

11. DDT, a _____ once widely used to kill insects, is now banned in many countries.

    (A) chemical (B) chemistry (C) drug chemist (D) medicine

12. Car owners today enjoy a five year _____ over the life of the car engine.

    (A) promise (B) warranty (C) authority (D) security

13. The student made a (an) _____ presentation; he had everything well organized.

    (A) realistic (B) strategic (C) systematic (D) automatic

14. Recent _____ show that there is an increase in the number of cars sold.

    (A) statistics (B) tactics (C) techniques (D) strategies

15. Your theory is too complicated. Can you _____ it?

    (A) signify (B) identify (C) simplify (D) intensify

16. The invention of the computer was a _____ in many ways, especially in creating documents.

    (A) rotation (B) revelation (C) evolution (D) revolution

17. As Christmas approaches, many people begin to make their New Year's _____.

    (A) isolations (B) resolutions (C) solutions (D) pollutions

18. The popularity of laptop computers is increasing _____; more and more people are carrying them wherever they go.

    (A) hardly (B) rapidly (C) sensibly (D) agreeably

19. The _____ of the suspect has begun; he has been identified by security cameras as a tall man wearing dark glasses.

    (A) pursuit (B) invitation (C) investment (D) transaction

20. _____, that is, saying the same thing over and over again, is necessary in language learning.

    (A) Association (B) Repetition (C) Assertion (D) Competition

Chapter 10
Legal Affairs & Tax
法務與稅務

Legal affairs encompass all tasks related to a company's operations and transactions. When business partners choose to collaborate for mutual benefit, they sign a contract that outlines each party's rights and obligations. Failure to adhere to these terms and conditions can lead to a legal crisis for the company. Tax issues are also critical; if a company reports lower earnings than it actually generates, it may face legal charges and be sued by the government. In such cases, it is important to hire qualified professionals to help avoid violations.

Chapter 10 Legal Affairs & Tax
法務與稅務

New TOEIC 1200

1 Contract 合約 ㉗

協議
1148 **agreement** [əˋgrimənt] *n.*

例 The two clients reached an **agreement**.
這兩家公司達成了 agreement。

條款；條件
1149 **condition** [kənˋdɪʃən] *n.*

例 Please read the **conditions** in the contract carefully.
請仔細閱讀合約裡的 conditions。

內容
1150 **content** [ˋkɑntɛnt] *n.*

例 My client did not agree with the **content** of the agreement.
我的客戶不同意協議書裡的 content。

合約
1151 **contract** [ˋkɑntrækt] *n.*

例 We need to meet the lawyers at 4 pm to sign the **contract**.
我們下午四點要跟律師碰面簽 contract。

配合，合作
1152 **cooperate** [koˋɑpəˌret] *v.*

例 If we don't **cooperate** according to the agreement, they could take us to court.
如果我們不 cooperate 履行協議，對方可能會訴諸法庭。

1153 **copy** [ˋkɑpɪ] *n.* 副本，影本

例 Make sure you keep a **copy** of all your important documents.
要確定你所有的重要文件都保留 copy。

1154 **correction** [kəˋrɛkʃən] *n.* 修正

例 There are several **corrections** that need to be made to the agreement.
協議書中有幾個地方需要做些 corrections。

1155 **counselor** [ˋkaʊnslɚ] *n.* 律師；法律顧問

例 As a **counselor**, he is able to practice law in this state.
身為 counselor，他可以在本州執業。

1156 **counterpart** [ˋkaʊntɚˌpɑrt] *n.* 對等者，雙方

例 Both business **counterparts** need to sign the contract.
交易 counterparts 皆需在合約上簽名。

1157 **countersignature** [ˌkaʊntɚˋsɪgnətʃɚ] *n.* 會簽

例 The document requires a **countersignature**.
文件需經 countersignature。

1158 **date** [det] *v.* 註明日期

例 Don't forget to **date** the contract.
別忘了在合約上 date。

Chapter 10 法務與稅務

253

細節	1159 **detail** [dɪˋtel] *n.*
	例 Please meet me at my office so we can discuss the **details** of the contract.
	請到我辦公室來，我們好討論合約的 details。

文件	1160 **document** [ˋdɑkjəmənt] *n.*
	例 Don't forget to bring enough copies of the **document** with you to the meeting.
	開會時別忘了帶足夠的 document 副本。

草案；草稿	1161 **draft** [dræft] *n.*
	例 This is only the first **draft** contract.
	這是第一份合約 draft。

缺點	1162 **drawback** [ˋdrɔ͵bæk] *n.*
	例 There are many **drawbacks** when proceeding with a business deal without a contract.
	進行一場沒有合約的商業交易是有許多的 drawback。

副本	1163 **duplicate** [ˋdjupləkɪt] *n.*
	例 Please make a **duplicate** of the contract for my client.
	請給我的客戶一份合約 duplicate。

持續期間	1164 **duration** [djʊˋreʃən] *n.*
	例 The **duration** of the contract is three months.
	合約的 duration 是三個月。

1165 **expire** [ɪk`spaɪr] *v.*　　　　　　　　　　屆期，滿期

例　The contract will **expire** before the work has been completed.

合約在工作結束前就會 expire。

1166 **negotiate** [nɪ`goʃɪ‚et] *v.* 　　　　　　談判，協商

例　We should **negotiate** the terms of the contractual before we sign.

在簽約前，我們應該 negotiate 合約的條款。

1167 **obligation** [‚ɑblə`geʃən] *n.* 　　　　　義務

例　You are under **obligation** of the contract to work for two more months.

合約顯示你有 obligation 多工作兩個月。

1168 **offer** [`ɔfɚ] *n.* 　　　　　　　　　　　報價；提議

例　She was disappointed with the **offer**.

她對這 offer 感到失望。

1169 **on behalf of** [ɑn bɪ`hæf əv] *phr.* 　　代表

例　I gave my lawyer the authority to sign **on my behalf**.

我授權給我的律師 on behalf of 我簽名。

1170 **partner** [`pɑrtnɚ] *n.* 　　　　　　　　合夥人

例　My business **partner** is not able to sign contracts without my approval.

我的 partner 沒有我的同意不能簽任何合約。

Chapter 10 法務與稅務

255

合夥關係　　1171 **partnership** [`pɑrtnɚˌʃɪp] *n.*

例　They have had a business **partnership** for years.
他們曾經在生意上有多年的 partnership。

延續　　1172 **renew** [rɪ`nju] *v.*

例　My boss offered to **renew** my contract.
我老闆表示願意 renew 我的合約。

修正　　1173 **revise** [rɪ`vaɪz] *v.*

例　Please **revise** the contract.
請 revise 合約。

簽名　　1174 **sign** [saɪn] *v.*

例　Please **sign** your name on the line.
請在橫線上方 sign 您的大名。

簽名　　1175 **signature** [`sɪgnətʃɚ] *n.*

例　The contract requires your **signature**.
這合約需要你的 signature。

條款　　1176 **term** [tɝm] *n.*

例　If you signed the contract, you are obligated to fulfill the **terms**.
如果你簽下合約，你就有義務履行 terms。

2 Legal Affairs 法務 (28)

1177 **accumulate** [əˋkjumjəˌlet] *v.*　　累積，積聚

例 The law firm has **accumulated** a fortune from winning so many court cases.

這間律師事務所因打贏不少官司而 accumulated 很多財富。

1178 **attorney** [əˋtɝnɪ] *n.*　　律師

例 My **attorney** said he would contact me with the court date.

我的 attorney 說他會聯絡我開庭的日期。

1179 **commitment** [kəˋmɪtmənt] *n.*　　承諾，保證

例 The company is being sued because they backed out of a **commitment**.

該公司因沒有履行 commitment 而被告。

1180 **case** [kes] *n.*　　案例，事例

例 In this **case**, I think you might be right.

我想在這 case 上，你說的也許是對的。

1181 **confidential** [ˌkɑnfəˋdɛnʃəl] *adj.*　　機密的

例 The company lawyer keeps all information **confidential**.

該公司的律師對所有資訊均保持 confidential。

1182 **consent** [kənˋsɛnt] *n.*　　同意，贊成

例 We need your **consent** before we proceed.

在著手進行前，我們需先取得您的 consent。

Chapter 10 法務與稅務

削減，減少	1183 **curtail** [kɝˋtel] *v.*
	例 The lawyer told his client to **curtail** his public appearances during the trial.
	律師告訴他的客戶在審理期間 curtail 公開露面。

協議	1184 **deal** [dil] *n.*
	例 Let's try to make a **deal** without getting lawyers involved.
	讓我們試著在沒有律師涉入的情況下進行 deal。

決定	1185 **decide** [dɪˋsaɪd] *v.*
	例 If you **decide** to plead not guilty, you'd better be prepared for a long trial.
	如果你 decide 不承認有罪，你最好要為接下來的長期審理做好準備。

宣告	1186 **declare** [dɪˋklɛr] *v.*
	例 After James was **declared** innocent, he took a long vacation.
	在詹姆士被 declared 無罪後，他放了個長假。

討論	1187 **discussion** [dɪˋskʌʃən] *n.*
	例 The attorneys are having a serious **discussion** in the office.
	律師們正在辦公室裡嚴肅地進行 discussion。

額外的	1188 **extra** [ˋɛkstrə] *adj.*
	例 We may need some **extra** time to prepare for your court appearance.
	我們需要 extra 時間準備你的出庭。

1189 **lawyer** [ˋlɔjɚ] *n.* 律師

例 If you are looking for an attorney, I can give you my **lawyer**'s contact information.

如果你要找律師，我可以給你我 lawyer's 連絡方式。

1190 **legal** [ˋligl̩] *adj.* 法律上的

例 I need to talk to my lawyer to get some **legal** advice.

我需要跟我的律師談談，尋求他的 legal 建議。

1191 **pirate** [ˋpaɪrət] *v.* 非法複製

例 You can be put in jail for **pirating** CDs.

你要是 pirating 音樂光碟是會坐牢的。

1192 **priority** [praɪˋɔrətɪ] *n.* 優先（權）

例 Please make this client's case a **priority**.

請將這位客戶的案子列為 priority。

1193 **privacy** [ˋpraɪvəsɪ] *n.* 隱私

例 Employees don't have much **privacy** because the offices have glass walls.

因為辦公室有玻璃牆，所以員工沒有什麼 privacy 可言。

1194 **promise** [ˋpramɪs] *v.* 承諾，保證

例 I **promised** my client I would meet him in the morning.

我向客戶 promised 我早上會跟他碰面。

Chapter 10 法務與稅務

重新考慮　1195 **reconsider** [ˌrikənˈsɪdɚ] *v.*
- 例 I hope you will **reconsider** our offer.
- 我希望你能 reconsider 我們的提議。

代表　1196 **represent** [ˌrɛprɪˈzɛnt] *v.*
- 例 It isn't a good idea to **represent** yourself in court.
- 在法庭上 represent 你自己打官司不是個好主意。

壓力　1197 **stress** [strɛs] *n.*
- 例 Court battles can cause a lot of **stress**.
- 法庭上的攻防戰會帶來很大的 stress。

緊張　1198 **stressful** [ˈstrɛsfəl] *adj.*
- 例 The situation was **stressful** for all involved.
- 對所有相關人士來說，情況令人 stressful。

3　Tax 稅務 ㉙

優勢　1199 **advantage** [ədˈvæntɪdʒ] *n.*
- 例 The luxury tax provides an apparent **advantage** to self-occupancy in the real estate market.
- 奢侈稅為房地產市場中的自住客提供顯而易見的 advantage。

總額　1200 **amount** [əˈmaʊnt] *n.*
- 例 What **amount** do I owe the government?
- 我欠政府多少 amount？

260

1201 **audit** [ˋɔdɪt] *v.*　　　　　　　　　　　查帳，查核

　例　The company will be **audited** at the end of the month.
　　　公司月底要 audited。

1202 **authority** [əˋθɔrətɪ] *n.*　　　　　　權，職權

　例　The judge has the **authority** to decide on the penalty.
　　　法官有 authority 決定罰款的金額。

1203 **authorize** [ˋɔθəˏraɪz] *v.*　　　　　　授權

　例　I did not **authorize** these charges on my credit card.
　　　我沒有 authorize 用信用卡支付這些費用。

1204 **calculate** [ˋkælkjəˏlet] *v.*　　　　　計算

　例　My accountant made a mistake when **calculating** my taxes.
　　　我的會計師在 calculating 我的稅金時弄錯了。

1205 **citizen** [ˋsɪtəzn̩] *n.*　　　　　　　　公民

　例　All **citizens** must pay tax.
　　　所有的 citizens 皆需納稅。

1206 **claim** [klem] *v.*　　　　　　　　　　申報

　例　You must **claim** the amount of money you made when you file your income tax.
　　　在申報所得稅時，你必須 claim 所得總額。

Chapter 10　法務與稅務

客戶	1207 **client** [ˋklaɪənt] *n.*	
	例 The accountant does taxes for all of his **clients**.	
	會計師替他所有的 clients 處理稅務。	
佣金	1208 **commission** [kəˋmɪʃən] *n.*	
	例 People who work in sales must claim the money they make on **commissions**.	
	業務從業人員必須申報 commissions 所得。	
扣減	1209 **deduct** [dɪˋdʌkt] *v.*	
	例 The company **deducted** too much tax from my pay.	
	公司從我的收入中 deducted 了太多的稅。	
到期	1210 **due** [dju] *adj.*	
	例 Tax returns are **due** at the end of the month.	
	退稅這個月底 due。	
經濟的	1211 **economic** [͵ikəˋnamɪk] *adj.*	
	例 The entire country is going through tough **economic** times.	
	整個國家正經歷 economic 艱困時期。	
經濟	1212 **economy** [ɪˋkanəmɪ] *n.*	
	例 The bad **economy** is causing stress for lot of people.	
	economy 不振讓許多人感到壓力。	

1213 **financial** [faɪˋnænʃəl] *adj.*　　　　　　財務的；
　　例 The company's **financial** security depends on　金融的
　　　 the success of this product.
　　　 公司的 financial 安全取決於產品的成功。

1214 **government** [ˋgʌvɚnmənt] *n.*　　　　　政府
　　例 The **government** audits people at random.
　　　 Government 隨機查帳。

1215 **impose** [ɪmˋpoz] *v.*　　　　　　　　　　課徵
　　例 Higher taxes are **imposed** on people who have
　　　 high incomes.
　　　 高所得者要 imposed 較高的稅。

1216 **insurance** [ɪnˋʃʊrəns] *n.*　　　　　　　保險
　　例 It is important to purchase home **insurance**.
　　　 買房屋 insurance 是很重要的。

1217 **penalty** [ˋpɛnḷtɪ] *n.*　　　　　　　　　罰金
　　例 You will have to pay a **penalty** if you file your
　　　 taxes late.
　　　 如果太晚報稅，你得付 penalty。

1218 **property** [ˋprɑpɚtɪ] *n.*　　　　　　　　房地產
　　例 **Property** taxes downtown are really high.
　　　 市區的 property 稅真的很高。

Chapter 10　法務與稅務

代扣，代繳　1219 **remit** [rɪ`mɪt] *v.*

例 Employers must **remit** income taxes from their employees' income.

雇主必須從員工的收入中 remit 所得稅。

增加，提高　1220 **rise** [raɪz] *v.*

例 Income taxes are expected to **rise** this year.

今年的所得稅預期會 rise。

提交，呈遞　1221 **submit** [səb`mɪt] *v.*

例 Don't forget to **submit** your taxes by the deadline.

別忘了在截止日前 submit 報稅。

關稅　1222 **tariff** [`tærɪf] *n.*

例 We need to pay a **tariff** on all imported merchandise.

所有進口的商品都必須付 tariff。

稅　1223 **tax** [tæks] *n.*

例 There is no sales **tax** on clothing in that country.

該國不課徵衣服的銷售 tax。

稅捐機關　1224 **tax authority** [`tæks ə‚θɔrətɪ] *n. phr.*

例 The **tax authority** is investigating our company finances.

Tax authority 正在調查我們公司的財務。

264

1225 **tax revenue** [ˋtæks ˏrɛvənju] *n. phr.* 稅收

例 A lot of the country's **tax revenue** goes to health care.

國家的 tax revenue 很多用於醫療保健。

1226 **tendency** [ˋtɛndənsɪ] *n.* 傾向，習慣

例 I have a **tendency** to wait until the last minute to file my taxes.

我有等到最後一刻才要報稅的 tendency。

1227 **violation** [ˏvaɪəˋleʃən] *n.* 違法行為

例 The company is being charged with several tax **violations**.

該公司因數件稅務 violations 遭起訴。

Exercises

請從選項中，選出最適當的答案完成句子。

1. The words lawyer and _____ are synonyms; they mean roughly the same.

    (A) practitioner (B) attorney (C) layman (D) intern

2. The police found the stolen car abandoned by a river and called the owner to _____ it.

    (A) claim (B) pronounce (C) compliment (D) raise

3. The _____ told his lawyer that he wanted an end to the lawsuit.

    (A) client (B) agent (C) informer (D) obsessed

4. After Pearl Harbor, the US _____ war on Japan.

    (A) claimed (B) announced (C) declared (D) determined

5. My parents told me not to make _____ that I couldn't keep.

    (A) comments (B) judgments (C) decisions (D) promises

6. Being the best salesperson, Jessie will _____ the company at the national conference.

    (A) represent (B) suppress (C) introduce (D) inform

7. If you do something wrong such as breaking the law, you will have to pay a _____.

    (A) ticket (B) penalty (C) punishment (D) payment

8. I am under no _____ to help you, but for old time's sake, I will help you one last time.

    (A) obligation (B) duty (C) responsibility (D) entertainment

9. My driver's license _____ on my birthday; I have to renew it.

    (A) provokes (B) despises (C) inspires (D) expires

10. People are more or less under _____; we must learn how to deal with it so that it won't cause much harm.

    (A) stress (B) frustration (C) setback (D) inflation

11. I have worked out a solution to the company's financial problems. I will _____ the solution to the president tomorrow.

    (A) submit (B) yield (C) postpone (D) tease

12. If you are married, you have a _____ to your spouse; faithfulness, that is.

    (A) restoration (B) commitment (C) conservation (D) reservation

13. After I brainstormed, I was able to write a _____, which later became a full essay.

    (A) abstract (B) briefing (C) scribble (D) draft

14. There is a _____ for dogs to have their own way; it is essential that the owner demonstrate leadership so their pets know what to follow.

    (A) certainty (B) continuity (C) tendency (D) responsibility

15. Without the applicant's _____, the application is not valid.

    (A) signature (B) symbol (C) metaphor (D) significance

16. My teacher said I had to _____ my composition because it was poorly organized.

    (A) resume (B) revise (C) contain (D) constrain

17. The owners of the company decided to continue their _____ by signing a contract.

    (A) scholarship (B) citizenship (C) censorship (D) partnership

18. Since the new law took effect, there have been very few _____. People either appreciate the order it maintains, or they are naturally law-abiding.

    (A) violations (B) intentions (C) indications (D) implications

19. My lease is due next week, so I have to _____ it in order to continue living in this nice apartment.

    (A) return (B) reverse (C) revise (D) renew

20. It's hard trying to take _____ of Jim; he is a businessman.

    (A) storage (B) calculate (C) advantage (D) transaction

Review 5

I Photographs (42)

Look at the pictures below and listen to the statements. Then choose the statement that best describes what you see in the picture.

1. (A) (B) (C) (D)   2. (A) (B) (C) (D)

II Conversations (43)

You will hear a conversation between two people. Listen to the conversation and answer the questions below.

Questions 3-5

3. What are the people talking about?
    (A) Product prices.   (B) Delivery options and fees.
    (C) A customer complaint.   (D) Ordering online.

4. When will a product be delivered that was ordered at 2 pm?
   (A) Within 15 minutes.
   (B) By 5 pm the same day.
   (C) Between 5 and 6 pm the same day.
   (D) The next day.

5. What does the company charge for regular delivery if the order is more than $100?
   (A) No charge.
   (B) $5
   (C) $10
   (D) It depends on the exact price of the order.

III Short Talks 44

You will hear two short talks given by a single speaker. Listen to the short talks and answer the questions below.

Questions 6-8

6. Who is the speaker talking to?
   (A) The board of directors.
   (B) Laboratory workers.
   (C) Company employees.
   (D) His boss.

7. What is said about the new badges?
   (A) They must be worn at all times.
   (B) They only need to be worn in the laboratory.
   (C) Employees need to submit a request to receive one.
   (D) The loss of a badge must be reported to the laboratory.

8. What is said about the laboratory?
   (A) It is accessible to all employees.
   (B) You need your badge with a magnetic strip to open the door to the laboratory.
   (C) You need written authorization to use the lab.
   (D) You need to make a request 90 minutes before entering the lab.

Questions 9-11

9. What type of announcement is this?
   (A) A safety warning.
   (B) An advertisement.
   (C) A press release.
   (D) A lab report.

10. How does the sunscreen work?
    (A) By getting under the skin.
    (B) By having a strong effect on the skin.
    (C) By combining chemicals.
    (D) By covering the skin's cells.

11. Why is it safer than other sunscreens?
    (A) It is made of non-allergenic ingredients.
    (B) It has been tested on lab animals.
    (C) It is made of new chemicals.
    (D) It is convenient to apply.

IV Reading Comprehension

You will read a text followed by several questions. Select the best answer for each question and circle the letter (A), (B), (C), or (D).

Questions 12-14 refer to the following email.

Mr. Kimura:

I am writing this to ask you a favor. Remember those designs you began last year and then you gave it to me to work on?

Well, I decided that I like them just as they are, so I plan to use them in the upcoming fashion show, giving you full credit. I know you told me I could use them however I want, but the lawyers at my company want me to get a signed statement from you.

I am sorry for any trouble this may cause you. Lawyers always want everything to be so official. In order to save you time and energy, I have written a first draft of the short document and attached it to this email. The show is next week, so could you sign it and send it back to me as soon as possible?

As always, thanks for everything.

Samantha Bird

12. What does Samantha want Mr. Kimura to do?

    (A) Give her some fashion designs.

    (B) Confirm that she has permission to use his designs.

    (C) Send her designs back to her.

    (D) Call her company lawyer.

13. Why does Samantha need him to hurry with the request?

    (A) Because the lawyers insist on getting it immediately.

    (B) Because they need it before the show.

    (C) Because it has to be official.

    (D) Because last time, his response was too slow.

14. What is attached to the email?

    (A) A document written by Samantha.

    (B) A letter from the lawyers.

    (C) A picture of the designs.

    (D) A signed statement.

V Text Completion

Read the text that follows. A word or phrase is missing in some of the sentences. For each blank, four answer choices are given. Select the best answer to complete the text.

Stanford University, the University of California in Berkeley, and the University of Michigan have all signed (15)_____ authorizing Google to scan books from their libraries.

The librarians say the initiative can give new life to books that have been forgotten.

However, there is some (16)_____ surrounding Google's project. Digitizing current books whose (17)_____ holders are known is not in dispute. Neither is digitizing older books whose copyrights have expired. Problems arise over digitizing books that are out of print and still under copyright, but the current holder of that copyright is unknown. Selling digital copies of those books could become (18)_____, and there are questions over who will get those profits.

Google (19)_____ the project is about more than money. A spokesperson said the greatest (20)_____ for Google and for all Internet users would come from improving its search system.

15. (A) lawsuits   (B) inspections   (C) damages   (D) agreements
16. (A) controversy (B) prosperity   (C) motive   (D) regulation
17. (A) design   (B) infringement (C) patent   (D) copyright
18. (A) profitable   (B) accessible   (C) suitable (D) gratifying
19. (A) claims   (B) denies   (C) enforces (D) provokes
20. (A) revenue   (B) benefit   (C) damages   (D) innovation

Answer Key

Chapter 1

Exercises (p.28)

1. D	2. D	3. A	4. A	5. C
6. C	7. C	8. B	9. B	10. A
11. B	12. C	13. D	14. D	15. A
16. C	17. B	18. D	19. A	20. C

Chapter 2

Exercises (p.46)

1. executive
2. advice
3. position
4. staff
5. founder
6. branch
7. secretary
8. division

Chapter 3

Exercises (p.95)

1. D	2. B	3. C	4. C	5. B
6. A	7. D	8. C	9. A	10. D
11. B	12. A	13. B	14. C	15. B
16. D	17. A	18. B	19. C	20. B

Chapter 4

Exercises (p.121)

1. A	2. B	3. D	4. A	5. B
6. B	7. C	8. C	9. C	10. B
11. A	12. B	13. C	14. B	15. C
16. D	17. A	18. B	19. D	20. A

Chapter 5

Exercises (p.157)

1. D	2. B	3. C	4. D	5. A
6. B	7. B	8. D	9. A	10. B
11. B	12. D	13. A	14. B	15. B
16. A	17. A	18. B	19. A	20. C

Chapter 6

Exercises (p.179)

1. C	2. C	3. C	4. A	5. B
6. B	7. C	8. A	9. C	10. D
11. D	12. D	13. B	14. A	15. C
16. A	17. D	18. C	19. B	20. D

Chapter 7

Exercises (p.200)

1. A	2. D	3. C	4. C	5. A
6. A	7. A	8. A	9. B	10. B
11. B	12. D	13. D	14. A	15. A
16. C	17. A	18. B	19. C	20. B

Chapter 8

Exercises (p.219)

1. A	2. C	3. B	4. B	5. B
6. B	7. A	8. C	9. D	10. A
11. A	12. B	13. C	14. C	15. B
16. B	17. D	18. B	19. A	20. D

Chapter 9

Exercises (p.248)

1. C	2. B	3. A	4. C	5. A
6. D	7. C	8. C	9. A	10. A
11. A	12. C	13. C	14. A	15. C
16. D	17. B	18. B	19. A	20. B

Chapter 10

Exercises (p.266)

1. B	2. A	3. A	4. C	5. D
6. A	7. B	8. A	9. D	10. A
11. A	12. B	13. D	14. C	15. A
16. B	17. D	18. A	19. D	20. C

Review 1

I. Photographs (p.47)

Picture 1

(A) People are giving away free food.

(B) People are asking about job opportunities.

(C) The woman on the right is wearing a mini-skirt.

(D) They are at a fancy dress party.

Picture 2

(A) A ship is picking up passengers.

(B) There is a beach volleyball competition going on.

(C) A man is flying a kite on the beach.

(D) Many people are sunbathing on the beach.

II. Conversations (p.47)

Questions 3-5

(Man)	So according to your résumé, you worked at Sunray Industries for two and a half years. Can you tell me about your work there?
(Woman)	Yes, I was a manager for new projects.
(Man)	Tell me about that. What kinds of things did you do?
(Woman)	Well, I made contact with our target company and discussed business opportunities with them. Then, after I had learned more about their abilities, I prepared and suggested new project plans.

Questions 6-7

(Woman)	I'm afraid we'll be late for the concert on Friday evening. The traffic in town is always heavy on Friday nights.
(Man)	Can you take this Friday off? Then we can leave early and avoid the traffic jam.
(Woman)	That might be hard. My boss is really strict. If we want to take leave, we have to give notice at least two weeks in advance.
(Man)	Well, see if you can just take the afternoon off.

III. Short Talks (p.48)

Questions 8-9

You sent in your résumé and you got a job interview. Now you have to make sure that you get what you want from the interview. Many people say it is best to tell the interviewer what he or she wants to hear. However, this is not good advice. You might get a job that is not suitable for you. Your answers at an interview should always be truthful. By showing respect and self-confidence, you will make the employer believe that you are the best person for the job.

Questions 10-11

Good morning, everyone. As you know, our baseball club has interviewed several candidates to be our next manager. Today, I am pleased to announce that Michael Hunter is the new manager of the Johnstown Bears. Michael was a player for the Bears and has been our coach for the last two years. Michael is well-liked by the organization and brings a lot of experience. Ladies and gentlemen, please welcome Michael Hunter.

Answer keys

1. B 2. D 3. A 4. B 5. C
6. D 7. C 8. B 9. A 10. A
11. B 12. D 13. B 14. A 15. B
16. C 17. D 18. A 19. B 20. C
21. B 22. D 23. B 24. C 25. A
26. B 27. D 28. B

Review 2

I. Photographs (p.123)

Picture 1

(A) The men are playing chess.
(B) The men are having a meeting.
(C) The man on the left is reading through his glasses.
(D) The men are in the middle of a presentation.

Picture 2

(A) People are boarding the train.
(B) A woman is getting off the train.
(C) This is an underground platform.
(D) There are advertisements on the side of the train.

II. Conversations (p.123)

Questions 3-4

(Man)	I know you aren't getting along with Claire, but please don't be so obvious about it.
(Woman)	It's really hard to be polite. She's so talkative. She distracts me from my work.
(Man)	I understand. But she looked really sad this morning. Just try to be nice.
(Woman)	Alright. I'll go apologize to her later.

Questions 5-6

(Woman)	You look a bit uneasy today. Is anything wrong?
(Man)	The managers from the head office will arrive in one hour, and I have to make an important presentation in the meeting.
(Woman)	Is there anything I can do for you?
(Man)	Could you listen to my presentation now and tell me what you think of it?

III. Short Talks (p.124)

Questions 7-8

We have had a lot of complaints about noise in the office. The main causes of this problem are people talking loudly on the phone or shouting to others to get their attention. Sometimes the sound on people's computers is also too loud. To create a better working environment for everybody, please try to be thoughtful of others. If you need to talk to someone, go over to their desk, instead of yelling across the room.

Questions 9-10

Thank you all for coming to this department meeting. In the last year and a half, we have seen the number of our customers decrease by 15 percent. Of that 15 percent, half came from our 25 biggest customers. We're here today to discuss what we can do to make sure that we are keeping our customers happy.

Answer keys

1. B	2. D	3. D	4. C	5. C
6. A	7. C	8. D	9. D	10. C
11. D	12. A	13. B	14. C	15. B
16. C	17. B	18. D	19. C	20. B
21. C	22. A	23. C	24. A	25. D
26. B	27. C	28. B		

Review 3

I. Photographs (p.181)

Picture 1

(A) People are waiting on the platform.
(B) The bus is departing.
(C) The train has arrived at the station.
(D) The man is carrying a suitcase.

Picture 2

(A) The people are having a picnic.
(B) The award ceremony has started.
(C) The man is proposing a toast.
(D) They are sitting outdoors.

II. Conversations (p.181)

Questions 3-4

(Woman)	Would you like a hotel room near the airport or would you prefer one downtown?
(Man)	What do you suggest?
(Woman)	You're leaving on an early morning flight and downtown traffic can be really bad at that time.
(Man)	OK, I'll follow your recommendation then.

Questions 5-6

| (Woman) | How are you going to take all that luggage on an airplane? |
| (Man) | I'm not flying. I'm taking a train. |

(Woman) What a good idea! Sure, it takes longer, but the scenery should be worth it.

(Man) Yes. I always take the train because it's better for the environment.

Answer keys

1. C   2. D   3. B   4. B   5. D
6. D   7. B   8. C   9. A   10. C
11. B   12. A   13. B   14. D   15. B
16. C   17. C   18. D   19. C   20. D
21. C   22. A   23. B   24. A   25. B
26. B   27. A   28. A   29. C

III. Short Talks (p.182)
Questions 7-8

Those of you on your morning drive to work need to be aware that a section of Route 101 has been closed. It seems that a truck carrying chemicals overturned about 15 minutes ago. Police are directing traffic away from the scene. At this time, we don't know what caused the accident, but it looks as if it will take some time to clean up. If that is your normal route, we suggest you make a detour via Andersen Parkway. We'll let you know when the situation has cleared up. And now we'll go over to Dave in the studio for the 8:00 am weather report.

Questions 9-10

To your left, we are passing the St. Monique district. This is a famous artists' community. As you can see, there are many painters still at work in some studios along this street. Even so, many of these former studios have now been converted into small art galleries. Now, follow me as we are going to stop and have some coffee at one of the cafés that many famous artists frequented to exchange ideas and recite poetry.

Review 4

I. Photographs (p.221)
Picture 1

(A) The woman is holding a receipt.
(B) The woman is waiting to be served.
(C) The man is standing in line.
(D) The man is carrying a box.

Picture 2

(A) The women are in a restaurant.
(B) The shop is full of customers.
(C) The woman is at the checkout.
(D) The boy is buying candy.

II. Conversations (p.221)
Questions 3-4

(Woman) This client's bill is overdue. The payment was due a month ago.

(Man) Have you sent him a notice?

(Woman) I've already sent him two.

(Man) This is a frequent customer. We've never had problems before. Try calling him to find out what's going on.

Questions 5-6

(Woman)	This phone bill is much more expensive than last month's, yet we actually made fewer long-distance phone calls.
(Man)	I know. If you look at the bill, they added some new fees they never told us about.
(Woman)	This is ridiculous. They could have at least informed us in advance. I think we should start looking for a new provider.

III. Short Talks (p.222)

Questions 7-8

Three days ago, the accounting department released the financial statement for last year. As expected, the numbers reflect a serious downturn. The economic crisis is affecting each region of the country. We have no way of knowing when the economy will begin picking up again. Therefore, the president has called this emergency meeting in order to come up with some ideas on how to cut back on spending. We're open to any suggestions.

Answer keys

1. A	2. C	3. C	4. A	5. A
6. D	7. C	8. D	9. B	10. B
11. B	12. C	13. B	14. A	15. D
16. A	17. C	18. C	19. A	20. A
21. B	22. D	23. B	24. B	25. C
26. B	27. D	28. C		

Review 5

I. Photographs (p.269)

Picture 1

(A) She is pushing a shopping cart.

(B) She is using a hand-held device to take inventory.

(C) She is moving boxes in the warehouse.

(D) She is distributing products.

Picture 2

(A) They are leaving the premises.

(B) They are investigating a patent infringement.

(C) They are wearing hairnets.

(D) The man on the right is interfering with their work.

II. Conversations (p.269)

Questions 3-5

(Woman)	Hello, I'm calling to ask whether your company provides same-day delivery.
(Man)	Yes, we do. We provide same-day delivery for all products that we have in stock. Products ordered before noon can be received by 5:00 pm.
(Woman)	I see. Is there an additional fee for same-day delivery?
(Man)	We deliver your order to you at no cost if the total value of your order exceeds $100. For all other orders, we

charge $5 for regular delivery and $10 for same-day delivery.

III. Short Talks (p.270)
Questions 6-8

Good morning, and thank you for coming today. I have some important announcements to make. Starting next month, new photo identification badges with a magnetic strip on them will be distributed to all employees. This badge must be visible at all times while you are on company property. Lost or misplaced badges must be reported immediately to the Personnel Department.

In addition, the entire Research and Development section of the main building will be accessible only to authorized laboratory employees. Should you be required to enter that area, a request must be made to division staff at least 90 minutes prior to your desired entry time. Thank you for your cooperation.

Questions 9-11

Now that summer is finally here, we are proud to announce the launch of a new sunscreen that will make your time out in the sun safer than ever before.
Some sunscreens contain chemicals, which may have an effect on more sensitive skin, but our sunscreen is made of safe ingredients. Lab tests have shown that it does not cause allergic reactions. Major active ingredients include natural plant extracts and anti-oxidants ground so fine that these ingredients actually cover your skin at a microscopic level, not letting the sun's rays come in contact with your skin cells. No other sunscreen will keep your skin healthier and younger-looking.

Answer keys

1. B	2. C	3. B	4. D	5. A
6. C	7. A	8. D	9. B	10. D
11. A	12. B	13. B	14. A	15. D
16. A	17. D	18. A	19. A	20. B

Notes